Murder in Germantown

Murder in Germantown

A Ravonne Lemmelle Mystery

Rahiem Brooks

Prodigy Publishing Group
Philadelphia, PA

ALSO BY RAHIEM BROOKS

Laugh Now
First Laugh (E-book Only)
Die Later

Con Test: Double Life

Truth, Lies, & Confessions

CONTRIBUTOR
ARC BOOK CLUB Official Literary Cook Book

Published by **Prodigy Publishing Group**

This novel is a work of fiction. Any references to real people, events, business, organizations, or locales are intended only to give the fiction a sense of reality and authenticity. Names, characters, place, and incidents are the product of the author's imagination or used fictitiously. Any resemblance to actual persons, living or dead, events, or locales, is entirely coincidental.

Cover and Author Photography by Gregory Goodwin
Typesetting: Rahiem Brooks

ISBN 978-0-615-69016-2
LCCN on File

PRINTED IN THE UNITED STATES OF AMERICA

[September 2012] First Edition

This book is dedicated to my close friends:

Nathan Anderson
Marcus Gary
Rudolph Jainlett
Daymon Blackmon
Khaim Hill
Kevin Woodard

ACKNOWLEDGMENTS

In my first published book (Laugh Now), I made clear that no author is an island, and now on book five confess that was very true.

My publishing career would not be possible without Envy Red, Kristofer Clarke, English Ruler (proofreader), Aaron Walker, Gregory Goodwin (graphic designer), Jenetha McCutcheon (editor), and Donna Saunders.

Much love and respect,

Rahiem Brooks

www.rahiembrooks.com

Murder in Germantown

PROLOGUE

CHAPTER 1

Actively engaged in a debate about the details of his wife's 40th birthday party on his cell phone, Mark Artis walked to his car in the parking lot of the downtown Philadelphia Gallery mall. Not paying attention, he dropped his keys. He put his shopping bag on the ground as he bent over to retrieve them.

"Sue, I am telling you. She'd adore white over pink. She's not..."

In mid-sentence, he was jabbed in his rib cage with a handgun. He paused and lost his concentration on the call and focused on breaking the wrist of the gunman, who dropped his pistol. Before he could gather himself, another goon placed an automatic weapon inches from the bridge of his nose. He didn't kill him. They wanted him alive.

February temperatures had been declining. Doppler radar claimed it was 35 degrees, but the weather felt more like minus 25 degrees. Mark used a wireless device, so that he could keep his hands warm in his pockets. He was a bulky man, not fat; made of muscle. He had a thick neck and strong, broad shoulders, and was enveloped in pale skin from a lack of sunlight.

"Come with me, Mark," the thug ordered. "I dare you to use any more jujutsu because I would have quite the time ending Samantha's beautiful life."

In the mist of the attack, his smart, confident secretary on the other end of the call, wanted to assure him that help was on the way.

"Mr. Artis, I'll contact the police. Maybe they can locate you using the tracking device in your phone."

Good girl, Mark thought, as the gunman snatched the earpiece and tossed it. Mark still had his secretary, as his clandestine ally.

At the outset of the attack, Mark thought he was being robbed, but the gunman knew his wife's name and that he had jujutsu training; he was a black belt. His mind spiraled uncontrollably searching for the place or date that he had wronged someone. There was no way he would be so negligent. He valued his life and the lives of his family, so he followed the man's orders and climbed into the back of a dingy van.

Mark rode with a black bag over his head and handcuffs on his wrists for 15 minutes, and his supposition was verified. The van door opened and the bag was removed. Mark was in the garage of a chop shop. He was escorted past ten or so exotic European vehicles to a doorway that led to an office. Everything in the office looked bland and resembled a legitimate mechanic's office. He knew it wasn't.

Mark was forced to the floor as an emaciated woman in need of tit-raise appeared. Her hair was slapped into a chignon, and she walked over to him and planted a military boot on his chest. She puffed a long fag and steel-gray smoke bellowed into the air. Certainly, he was not invited to meet her. He did not recall gangsters handing duties down to women.

The woman informed him, "I see you're quick with your hands. Broke Mikey's wrist. That's why I invited you. I hope you respond as hastily to my $200,000 question."

She invited me. Really! *It was more like a warrant for my arrest*, he thought. He elected to keep that confidential.

"What is the question?" he asked the bitch sincerely. He could be sincere.

"Shut your cum dumpster mouth!" the man who brought him to the little *tête-à-tête* suggested.

Mark would bet that man’s tone would change if he weren't handcuffed.

"Lex, you're free to go," the hostess told her flunky.

She then squatted over Mark, ass on his crotch, and warned him, "Do not patronize me, Mark Alexander Artis."

A thick cloud of smoke fulminated into his lungs to punctuate her point.

"The name is Jewel."

"Okay, Jewel. Why am I here?" he asked getting down to business.

She stood and threw him a sardonic grin.

"Here's the deal," she said and then added, "your wife Samantha has been kidnapped."

"No! No! No!" He barked.

It was more of a scream than a masculine yell. Mark began to rise from the floor and Jewel flashed a chrome Colt .45. Mark thought long and hard about getting up off the floor. Hopefully, Sue was recording all of that. The thug had activated the hand set when the ear piece had lost signal.

"It's 10:30 in the morning, Mark Artis. I shall have 200,000 unmarked, non-sequential, American dollars in my possession by the close of the banking business day. That's traditionally three p.m. And I adore tradition, Mark."

"I do not have that kind of cash," he warned her earnestly.

"Then you no longer have a fucking wife!"

CHAPTER 2

Mark Artis drove his Jaguar XJ8 to his Victorian manse on Presidential Boulevard in suburban Bala Cynwd. The small area was 20 minutes from downtown Philadelphia. He pulled into the rotund driveway, disembarked, and was greeted by FBI and the Lower Merion PD locals.

Communication specialists from the FBI hastily equipped his home with enough devices to converse with Pluto denizens. One device assured the conversation between the FBI and Jewel would be made available to everyone in the dining room. Another device would record the suspect's voice. A third whatchamacallit would trace all incoming calls to the callers' location within minutes.

All of that transpired while Mark was in the picture-less family room. A woman joined him and identified herself as Jane Duval, FBI. She assured him that the FBI would lend their expertise to him. She said it as if he should bend over and smooch her ass. His tax dollars had insured this service.

"Ms. Duval, I appreciate the blessing, but my wife is missing. If she is harmed, I'll find the sons-of-bitches and I'll annihilate them one-by-one. And the result is not my concern. This is unimaginable."

"You're venting, Mr. Artis. That is to be expected."

"Venting!" He hissed venomously. *The good old*, FBI, he thought.

"They want money. By three. Period! Didn't you hear the recording from my secretary? I am not rich. This place is time-shared. I am here on business. The Jag is from Hertz."

"Don't worry about the cash demand. Our Wells Fargo crisis liaison is prepared with the cash."

"It better not be booby trapped, because if my wife is harmed due to your chicanery..."

The telephone rang and interrupted him. Mark raced to the telephone along with a half-dozen suits. The FBI Special Agent in Charge instructed Mark to keep the napper on the line as long as possible. He handed Mark a script to follow.

Mark said, "Artis residence." He wanted the caller to know they had the correct number.

A Brooklynese female voice: "I see you've made it home safely in your car." The word car sounded like "caw".

"Where's Samantha?"

"Sammy's fine."

"Where do I find you to exchange the cash for my wife?"

"We will get to that, but first..."

"I want proof now!" Mark demanded.

He hadn't heard much, but it had been enough. He tossed the script to the floor and dared any one to question him.

"Bam, Love. Drag her over here. Sammy say hello to your hubby."

"Mark, oh Honey..."

"Baby, I'm going..."

"I said say hello. No coo loving quip in my ear," the kidnapper said.

"You better not harm her. I swear..."

"You swear what?" Jewel asked. Her words leaked contempt. Everyone was silent and Jewel went on. "Have the agents tear down their tracking and recording crap. I'll have further instructions for the cash pick up and drop locale when that's been done."

Click!

The call was over. Dead. The end. And not traced. Mark was pissed.

The FBI agents were awaiting a professional to call back. For them a good thing. Maybe Jewel was known to them. No one gave a rat's ass that some lamebrain had just ordered them to tear down the spyware.

"Tear that shit down," Mark Artis demanded.

"Mr. Artis, we cannot do that. Surely, she or he knows that. They have no way of knowing if we have complied or not. She simply wants us to be martyrs to her caveats. We do not and will not negotiate with thugs. When she calls again simply convince her that we met her demand."

All Mark heard was blah, blah, blah. The phone rang again and Mark was jolted back to reality.

"Am I being traced and recorded, Mr. Artis?"

"Yes," he replied honestly. *Screw the feds*, Mark thought.

The ASIC was infuriated. He snatched the phone from Mark.

"This is..."

Jewel cut him off, "Assistant Special Idiot in Charge Donald Malloy. Thirteen year vet. Yale law. Two boys. One dog. And a partridge in a pear tree. I am colder than a polar bear's pussy, simpleton. I'll snatch your twins and Toto, too, as my next move, if you obstruct my plan, Mr. Malloy. Now be a good boy and turn on the living room TV."

Click!

The feds and locals rushed to the TV. After a brief inspection for a bomb, they decided to summon the bomb squad prior to touching it. Too bad. Mark grabbed the remote and turned it on. The ferocious surprise was contagious. Everyone looked distraught. Each expression on par with being delivered the news their baby was still-born. They all watched themselves on the TV. The picture quality was pristine.

The telephone rang.

The kidnapper was chuckling.

"Why so glum, chum?" she asked no one in particular. "Now that the cat's out of the bag, we are clear who the boss here is. Let's get down to business. You know what I mean by that," she said in a South Philadelphia Italian mobster drawl.

"I'm listening," Mark told her genuinely.

"All of the fags, I mean feds, should be listening, too. Carefully. The home is severely enveloped in enough dynamite to sink the Virgin Islands. All of them! Look at the television."

They looked and the screen flashed from room to room and all points outside the house.

"I am Big Sister, lads. No one leaves. No one makes unauthorized calls. No one sends text messages. Or there will be a lot of hymnals and carnations bought. Are we clear?"

No one replied.

"Are we fucking clear?" she barked wickedly.

"Yes," everyone in the room said.

They shook their heads up and down.

"So subservient. I love it!" Jewel said jubilantly.

"Malloy, you're authorized a call to Katherine Donahue. You may inform her that you have an agent arriving at the Broad Street and Samsun Street branch to retrieve the cash. She should stow the cash in a duffle bag that was dropped to her desk 26 seconds ago. She forks over the currency and I will let you know how to get back Samantha. Capeesh?"

Once again, click!

CHAPTER 3

Mark sensed the haughty FBI had been deflated. There would not be any hoots of celebration and champagne popping after solving this capper. They had been beaten by their own game. It was rumored that a lot of successful busts and cracked cases were the result of sloppy criminals, and not adroit police work. Perhaps, Jewel had proved that.

Mark dithered on the sofa. He rocked and folded his arms. His shaking was noticeable. He needed hard liquor and he found some at the bar. His every move was showcased on Mark-TV. It was such a home invasion of privacy. He began to talk about his wonderful wife. He spoke of stowed memories that he had totally forgotten. The kidnapper heard every damn word. Prayerfully, the telephone rang.

"This is Malloy," ASIC Malloy answered. "Hold a second. It's for you," he said, extending the phone to Mark.

"Yes, Jewel."

"Mr. Artis, I want you to collect Mr. Malloy's badge and gun. Holster and all."

"Why would he do that?" Malloy asked.

"Because I said so. How else will I recover the cash from Donahue? You didn't believe I'd send one of my guys into your trap, did you? Maybe you did? Sucks to be you then? Now tender the costume clown."

Malloy handed over his bona fides and Mark donned them. It was all displayed on Mark-TV.

"Don't look ashamed, Mark. Think of today as Halloween. You're dressed as an asshole." Jewel broke into a Broadway chuckle.

"Mr. Artis, you will take the quickest route to downtown Philly. Get the cash and deliver it to mama. You will leave by yourself. Any tricks and you'll be jettisoned to Pluto. There's a bomb on your car that would do that easily. Get it? Got it? Good."

* * *

Two minutes away from the house, Mark cruised in the XJ8 down City Avenue. He pulled into a Target parking lot and pulled off his artificial hands along with his faux mustache and beard. The widened snout, Dumbo ears, and thick neck came off next. He removed the dress shirt, pulled of the 40 pounds of excess body mass, and revealed his true size. He was parked next to a very low-key Ford. He hopped out of the XJ8 and into the Ford Taurus and commenced his getaway.

"How'd getting the cash go?" Mark asked Jewel.

"It went great. Bam walked out with the cash as Malloy handed you his badge."

"So all is well?"

"Yes. Well Mickey still doesn't think you had to break his wrist for mall parking lot cameras."

PRESENT DAY

FRIDAY, JANUARY, 5 2007

CHAPTER 4

Sometimes, my criminals are likable, but oftentimes they're not. The current one I hated, but I represented him (and his money) without prejudice. His name, Mark Artis. I was interested in Artis' trial verdict. More than the norm. He was an alleged con man and believed to be a serious threat to the Department of Commerce. I doubted that, and my investigators found evidence to prove me correct. But hey, I was bound by attorney-client privilege so I kept those details quiet. I credit my investigators because I actually did more than try one case per year. I did not suffer from the boredom of the unfolding discoveries of one case for months at a time.

I am busy on the Philadelphia criminal judicial circuit, and on the tip of every criminal's tongue in the Federal Detention Center (FDC) in Philadelphia and in the Philadelphia Prison Systems. It was not the same as being chased down by paparazzi, but.... I could not report to every crime scene, interview every witness, or verify every alibi for all of the clients. I multi-task. So big ups to my detectives. The police have theirs and I have mine.

I just defended Artis in a trial on the 9th floor of the United States Courthouse at 601 Market Street. The jury deliberated for two days and requested the transcripts of the government's key witness: Tanya "Jewel" Stalin (Russian, but no relation to the communist). Too bad the jury could not have her transcripts, and had to rely on their memories. I managed to get them the police reports and notes to compare to her testimony, though. I imagined they believe her to be a vicious liar--she was--and I had brought out her lies. Called her a terrorist, too. Yes, I was way out of line, but hey, an acquittal was acquired by any means necessary. The jury had a verdict, and I had to wait for them to deliver it.

At 9:30, Artis had found me perched at the defense table. I had known I would be in the courtroom holding my breath, so I had downloaded the sports news on Carmelo Anthony returning from his famous 15-day suspension. He would join the recently-acquired Allen Iverson with the Denver Nuggets. I did not have to see Artis approaching me. The heels of his loafers crashed the hardwood and his handcuffs echoed. The unarmed Marshal sat him next to me.

"It does not take a rocket scientist to find me not guilty of all charges." He proclaimed. "No prints or DNA of mine was found at the scene. Their whole case hinged on the testimony of a sleazy coke whore who would have sold her mother out. The jury is taking long. Does that mean anything?"

"What do you mean?" I asked with a subtle hint of sardonicism.

What happened to a good morning pleasantry? This was one of the reasons I knew he had not played the federal agents. He had no class. Or grace. Mark, or whatever his real name was, had proven himself to be a pompous, self-centered bastard. I thought I needed my black ass fanned and fed grapes like royalty considering no Philadelphia tri-state area barrister wanted to touch him. I defended him. Offered my Harvard Law bookishness and sound experience to the noodle despite my disgust at how he allegedly devastated the government designed to protect *moi*.

"Could they be wrestling with finding me guilty?"

What the hell did he think? Yes, they were. Guilty or Not Guilty? That was the question.

"Mark," I replied. "The length of time they deliberate means nothing. My best conjecture says they are worried about Jewel's testimony."

"Ravonne, she botched a kidnapping after she had already gotten away with five others, and when the FBI swooped in on her for the mastermind, she fingered me. We had a one-night stand and my voice...." He paused and looked into the air. "My goddamn voice sounded like the man that had hired her. She should be on trial alone!"

"Mark, please! I know the facts."

It was my way of screaming shut the fuck up. After the comment, I studied him for a second. I checked for a sign that he was upset. He had a cold stare, but I stared back. I won the stare down and had no fear of him firing me.

"So, you wanna hear about my date last night?" Mark asked me as if I desired to relive some bimbo flashing him her boobs outside the FDC cell window overlooking Arch Street.

Picayunish should've been his last name.

I stayed up countless nights constructing a solid defense, and he did nothing but eat commissary, watch Sports Center, see enough flesh to play with his wiener, and had the audacity to think I wanted to hear about it. It was not easy to restrain my position, but I reduced my reply to, "Mr. Artis."

I stopped and breathed deeply. He hated the nom de guerre and was adamant it was not his.

I continued with, "I am on trial for my life. So, no, I do not care to relish your twenty-five cent booth experience."

"On trial for your life?" he asked and paused. "Since when?"

Marky-Pooh's words dripped with disgust. Jewel's pet name for him, not mine.

"I will be further ostracized from practicing law in Philadelphia if I lose this case. And that is my life," I said candidly. "Even if I obtain an acquittal, I'll be the attorney who freed a con artist and duped the US out of $200,000, not including trial expenses."

Refreshing.

I had upset my client and then left him at the defense table. I walked to the window and peered down at the Mark Artis Circus taking place out on Market Street. The press had wanted the verdict. I was not usually perturbed by my clients, but there was a time when sound seriousness was mandatory. Being inside of a courtroom staring stoically down the barrel of a life sentence was a qualifier.

I had seen the press going mad outside. All of them pissed because they did not get a seat in the courtroom. The press seating was done by lottery and the stars were not with the press outside. I took an imaginary bow and smiled. I had captivated an audience again. After my performance with the Bezel trial, I loved to perform for the local media and I looked for an E-mail from CNN to come.

I then sat back down at the defense table and put on my smart pince-nez. They made me look fussy and intellectual. A man passionate about my craft of criminal defense.

I was!

I whispered to Mark to behave when the verdict was read.

Reporters rushed in to fill the available seats.

The judge hit the bench with the jury in tow. They looked forlorn. Shameful. My mind immediately began to ponder errors and plot appeal strategies. I doubted if I would represent Mark in the appeals process because I was aware the he would conjure a reason I, Ravonne Lemmelle, was ineffective. Yes, that was the number one appeals ground, and Mark would desperately want to get back to the streets if he was found guilty, so he would try to make me the fall guy. It was highly doubtful that would work out for him.

"I've come to learn you, the jury, have reached a verdict," the judge said to no one in particular.

She was looking around at the media mongers taking their seats. However, her voice was stern and appeared to be elated.

"We have, Your Honor," the foreman reported.

CHAPTER 5

The piercing scream sliced through Aramis like an arrow. He ignored it, bunched his pillow into a new shape and snuggled it around his head. The ringing from the house phone then started and stopped. The cell phone immediately began to ring again. The Lil' Wayne *Fireman* single identified the caller. Aramis rotated the pillow and hoped the caller would call back later. The caller did, and it took seconds. His watch read 10:30 a.m.

Aramis curled his palm around his cell phone and flipped it open.

"You better be dying. I mean literally dead!"

"Aramis Reed! I know damn well you're not still in bed?" Ravonne asked.

"What's the matter, Ray-Ray? I'm sleep."

"Noooo, you're talking to me."

Aramis slammed the phone shut.

Ravonne called right back.

"Look!" Aramis barked. "I was up all night. I'm tired."

"We have a problem. I had Artis acquitted and was doing a live press release, which you missed--"

"Why the hell are you making that a problem?"

"It's actually not. As soon as I began to walk away from the reporter madness, my cell phone rang. It was John B. Kelly's Home and School Association president, Tina Burton. She..."

"She reported they're having a bake sale and she called on you to ask me to report it? Look, Ray-Ray, when I get up, I will call you."

"Actually, smart ass. She told me there was a shooting on the corner of Wayne and Seymour in front of the convenience store. Real convenient, huh? I know the kid that was shot, too. I'm on my way there and I'll call you back in a half because I want you to report the shooting."

Ravonne hung up.

Aramis had spent the night on the sofa with his jeans wrapped around his ankles. After an anonymous bout of oral sex, he fell asleep right where she had left him. When she had reported for duty, Aramis stared at her through the camera mounted by the door as she stood in his apartment foyer. Not much to talk about, but he needed to explode in order to fall asleep. And awake, for that matter. He was a bona fide sex addict in need of therapy. The woman had left him comatose on the sofa. Many women like her were all over the Party Line and Internet dating site's chat rooms. Aramis took full advantage of the sex networking sites.

His eyes roamed the living room. The room was quaint and modern. It escaped looking like a struggling free lance reporter's pad. Hardwood floors and white doors ran everywhere. The ambiance was serene.

Aramis' dog, Taurus, had continued to sleep while Aramis and Ravonne had chatted. Aramis had won Taurus after an indecent break-up with his ex-fiancée. She relocated to Virginia with a new lover. Now Aramis lived with a Welsh corgi and dedicated his life to his job and harlots.

"Move!" Aramis barked at Taurus, as he walked to the apartment window.

Taurus barked an obscenity back and didn't budge. Ten stories below, snow densely blanketed the asphalt of the complex parking lot. He padded to the bedroom, and found neatness and order. He had a queer guy for the straight guy home.

He cued P. Diddy's *Last Night* featuring Keyshia Cole to play repeatedly while he showered. He was a slim, caramel man with voluptuous lips and bushy eyebrows. He had a commanding sex appeal and the best report in Philadelphia smile. Out of the shower, he did the deodorant and lotion thing, and then splashed Romeo Gigli on his wrist, neck, and pelvis. He never knew when a woman's face would venture down there. He didn't want to be musky. He slipped on a crisp, white button-down, well-tailored grey trousers, and soft leather Prada ankle boots.

In the kitchen he popped a multi-vitamin and drank two bottles of Ensure. Breakfast was served. He had to eat healthy to prepare for the garbage he took in daily on the beat.

Twenty minutes later, Aramis commandeered his Audi A8 out of the Park Drive Manor complex and headed south on Pulaski Avenue. The homes he passed were all connected. They were mostly like that in the city, even in some of the tonier areas. Some people hushed all of the noise in one home and spied on the happenings in a neighbor's. What a neighborly bond?

Aramis reached Penn Street and passed the high-rise Pulaski Town projects. He drove and had an epiphany. What mind boggled him was that Los Angeles, the gang-bang headquarters of America, had a more ferocious reputation than the most rugged out area of Philadelphia. Albeit, the Los Angelenos lived in ranch homes. In LA boys washed their parents' cars in driveways and mowed lawns. What a luxury, he thought. Grass and driveways in Philadelphia were rare in the ghetto. On the East Coast, period. Even the lawyer/doctor Huxtable team didn't have a lawn or driveway.

Philadelphia had the Italian mob and Black mafia who remained fairly stealth, unless their dollar was disturbed. They didn't have colors, hand signage, bald heads, or sports apparel to identify themselves. They were about the mighty dollar.

Philadelphia.

Aramis crossed Hansberry Street and passed the clover shaped John B. Kelly Elementary School. He surmised one of the school's student's lives had ended, caught by the stray bullet of an asshole. He drove two more blocks to Seymour Street and wanted to make a left, but a police cruiser wasn't having him make that move. He parked on Pulaski and his cell phone rang.

CHAPTER 6

Aramis picked up on the second ring, and I said, "I hope you're not still in bed."

"No," he replied, "I'm parking at Pulaski and Seymour. Where are you?"

"I am already on Wayne Avenue in front of Happy Hollow Playground. Walk down Clapier Street and meet me."

What could I say to him, but welcome to Germantown. I stood outside my car and shivered a little from the cold. Winter in Philadelphia was no jester. At night, in the summer, the two-block tract was lively in the Germantown section of North Philadelphia. Wayne Avenue had everything the Happy Hollow residents needed, but everything wasn't happy.

Starting at Wyneva Street was the Happy Hollow Playground. The playground had a sliding board and swing arena, an indoor gym, and a boxing training facility. The basketball court hosted summer basketball league games. Directly across the street stood Charlie B's Sports Bar, that new bitch, considering the legendary Moe & Curly's was now an Asian-owned beer distributor. Moe & Curly's was the spot a few years earlier and they sold the largest hoagies on the north side of City Hall. The bar drew patrons from all over the city.

The Avenue had a thriving Jamaican store that sold more weed than groceries. Right next door, was another grocery store owned by Asians. Amidst this debauchery was also two churches and an Asian-owned laundromat. It seemed everything had been conquered by the Asians. I looked forward to an Asian or Hispanic United States president. Maybe even a Black one.

On the corner of Seymour Street were, a soul food joint, cell phone store, exterminator, and an independent African School taught pre-K to third grade. Next to the school stood, a hardware store, discount store and dry cleaner. Yes, everything was on this strip for the Germantown residents.

Aramis found me and we traipsed together, skipping the handshake. We were on business and not best friends. I had grown up on Seymour Street and my grandmother stubbornly remained there. I also gave pep talks to the area teen bad asses and taught boxing lessons one night a week at the playground gym. As far as the crime scene, officially my job was nothing but showing my face and encouraging the police to do their jobs. For their benefit, it behooved them not to prove themselves as lazy characters.

Long, long before Rev. Dr. Martin Luther King, Jr. learned to boycott, some tenants in Ireland (circa 1890's) ostracized their land agent. His name was Charles C. Boycott. Something to take to your next dinner party, but for the purpose of this recounting, I planned to boycott the 14th police district as ferociously as the Irelanders.

At Germantown High School, I was an honor student in the Social Studies Law and Government Magnet Program. I had won my mock trials in high school and at Harvard. I crushed opponents during debate tournaments. I had no siblings with demanding parents, so I became a school worm. I was involved in everything.

In the tenth grade, I formed a rally outside of the Mayor's office because he allotted more money to the Philadelphia Police Department for more powerful vehicles, but not a dime for new school textbooks. The way I saw things, then and now, better educated Philadelphians meant less police cars. My father was guided into the Mayor's seat the next election.

In my senior year, I raised money and chartered five buses to Harrisburg, the state's capital. My followers and I asked why the City of Brotherly Love had been short changed on gentrification funding. My "hold the politician accountable" motto did not prevent me from challenging Mayor Joshua Lemmelle, either. Father and all. He promised salary raises for Philadelphia's finest--the teachers--which the budget proposal did not reflect, and I called him on it in public. We're estranged now, but one day he'll need me for a lung or kidney. I would be waiting, too.

With Aramis in tow, I lifted the yellow crime scene tape which identified where the crime scene had begun. I wouldn't dare infringe on the evidence to convict the senseless derelict responsible for the murder. Aramis waved his notepad and press pass in a detective's face. I had no business doing that, but this was different.

The first thing Aramis did was record the detective's name. He wouldn't want to misspell the name of the man having ignored a reporter trying to bring a crime to the public. Aramis wanted to get the public looking for the killer immediately. He asked a preliminary question.

The detective replied, "From what we got, a guy named Suspect was the intended target. The shooter missed by a mile. Hit the kid. He's over at Germantown Hospital now. One other is dead."

Detective Spencer had a stiff charcoal and white crop, and wore a wrinkled uniform. His shoes didn't shine. And I'd swear his breath smelled like Certs over vodka.

"What's his status? Who is the kid?" I asked as if I hadn't known.

"Fair. Quincy James. It was a leg shot."

"Wydell's brother. You know this will be a war, right, detective? I can assure you. Quincy is a straight-A student. He's going to Fitler Advanced Placement next year," I explained. "He's one of the kids I train. Wants to be a teacher and he's only in the fourth grade."

"What's going on here?" Aramis asked. "This is the third shooting since Christmas. It was only a matter of time before someone was hit."

"Apparently, Suspect has a bullet on his head. Supposedly, he raised the prices of his product and clamped down on being liberal. He has a beef with Big Boo brewing, too. Why? I dunno, yet."

"You should. You are a detective, right?" Aramis said. Aramis was about as nasty as me at times.

"Watch it!" The detective said. He lifted his glasses and put on a blank face.

"And you're doing what to curb this disaster unfolding? Or lock down the men that want him dead?" I asked.

"Listen, Ray-Ray. You know Suspect has Miller to protect him. The man is smart and very methodical. The DEA is on him, and we can't compete with him. And as far as the men wanting him dead, no, I am not pressed to lock them up and I am sure Quincy James understands why."

"Spence, Miller is an attorney. His powers aren't greater than yours, sir. You're a detective." Aramis had drew another blank face from the detective.

I was being the good guy and letting Aramis be the bad guy this day. It wasn't planned like this. It just unfolded this way.

"I am no cop, but for me, make a concerted effort to find Quincy's shooter. I understand your lack of concern for Suspect, but they've hit an innocent."

"Yeah," Aramis chimed in and gave the detective a wicked raised eyebrow.

"They've upped the ante, don't you think? Even if by accident. They need to be addressed."

"I'll do what I can."

"I am sure you will, or I will do all I can."

"Is that a threat, Aramis?" the detective asked with a smile.

"Nope. That's against the law."

CHAPTER 7

At the turn of the millennium, he was Gordon Odell, masterful art forger. He had duped billionaires out of millions. By the 9/11 conundrum, he was Sylvester Bailey, extraordinary international hacker. During the 2002 winter Olympics, he had become Donald Holloway, an expert jewelry thief. In 2006, he was Mark Artis, a saucy con man. Alas, after a brief hiatus he began 2007 as a robbery aficionado, Skyler Juday.

All of him was an alias.

A lie.

An embellishment.

A pseudonym.

Which was why he posed as Mark Artis and paid Jewel a bonus to finger an innocent man. He smiled at how he made seasoned FBI agents look like children playing cops and robbers. He was a modest man. He would respond to any acclaim with a yawn. He had no remorse for the man Ravonne represented spending time in jail before Ravonne had gotten him off.

Many wanted his government name. So did he. He had long ago forgotten. His country of origin? His vices? They all needed a number behind Interpol, FBI, CIA and the rest of the alphabet clowns, all of whom wanted a piece of him.

Mr. 357 was his moniker.

Mr. 357 was one gargantuan tandem of mystery, suspense, thriller, and a dose of comedy. He believed the FBI caper was comical. A parody. The joke was on...

...Who cared?

He was by no definition invincible. He did strive for intelligent crimes, though, which helped him thwart arrest. His crimes were plotted with droplets of sex, brilliant gun play, and Hollywood pandemonium. A web site--www.mister357.com--was devoted to theorists, propaganda weavers, and conspiracy mongers regarding his identity. He was as famous as Deep Throat. He was fortunate. He was also a slick bastard who mailed bodies to the local FBI, Interpol, and Scotland Yard at his discretion.

Like Jewel, Mr. 357 always needed personnel. No one had a recurring role in his productions. He did his own screen tests, too. He targeted a prospective thespian and then scrutinized their strengths, deducting for weaknesses. Those making the cut were compensated.

He was considering an attorney. The one he would contract when he was caught. He would be caught. Not because he would get sloppy and the police would clean up. Nooooo! He planned to get arrested on purpose. He wanted to beat the beloved American judicial system. Particularly, federal prosecutor, Matthew Meehan, for allowing Mark Artis to go free.

Mr. 357 would cast one Ravonne Lemmelle as a puppet in this production.

Ravonne was perfect for the job of the attorney in his upcoming master piece theater. Skylar Juday had studied Ravonne in court and adored the man. Ravonne proved to be smart, quick on his feet, and the man acted. Ravonne was second in his law school graduating class with job offers from New York, Los Angeles, Chicago, and Atlanta. Yet, he remained loyal to his city, and Skylar Juday loved him for that. Ravonne was not moved by the money that was thrown at him in law school. He had his own money, and wore it confidently, not cockily. Talks were held about adding him to the White House staff. Skylar figured that was a cheap ploy to add color to the Capitol. They wanted the crème de la crème of the coloreds. Ravonne didn't fall for that ruse, either. Skylar had vetted the man and planned to continue to. To his estimation, Ravonne had one character flaw, which would work for his scheme. No one would believe Skylar Juday hired such a gross sinner like Ravonne Lemmelle.

Mr. 357 watched Ravonne walk away from the Wayne and Seymour Streets crime scene. He then walked to the Wayne Junction SEPTA regional rail line station, and vowed to make everyone believers.

CHAPTER 8

By early evening, I was in my office and tired of being on my feet. I had counseled a few of the area kids and went to the hospital to visit Quincy, but I only spoke to his mother and brother because he was in surgery. He had been shot in the thigh, and would be fine.

Some men were out in the arctic winter winds and heading home to their adorable wives. Some to their mistresses or the bar first, but none the less, home to be loved. I was legally married, had a son, and a relationship (not with my wife, I'll explain later) that was on a shaking boat, which I was in no mood to rush home to until the current calmed. My comfy office would do just fine. I worked for Martir, Savino & Associates and they always welcomed me in their billing nursery. Litigation always needed nursing, and I had plenty of diapers and bottles.

Finally, I had a celebratory jubilee after winning the Artis trial. My second huge case. The first was the Bezel Brothers and that case required me to have a personal body guard. The controversy was delightful for my career, but I'll spare the details of the case.

At the mahogany bar inside my office, I stared at myself in the mirror. I had a face that lied and claimed that I was twenty. I was thirty. No, I had not drunk from the fountain of youth. I attributed my African descent for the youthful honor. I was also exposed when I spoke. I had been accused of being a twenty-dollar word showoff. I read every night and I asked Mr. Webster to define any foreign wordage. My adjective and adverb coffer was corpulent. See what I mean.

I am five feet eight-and-a-half inches tall. Five-nine in footwear (today wing tips), and if you asked my height, I would say five-ten. I'm sleek and slender and had been hitting the gym, two , sometimes six, times a week to chisel my physique in a daring attempt to rival a Donatello. That was all coated in a Hershey Kiss chocolate complexion and expertly packaged in a European cut suit, double cuff dress shirt, and a funky tie. It had been said that clothes made the man. I begged to differ. I had a gorgeous smile, but it hadn't always been that way. In law school I had cosmetic dental work done. That was the ticket that had gotten me into many women's beds, but that was not where, I, Ravonne Lemmelle, wanted to be, though.

There was a light knock on my glass door before it opened without my permission. I planned to create a verbal agreement with the space invader to assure that breaking and entry did not reoccur. Recognizing the throwback took me a moment. I hadn't seen it, I mean, her, in years.

Five.

"Yoo-hoo. It's me. Ariel Greenland," the woman told me as if I gave a damn.

She was all toothy, and showcased a better veneer job than my own. She had a smile that mirrored Oprah Winfrey's. A smile suited for a coy woman who was refined and not murky, just like archaic wine. Her beauty rivaled a muntjac. Behind her emerald eyes were not a pretty deer, but a serpent, though. I could have gone another half-decade without her return. Or her silky ebony hair and svelte frame which carried a gargantuan ass.

"Hello, Ariel."

I imagined that I said that as smoothly as Dr. Lecter.

"What brings you here? It's only been ten years," I told her and proffered her the same smile that I passed along to prosecutors.

I wanted to gag off the politeness.

She glanced around my marble and glass office. "Impressive. And it's only been five years, smart ass!" she corrected me.

"Oh. My apologies." I had to humor myself. "I spend 70 plus hours here a week and, well..." I stopped talking because, I asked, "You know, what brought you here where it snows?"

Skip the small talk. I offered her a seat on a mohair sofa and then commanded my surround sound to quietly play Robin Thicke. What I really needed was that drink that I was after before she barged her *beau monde* ass into my office, but I sat at my desk with no desire to offer her cocktail. She didn't deserve one.

"Well," she said, and squirmed in her seat. Her shifting came as a shock to me. "Let's go for dinner and drinks."

I needed an ear waxing. She was kidding, right? "What's on your mind? What brought you into my office? The real reason."

That meeting had started interestingly. Ariel Greenland, head cheerleader of the Georgetown Hoyas needed help, I presumed. And of all people's, Ravonne Lemmelle's. Help which brought her crawling 3,000 miles from her sunny Los Angeles digs to mine in Philly. I was so uninterested in the whole shebang.

"What happened to the phone-a-friend lifeline?" I joked reluctantly.

I had to refrain from exploding.

"I need you."

"Nice!"

"My life is not what it used to be."

I was perplexed.

"And what might that have been?"

Evil me playing a con on her emotions. Her earlier decision had rendered me a single father.

(The only reason I've decided to privilege you to the balance of this exchange was to give you an understanding of my complex life. I have decided to be brutally free from deception with this outline of my life.)

"You know..." she stammered.

"I don't." I lied.

She wanted my help. Needed it. But was morbidly pained to ask for it.

"Oh. Alright," she said boldly. "Kimmie is missing."

"Translation. She's been kidnapped? Or she dumped you and now you're living on the dole?"

"The latter."

"Now you..."

The bitch cut me off.

"Now I need help from my husband!"

CHAPTER 9

"Pump your breaks," I said and stood. I really needed that jubilee. "Ex-husband. Drink?"

"We're still married." She corrected me and waved her ring finger in the air. "Gin and tonic."

"Only on paper. Rocks?"

She nodded. I mixed our libations and passed her a G&T with ice. I then went to my mirror. I wanted to watch myself when I said, "Like I needed you to leave my world with a baby during the fall semester of my last year at law school. I had to drop out a semester, you know? I had to set the baby up at my grandmother's."

"Look!"

I nipped that attitude in the bud.

"Don't come in here being disrespectful, Ariel. I've been congenial. It's best that I don't turn into a chimera."

"Okay! Our marriage was one to accommodate both of us, and I thought that you would leave me. I just beat you too it."

(If you're on an empty stomach right now, fix that. The rest of this exchange was en route to chaos and the revelations were best served on a full tank.)

I sat next to her and looked deeply into her eyes. "We were inseparable friends. I loved you, Ariel. You walked out on me with a baby. Now you have the heart of a lioness to come in here as if everything is just great. You have a lot of nerve."

"Look, Ray-Ray. I was childish. Immature. And a wreck in college. I am sorry about Harvard, but I thought that you would leave me for one of your boy toys."

I warned you, but anyway.

I replied, "Please!" with a chuckle.

It was hardly a laughing matter, but I needed it, though.

"I needed and loved you more than I needed any expression of lust for a man. True our marriage was one of convenience, but I remained loyal to our agreement."

"Bravo for you. I need you now, though. My husband."

"Like my son needs you. Now! You have some dildo strapped on to come in here demanding help. Did you help my son learn his ABC's or how to tie his sneaker? You know--"

My news flash was interrupted by my legal assistant. She tapped on my office door and I signaled for her to come in.

"Sorry. Didn't know that you had a client," she said and batted her thick lashes at me.

Marsha was no ordinary legal admin. assistant. She commanded admirers and had blonde hair and blue eyes. Cliché, I know, but Marsha was brilliant.

"Oh, this is no client. She's Brandon's mother. The absconder."

Marsha's terrific tan had blanched. She said hello to Ariel and then stated her business. "I completed the Johnson motion. You-know-who is on the line. I informed him that you were in the library. He countered and told me that he knows I'm covering for you, and he knows that you're in your office ignoring his calls. I'd have security sweep for bugs." She joked and chuckled.

I laughed.

Ariel would swear that I was fucking Marsha, but she would be wrong.

"See you Monday."

I knew she would call me for that 411 later that night, though.

"Eight sharp, Marsh," I warned.

She was beginning to set her own schedule, which was tardy.

I turned to Ariel and told her, "thanks to you I have to deal with this bullshit," as I sat down at my desk.

(The conversation that transpired is going to be mind blowing. I assure that. I also assure you that I am in a very serious homosexual relationship, which I have proven not to be monogamously challenged. My DNA did not have that defective strain. All of us are not promiscuous club hoppers, who live ten deep in an efficiency. Some of us gays do reside in the top drawer. And by the end of this narrative you would have learned that and a few other factoids to win a battle over common gay myths. My purpose of this warning was to promise my lifestyle has never stolen the thunder from my career. I could've kept all this a secret, but why lie? I am a grown ass man.)

I hit the speaker button and asked, "Can I help you, Mr. Jones?"

"You're ignoring your cell. Your secretary lies to me. At your command, I am sure. And you have an attitude."

It was as if he had founded a medical breakthrough on par with a breast cancer vaccine.

"My cell has been off since court. I forget to turn it back on." I lied.

He gave me a you've-gotta-be-kidding giggle, which I happily volleyed.

"Why haven't you come home? I've cooked sautéed chicken breast with grapes and grilled corn on the cob and cheese cake with fresh chocolate sauce to celebrate your win. I mean, acquittal."

"Working."

He hated one word answers.

"You know what?" He snapped.

"No, I don't. Tell me, sir," I said smiling.

"When your so very busy schedule makes room for me..."

"Okay. Bye."

I hung up. Believe me. He would have gotten me. Besides, I had company (You included) and he was making me out to be the bitch, as if both of our costumes did not consist of pants. There were no queens in our condo.

I looked over at Ariel Greenland, absconder-at-large, having forgotten momentarily that she was there. My angry level was code orange. Or whichever color Homeland Security had assigned the highest security threat level. I begged myself to downgrade a bit. At that point, I was in my professional raiment, but I would brandish my inner thug as soon as I exited the office. Couldn't let the white folks see me act a fool outside of the courtroom.

"Damn," Ariel said. "What was with that?" she asked. "Five years passed, but I know you, Ravonne Lemmelle. You love hard and do not take shit. You tolerate very little."

"Did you think of that before you flew here?"

"Anyway. Who was that?"

"Dajuan. And if you know so damn much, why am I a gay man and no longer bi?"

"Dajuan Jones, as in the singer?"

"Great catch, huh?" I joked with a mock smile on my face.

Her little recital moments ago showcased concern, but I wasn't fooled. Nor did I miss how she slithered away from my question.

"What did he do, cheat?" she asked.

I looked at her perplexed and she concluded, "He cheated."

She then asked, "Why" as if she cared. I hated fakes.

"My work habits are a tad avaricious. He thinks that when he's not on tour, my law career stops. Thinks that I should go into private practice rather than slave at the largest firm in the city, so that I can make my own schedule. Around his schedule. That and he was drunk."

"Everyone cheats when they're drunk. Even..."

"You!" I snapped and pointed an index finger at her. "You can say it. You left me for the same reason that he may. I'm too ambitious. Why that is so profoundly obnoxious to my paramours is insane. When NASA finds life on Mars, I pray that planet has appreciative denizen." (Or, Isaac Asimov's Solaria.)

She sat there silent, which was expected. I knew she was never prepared for me. She should have stayed in LA.

I dashed to my walk-in closet, shut the curtain and left her there to ponder.

I had dreaded that encounter, but I had handled myself remarkably well. I emerged from the closet sans tie, trousers and wing tips. They were replaced with Jeans and sneakers. I un-buttoned my dress shirt two buttons, and kept on the blazer. I am a great chameleon.

"Where are you staying?" I asked and grabbed my briefcase.

I tossed on a Yankees fitted cap. No, I am not a Yankee fan, but I loved the stripes.

"The Lowes."

"Let's take this chat there. I would invite you to my home, but I need to prepare Brandon for the shock," I said, walking toward the elevator.

"Uh..." she stammered dumbly.

"Um, my ass! Surely you had plans on meeting Brandon?"

"I'm not sure that I am ready for that. I am scared," she said as we entered an empty elevator.

"Scared of what?"

"Him hating me, Ray-Ray," she said, as we exited the elevator.

"I'll talk to him," I told her. "Good night, Frank," I told security of the Prudential Building and wondered how Ariel passed him and Marsha unnoticed. "He won't hate you. He's still waiting for you to turn up on TV."

On 12th Street, we walked out of the building toward Market Street. My coat and scarf was in my car, which was parked in the underground garage of the hotel where she stayed. It was directly across from my office. I parked there for free. A perk that I wrote corporate and asked for as a shareholder.

Before we entered the hotel's 12th Street entrance, I stopped and warned her, "If you have no intentions of meeting Brandon, then we can terminate this now."

She looked at me. Her eyes brilliant. They reminded me so much of Brandon's. Had she replied no, my world would have come crashing down again. I didn't collapse at that point. Later, Ariel definitely flew Heartbreak flight 8774 searing through my heart.

CHAPTER 10

Ariel stayed at the hotel whose anchor restaurant was host to my lunch dates. Prior to going into the gut of the enchanting Lowes, I stopped at Sole Food, the eccentric, crustacean restaurant. I had the waiter send a few of my favorite things to Ariel's room. Oprah had her favorite things, and I had mine.

My hostess looked horrified and seemed standoffish as we sat in the luxuriant hotel room. She had a tight petite body that I used to ravish abundantly. True, I should have still been, but things happened. I flipped the TV on and flopped on the bed. She looked at me dumbfounded. She should have been grateful that I was there and calm. I was miffed to the nth degree. My emotions were not describable, and please forgive me, I am not going to try to explain them.

I heard a knock and opened the hotel door. Luke handed me a decorative tray. I tipped him and he exited. He had prepared me a Bloody Mary with fresh horseradish, and I drowned it. My uvula was set ablaze and I was ready to breathe fire. Until then, the chit-chat was trite, and I'd spare you the contents and get right to the meat.

"So, Ariel. Let's have it," I said and joined her on the sofa. I handed her a gin martini.

"What?" she asked coyly. She sipped. A cool smirk on her face.

If choking her had been an option...

"Listen," I dug into my wallet and spoke. "Games have an appropriate time to be played. In fact," I handed her three photos of *my* five-year-old. "Tonight is Brandon's and my board game and pizza night, but he's spending it with Constance."

Tears welled in her eyes as she looked at the photos. I reached over and pulled her closer to me. The fit was still snug.

"This is too much. I shouldn't have come here."

"That's absurd," I whispered. "I've missed you terribly. Brandon is a reflection of you." I had kissed her forehead in an attempt to comfort her.

"He looks like me."

"He is a masculine version of you. Very creative and too damn smart. Rumored to be a child prodigy. He is in Judo and boxing classes, too. And he is very attractive to pretty little girls and women, too. Just like you."

"Funny. He's five, Ray-Ray," she said and sank deeper into my arms.

We were conjoined twins just like the old days.

"He's five and very understanding. I promise he will forgive you. Sometimes, I pull out our photo album and I'll point to you and ask him, who's that? He replies that it's his mommy. He thinks he has an advantage over other kids because he has two dads and a mom that lives in Hollywood."

"Brandon may become gay and it'll be all my fault. Had I stayed and we had our perfect marriage, with our candy on the side, this wouldn't be happening. But I was scared."

"I still have no idea what you were scared of. And after five years, I don't even care. I miss you. And trust me, Brandon likes pussy. He'd love to meet you, too. He has never asked why you left. He gets that. He had demanded to take acting classes to be an actor like his mommy. He's at the ripe age to be rescued from ever hating you."

"But what about us?"

"Ariel, let me be frank," I said and sat up.

I wouldn't be fooled twice.

"There is no us. We are parents, though. I am not five, nor as easily forgiving as King B. I mean Brandon. And besides..."

"I bet you fucking forgave D. Jones, faggot!" She exclaimed sarcastically.

She stood and walked to the window overlooking Market Street.

I was not pissed that she called me a name. That was what everyone called me when they were mad at me. It was laughable. I really didn't have to explain myself to her, but I wanted revenge.

"He shared a meaningless kiss and confessed to me, and I was angry at him for it. Accidents happen and can be fixed. Tragedies, though, are unrepairable. I do not need to tell you who did what. I do not play the break up to make up bullshit. In five years, I have grown considerably."

She walked over to me and pulled me to my feet. She looked seductively into my eyes and ran her hand along the length of my penis.

"Has all of you grown considerably?" she breathed.

Then would have been an excellent time to reveal that I haven't grown, but I was still a frightening size down there, but she didn't deserve the pleasure. Besides, I could not give her the satisfaction of believing that I was pussy-whipped. I could've lain her down and punished her atrociously for revenge. Got my nut. And left. But I didn't for one very good reason: I still loved Ariel Greenland.

I pulled away from her and said, "Ariel, now is not the time to pretend that we are all good, so let's patch up and have succulent make-up sex to start anew. Like you, I was bogged by immaturity five years ago, but I'm sure you understand not having a real social life, not being able to party, and travel forced me to grow up real fast. Maybe had I shared my parental obligations with..."

"Don't take this and turn it into a major guilt trip. I feel bad enough."

"Well, don't try to come here and fuck me as if this can be patched. You can't put a Band-Aid on a bullet wound."

"Fuck you, Ray-Ray!"

"I'm sure you'd love to."

I caught myself. I had a litany of haughty things to verbally pass along to my wife--soon to be ex. I would not dare dumb myself down, though. "Listen, Ariel. Where is this going? You said you needed something. What do you need? You didn't fly here for dick, I'm sure."

"I fucking hate you! You arrogant piece of shit. That's why I left you. Fuck you. Get out!"

"What? I haven't done shit to you. Then or now. I have been kissing your ass for two hours, when you should be French kissing mine. I'm not getting out. Put me the fuck out!"

"Oh, you're getting out." she raved and raced to the hotel phone.

I grabbed her, twisted her around and looked her deep into her eyes and hissed. "You're dead wrong, Ariel. You know damn well I do not deserve this. I've never hurt you, and I don't intend too. You could have stayed in LA and not brought this whole thing to fruition. Let's get to the point. You need something and you can probably get it, if you agree to see our baby, because you and I have nothing to iron out, but you owe him!"

I let her go. Well, I flung her like a flea. She dropped onto the bed.

"You're trying to blackmail me."

"Blackmail? Are you kidding me? I haven't asked you to free fall from an airborne Boeing jet. I asked you to see a child that you gave birth too, you stupid bitch!"

"I want a divorce. I only wanted half your shit, but I want the condo you live in with Dajaun and your car, too. And my son. I also want..."

"Is that why you came?" I asked laughing. "LA has excellent attorneys. Just marvelous when it comes to divorce and celebrity murders. You should've saved the airfare and hotel fees. My son. You're crazy! No court in America would take Brandon from me."

I was cracking the hell up.

"I'mma suck you dry, too, since you find me funny."

"What, this dick? That's 'bout all you'll be sucking dry. Cause I'll guarantee you will get nothing but dust, babe."

I grabbed my briefcase.

"We will see. Get out before I scream rape."

"No one in this entire city would believe you. Do you know who I am? You're an insane bitch. And I suggest you do not come near me again," I said and let the hotel door close behind me.

CHAPTER 11

I reached my car and threw myself and briefcase inside. I beat on the steering wheel. I was angry, and so much that I could not muster a tear. She did not have to come and interrupt my world. I didn't deserve that. That was why I was sure you have more faith on a higher power than your storyteller. If there was a God and he had a *soupcon* of love for me, perhaps he could send a messenger to tell me the reason for the unwarranted *casus belli*. I knew my behavior was verbally injurious, but she attacked me first. While, I should've remained calm, I couldn't lie to my heart and convince it that I was not hurt. I tried and that counted for something, right? Right.

I was not going to allow her to eat me alive, so I popped in *TP3* (*12-Play Part 3* by R. Kelly for all of the R&B remedial) and commenced a lonely drive to nowhere.

CHAPTER 12

I was calmed after another trip to Germantown. I had gone to Maplewood Mall, which was the epicenter of the area when the area was being developed. The one block had a law firm, insurance company, literacy project, clothing boutique, nutrition emporium, hair salon, and barber shop. That was why I was there to see Vergil, my barber at Clipperz. Vergil had been named after the Italian poet. He was more like the Greek God of Male Hair Precision.

Later, I pulled up to my street in Olde City and drove my blue-black BMW 750LI into the driveway. Don't be fooled. It was not a long driveway. It extended from the curb about the length of a SUV and led to a two-car garage beneath the living room.

The downtown Pine Street condo was darkened. I knew that Dajuan was home, thanks to his Range Rover being parked in it's spot. I was sure that he had been rehearsing the apologetic lyrics that would ebb in one of my ears and flow directly out of the other one. Of course, I was not rude or pompous. I was very demanding and expected the best. I came into this world in the ghetto, and I crept out of there with no intentions of returning. More importantly, I detested being cross and violated. Cheating was a major violation. Sure, I practiced law and mastered the art of deception. Not in my home, though.

Before I disembarked, I decided it was a good idea to apologize to Ariel Greenland. Make amends, you know? For Brandon's benefit, certainly, not my own. I dialed the Lowes and asked for room 917. I heard the desk clerk tap, tap. Then tap, tap, tap.

"I'm sorry, but Ms. Greenland has checked out, sir."

"Are you sure?" I asked disbelievingly.

"Of course, sir."

"Could she have changed rooms?"

"Let's see. No, sir."

Before I could fully thank her, she had hung up on me. Deliberately, I was sure. Served me right for treating her like a hostile witness.

Out of the car, I grabbed my briefcase and walked up the five stairs to one of the living room entrances. The other one was accessible from the side of the condo. I opened the door and was greeted by Ms. Pearl circling my feet. Her stocky, round head, and white, silky coat was adorable and she wanted her routine hug, but I was in no mood to grope her. I kicked off my sneakers and slipped on comfortable moccasins. No outside shoes were allowed on the white carpet. I glanced at the large clock that had been created by a drummer cymbal. It was 11:30 p.m. I perused the wall covered with photos of Dajuan in the company of R&B crooners and diva's. I stared at the baby grand situated as the living room centerpiece. I desired to take a saw to it. One wall was taken up by a gold leather sofa. I plopped on it and shimmied out of my blazer and shirt. I planted my feet on the earth toned marble coffee table, choc full of music tomes. The entire living room screamed, Dajuan Jones. I had to escape to the bedroom.

The futuristic, electronic master bedroom was where I found Dajuan feigning to be asleep. I knew that he couldn't wait to find the best moment to broach the topic of my disrespect from earlier when I hung up on him. I slipped out of my gear and took a quick shower. I stepped out of the shower five minutes later and all of a sudden the brass quarter notes as shower curtains said "Dajaun" and they too had to get the saw.

I was actually tired, but did not want to get into the bed considering I would have to share it. In the living room at the marble-topped sideboard, I fixed a double vodka gimlet. I sat at the kitchen table and enjoyed a slice of rum cake topped with maraschino cherries. It was palatable.

With the remainder of the cocktail in hand, I retreated to my den, aptly dubbed my home office. At the desk, ensconced in a comfortable executive chair behind a mammoth desk, I checked my personal E-mail. I then logged into my PEPCO account and paid the electric bill, and then on to the daunting task of deleting spam mail. I had Beyonce's Irreplaceable booming as Dajuan walked in. I pretended not to see him and continued to sing the break up track.

Dajuan's smooth and creamy peanut butter complexion glowed. His curly, close-cropped hair was disheveled and his bushy eyebrows rivaled Einstein's. He sat with his exposed six-pack on the love seat and hid his deep brown eyes in the palm of his hands.

"Ray-Ray, come here," he said.

It was more of a mumble, but I ignored him, nonetheless. Yes, I was being obstinate, but I felt obligated to be. Some people needed to be taught a lesson. He asked me to join him again, but added a "please" at the beginning and end of his request. Talk about redundant.

"I'm getting the bills paid before my son is utility-less. What's crackin' though?" I asked, having brought the Ebonics from Germantown with me downtown. I spoke as if I didn't have a worry in the world.

"Blackface, that can wait."

He called me a pet moniker during a time of war. I guess I should have said that everything was okay.

"Really?" I asked dragging the word out sardonically.

"Look. Can you please come and talk to me?"

He must have just played a Jodeci CD, or something.

"I am talking to you, DJ."

"I need to holla at you. Straight up!" He growled with a touch of aggression in his voice.

I desired to be a kid and lay out all of his cheating, filthy antics, but I decided to remain calm.

"You should've been hollering about us when you made your bed. Now lay in it," I said right on cue with Beyonce.

I wanted to laugh, but I held my composure. I was talking to him and replaying what I should have said to Ariel Greenland.

He stood and slithered to the desk and looked at the computer monitor. After careful review, he hissed, "This bullshit can wait."

He then pushed the power button on my PC. He reached to turn off the monitor and I grabbed his hand. I violently tossed it aside.

I huffed and angrily stood to leave the office when he put his hand on my shoulder. I yanked away, and turned around. I stepped deep into his space, and said, "Do not fucking touch me, dude, or..." I turned to leave and then added, "Try me!" I had had enough of being tested in one day.

In the bedroom, I found Brandon asleep in our bed. He was obviously hidden under the covers accounting for how I missed him earlier. He was supposed to be at my grandmother's for the weekend. Had I known he was home I would have been home for our Friday pizza and board game night, and not in a hotel arguing with his mother. Rather than argue with *Buck Rogers*, I took Brandon to his room and lay him in his red Ferrari bed. I returned to my own water bed and found my enemy on the other side of it with his head rested on his lap.

"You're not going to sleep," he told me, as I put on my *Waiting to Exhale* CD.

The CD severely irritated him. He knew that I loved to send subliminal messages via music.

"Look, fall back," I told him.

I had left my tax-paying citizen persona in the garage. I relaxed, pulled my luxe sheets over me and opened James Patterson's latest thriller, *Cross*.

Albeit, I was not comprehending the words fully, I was on the second paragraph when my novel took flight across the room. Before it landed, I was on top of Dajuan and prepared to drop a barbaric blow to his eye socket when my eyes looked deeply into his. I could see, feel, taste, touch, and smell his sorrow. He was hurt. Badly! Hurt that he'd hurt me. Hurt that he tore a hole into our already controversial home.

"Hit me." He seethed. "Go ahead. I'm not going to fight you back. Go ahead. Fuck me up!"

His eyes reddened and tears rained down his face.

All I could do was let all of my bottled up tears break through the dam and look directly into his eyes wholeheartedly and asked, "Why me?" And I seriously needed an answer.

He pulled me to him and embraced me tightly.

"I never meant to hurt you, baby," he whispered, and kissed my ear lobe. "I am so sorry."

He kissed my lips gently. Once. Twice. And then we shared a passionate kiss. I immediately had a flash back...

CHAPTER 13

...It had been a game of cat and mouse. It had been lovely. It had made me feel sixteen again when I was a Germantown boxing star, and had accepted that I was at least bisexual. Our meeting each other couldn't have been written any better by Shakespere.

It was spring and Aramis and I had been at a cocktail party amongst the tri-state area rich. We had been celebrating the first issue of *Brotherly Love*, a rag for the affluent African American Philadelphian man. The old money was there. The movers and shakers, too.

We left them at the downtown Ritz Carlton and walked to the Tower Records store at Broad and Chestnut. Inside Aramis perused rap albums while I searched the upstairs DVD new releases. I found nothing and went to the rap section. Yes, I immediately noticed Dajuan, but I typically ignored what I couldn't have. I never stalked straight boys or forced them to feel uncomfortable around me. However, Aramis informed me that Dajuan was admiring me. Allegedly. Aramis loved to point out down low men or prospective ones. I ignored Aramis' wishful thinking, and casually checked for myself. He may or may not have been right.

I had been taught that you didn't have evidence, if you couldn't put it through the five senses test. So I proceeded with Aramis in tow to the check-out counter.

The clerk bagged my Lil Wayne *Carter 2* CD as Dajuan exited the store.

It was night, Sunday, and downtown was not a ghost town, but if you did not live in the area, you were not there. Aramis cooked up the idea to stalk Dajuan. I was committing a crime before I took the bar exam. Dajuan looked back occasionally and Aramis assured me that Dajuan adored the chase, but being the coy guy that I am, I did not comprehend my straight best friend's ideology.

Two lights down on Walnut Street, Dajuan turned right and one minute later so did we. Boy were we in for a surprise. Dajuan was thirty feet from the corner looking at the Banana Republic display and I was prepared to continue past him, but his eyes were locked onto me like an Iraqi stealth bomber behind Air Force One. Aramis counted to three very quietly, and he then said, "What's up?"

Not to me.

To Dajuan.

I wanted to disappear.

We ended up exchanging numbers and the rest was history.

CHAPTER 14

Back from memory lane, I had to face that daunting demon. I rolled from on top of Dajuan and was still shaken up. He glared at me and then scooted closer to me. He wrapped his arms around me tightly. I was glad that he didn't talk. I didn't either. We both needed a drink and to think. One careless word and someone was going to be choked out. And he knew it, too. He did not speak. There was a loving sway to our embrace which screamed so loudly at us. The million dollar question was, were we listening?

I sat back on the headboard and Dajuan rested his head on my lap. He could not face me. I knew that the music taunted him, so I grabbed the remote control and cued R. Kelly's *Chocolate Factory. I Will Never Leave* played and I cued Ginuwine's *Differences* to follow. Dajuan began to tremble and held me tighter. He spoke to me. He did not look at me and his words were a whisper.

"I do not know what happens after this, but know that I am sorry and if we end right now, do not ever meet with a nothing-less disgrace like myself. And if you do, don't fuck with him."

"I know that I said some crazy things, but I didn't mean them. And I am sorry that I called you nothing-less."

"Don't take it back. You meant them and if I look deep within, you would be right about them. I have never loved anyone, but my mother, more than you. When I met you, you gave me the drive and determination to conquer any goal and encouragement to achieve anything. You became my rock and I threw that all away when I cheated."

"You fucked up, man. Bad. Naturally, you're more than nothing because you are everything to me. And, you're not a disgrace. Sorry about them crazy comments."

"You're out saving the asses of criminals and grinding hard to own your profession. You don't bother me with my tours, so I need to grow up on that note. You always tell me that I am the best thing that has happened to you, but sometimes your mouth can be nasty as hell. You're such a contradiction. Only the understanding can understand the confusing. Telling me that Aramis was mad at me meant nothing, only your words did, and only to a certain degree. I have been through a lot. I have a heart built of Kevlar, which means it's hard to get in, and not much that I care about."

"See that is the problem. You called me a contradiction, but you never fully open up to me, Dajuan. You tell me what you want me to know and keep the rest bottled up like I am a mind reader. Keep things real and we can avoid a lot of things. It's been four and a half years now, man. I can be trusted, you know? I hate that you be on this psychopathic avoidance kick. You have to trust me. I have earned it. You often elude that something happened to you when you were a kid, but you never tell me, and I never push you too tell me. When you're ready to tell me, you will."

"Look, going back and forth is for girls. Even though I am a Taurus and we're hard as hell, but I give in. I'm the best lover you have ever had and, the truest, by the way. At least, I was straight up and down and told you that I cheated. I mean, I commend you 'cause you will destroy a person's feelings and try to rebuild what you have destroyed. You inevitably crush them, but at the same time you cater to them. If I get any deeper, I'll begin to sound like a psycho and if I do that, you'll think I'm trying to challenge your intelligence, and besides getting deeper will only permit me to unearth more of myself, which I certainly cannot do. As a loner, I keep everything to thine own self."

He gave me a conspiratorial smirk, which I wanted to slap off his face.

"See that is the shit I'm talking about. How are you in love with me and be alone? You really need to get that straight if..."

"Anyway."

"See, there's the avoidance."

"Hopefully, you accept my apology and we can move on. Just dwell deep into the words and understand what's mixed in this soup. You showed me a lot of things I had never seen and took me places that I had never been. A lot of your friends never show you gratitude, but I do. If you have my old letters and poems at your grand mom's, I bet you could read any one of them and still smile," he said and totally ignored my comment. "Can you please forgive me?"

That was the typical fashion that he avoided the real problem. Like a lamebrain, I always gave in despite not wanting to. I have an avoidance problem too. I avoided conflicts with family and friends. Sometimes I pampered them just to keep the peace. And when I spoke my mind, I was called mean, cold-hearted, and shiftless. My harsh words were usually just very honest, blunt and direct. They were to encourage better behavior and to build the receiver. Sometimes the ones I really loved felt that I was always talking down on them, but I would never intentionally do that.

"I'mma let this go," I said to him. "And..."

He pressed his lips to mine to silence me. "No, ands. I can handle this. And don't ever act like you want to fight me again. I am still a canon."

Nothing else needed to be said.

But, wait there was more. The inevitable make-up sex. I shall refrain from narrating the delicious details of that encounter, considering I am sure you're not interested in all that. In fact, I will keep that policy until, THE END.

CHAPTER 15

Dave and Busters shut the games down at precisely midnight. The family entertainment complex crashed loudly onto the Delaware Avenue waterfront nearly ten years earlier. In January 2007, Dave and Busters had two restaurants, pool table area, poker tables, sports bar, and over 200 arcade games that remained active. No dollar amount was spared to attract hamburger- and FF-crazed kids who adored gaming. The same was true for the relaxing porterhouse type.

Outside of Dave and Buster's, a short stroll to the north, adults partied at nightclubs featuring crowds that ranged from techno, house, hip-hop, and country. On every night of the week, Delaware Avenue and Spring Garden Street were choked with inebriated club hoppers creating an adorable atmosphere for a robbery diversion.

Ordinarily, Dave and Buster's financial auditors were notorious for counting the receivables, verifying that all employees' time cards were calculated, updating inventory and securing cash in the cash room on the main level of the compound, all by two a.m. Too bad that that night was anything but ordinary.

Before the cash room door buzzed, the building lights faded to black, and emergency back-up lights flickered to life. They were immediately murdered.

"Power failure. Everyone respond accordingly," an off duty FBI agent said into a walkie-talkie.

Thirty-one-year-old Quadir Gibson, a four-year hard-nosed gumshoe, was privately hired by Dave and Buster's for protection. He was never without the Burberry trench, sneer, ethics stamped on his yellowish forehead, or adroit police impracticalities glued to his aura. He had deep eyes that were slanted. Not Asian slanted, but African American slanted. In the Germantown neighborhood where he had grown up, he had been given the street moniker, China. He even continued to play basketball at the Happy Hollow Playground.

In addition to orchestrating Dave and Buster's shut-down program twice a week for the extra cash, he had a serious case of helping free-spirited women with their nightly shut down programs, as well. They couldn't resist his six-feet-four-inches of stone.

Agent Gibson hopped up from his chair and told security, "I need these cameras up now!"

He violently slammed a paw on the table and caused it to collapse. Everything was all over the floor. He did not want that problem, but it was solely his problem.

Dave and Buster's security could have rivaled the Secret Service duties at the White House. They were heavily armed and patrolled the outside perimeter in uniform, but inside they donned suits and ear pieces. All of the men had confirmed that their areas were secure. That was a bold-faced lie. An impressively dressed hoodlum was in stairwell two using an unconscious sentry's walkie-talkie to radio in the clear signal. The goon carried a SIG Sauer P226 semi and was prepared to put it to carefully trained use.

Agent Gibson barked into the walkie talkie for the accountants that delivered the cash intake to the cash room to, "Get that cash secured, now."

It would be secured, but not by any Dave and Buster employees, though.

CHAPTER 16

It was hard for Aramis to go back to sleep. After his bladder needed emptying, he could not get back to dream land. He turned on the TV and entertained himself with a debate about which teams would reach the Superbowl on ESPN. Certainly, that would bore him to sleep and render him paralyzed. He snuggled in his bed to get back asleep.

Not!

He flipped the channel to BET and became immediately aroused. Uncut was on and the females in the video being shown had on risqué bikinis, which were artfully two sizes too small. One girl just had two pasties over her nipples. Another was bent over and forced her ass cheeks to applaud the rapper who was spitting lyrics behind her. *Wow*, Aramis thought. A caramel-colored vixen was on the hood of a 1958 Cadillac with her legs wrapped around her neck; her hairy bush packed neatly into a red thong, which would prompt any man to do what Aramis did next.

He slipped his boxers and tank top off and began to grope himself. He became swollen and was about to pleasure himself and the video ended, like a five minute lap dance. To add to that damage, BET aired a commercial and not another video.

Times like that forced Aramis to call up memories that he wished to blow into oblivion. Her name was, Marisa Davenport. Her occupation, hair stylist. Her last boyfriend, Aramis Reed. Had she been there still investing in their relationship, he would not need heat from Philadelphia Gas Works, nor long johns from JC Penney. She would be right there to keep his body warm and she had a special hideaway to cool his erection.

Aramis looked around his bedroom. The bedside clock read: 12:12. He was engrossed in his career so much so that all he had time for was casual dating of the one night stand variety. He wanted to prostrate himself at the feet of the pioneers who gave the world the Internet. It was those times that he could log onto a plethora of Internet sites to engage in exhaustive, animal, love-making with someone's wife--the best kind because they were very discreet with no strings attached. Just the way that he wanted it--very casual and non-committal.

He reached for his laptop, which was on the side of the bed where Marisa used to sleep. His laptop was his life. He pushed a key on the key board, and looked to see who of his buddies were online. His Buddy List was broken down into the following groups in descending order: Family, Close Friends, Internet Homies, Philly Booty, NJ Booty, DE Booty, ATL Booty, Miami, Booty, Detroit Booty, Chi-town Booty, and LA Booty. He had booty calls in all of those cities, ready in the event that he visited there. The Internet Homies were all males and a token female that he had met online and shared photos of Internet harlots. No longer did he have to scour clubs, bars, grocery stores, or even church to find a woman. All he needed was the world wide web, and at that time of night, it was choc full with co-ed prowlers who desired to misbehave, and he was ready to join them.

Aramis had 26 photos of himself on his computer to send to any chick who wanted to play. In 24 of them, he was nude. He was a lanky, well-built, 31-year-old man. He had soft, black, curly hair, a thin mustache and was otherwise clean shaven. His beard was optional. A sinister physique was clad under smooth caramel skin, with a penis that was porn-industry worthy. If asked, he would confess that he perceived himself as: A journalist, free-lancer, greenhorn, specializing in investigative reporting and desiring to crack a case that he could write a novel about.

He was a club hopper, who knew all of the popular hang outs in all major cities. His unconditional best friend was Ravonne Lemmelle, the up and coming ruler of criminal defense. A transplant from Newark, Delaware after his adoption at age 14, he was an aggressive person, blessed with the drive to excel.

All of that would be true. But none of the women he met on the Internet would learn any of that. To his Internet family and all of the women that he had met, he was: Handsome_Caramel1. If first names were required, he was Antonio, Ant for short. No last name was required. Antonio claimed to be 23, a Temple student, a drinker, not drug user, always used protection even with oral sex, and never kissed and told.

It only took 23-minutes for him to become bored with typing, so he went to Operation Mr. Telephone Man and called a phone chat line.

CHAPTER 17

The bookkeepers inside of the cash room heard a single knock at the door. One of them looped the table full of currency counters in pitch darkness, and knocked three times in response. That was the protocol for a power failure situation. After a precise three-second pause, there was the same three knocks with the same melody as the bookkeeper's. Only in that situation were keys used to open the door.

As the steel door pushed open, all of the Dave and Busters employees in the room were in a dead-like sleep before they hit the floor.

The three robbers were dressed in dark Kevlar armor that covered their entire bodies. They wore night vision goggles and masks. The masks protected them from the gas distributed through the room by the fourth robber who posed as a bookkeeper. All of the Dave and Busters employees were useless. The gas effects would wear off, but by then the knaves would be gone with the cash. All of it.

Cowered in the corner of the room was Destiny Fernandez, a half-black half Puerto Rican, recently employed by the gaming establishment. She too wore a mask provided by the man who hired her to betray her employer. The thieves began to stow the cash in waterproof backpacks.

When all of the cash was safely packed, the robbers slithered out of the complex to the parking garage, which partially hung over the Delaware River. The river separated New Jersey from Pennsylvania. An idling boat awaited them. They reached the end of the garage and in synchronized fashion, they leaped over the four foot barrier and dropped six feet into the boat. They all landed feline-like on all fours. They were all women.

SATURDAY, JANUARY 6, 2007

CHAPTER 18

At 11a.m., the three of us looked like three buddies--the kind of baby boomers accepted as members of a fancy, exclusive men's-only club. At the kitchen table, beneath the exquisite cookware-chandelier, we wore comfortable pajamas and enjoyed breakfast prepared by Daddy D. We were the kind of pals who worked on Wall Street and shared insider secrets habitually. We had a bond that was unbreakable.

"Can we go to the Art Museum?" Brandon asked.

He knew that Saturday was a father and son outing day.

"And, Daddy R, can I have my pizza, too? I waited up in your bed, fell asleep there and all of a sudden I woke up in my car."

He flashed me large, bubbly, brown eyes like his horrible mother's and tiny white teeth. For a five-year-old, Brandon was beyond normal comprehension. He was not a child prodigy, but beneath his tight curly hair, a prodigious development loomed.

"And, Daddy D, you fell asleep on my favorite part of March of the Penguins," he added and sipped his pineapple/orange juice.

Was this five-year-old, going on 35, chiding us? He probably was, knowing him. "'Pizza too," as if I was going to get my ass kicked if I didn't buy him pizza. Brandon thought being enrolled in boxing and Judo class meant that he could beat the world.

I reminded him, "King B, we went there last week. How 'bout a different one?"

"Besides," Dajuan added. "We are going to see Dream Girls with Beyonce in it and then the arcade."

"But I don't want to go to those places and I have a good reason. Last week, we missed the basement Egyptian part, Dad," Brandon reported to us.

He had a whine in his voice, but the adults at the table were not fooled one bit.

"King B, next week we are going to see a play at Freedom Theater about Egypt," I reminded him. "You'll get to see it live then."

"Will I get to see Nefertiti," he asked, excitedly. "I'm going to marry a girl just like Nefertiti when I turn 13. Right, Daddy D?" he asked, and looked for confirmation.

"Eighteen," Dajuan told his son, which informed me that they had already had this chat.

And I really wanted to know why my five-year-old was looking forward to marriage and not second grade.

"But I thought African boys had the rite thing at 13. I'm African, so I'll marry then."

"Slow down, Casanova," I interjected. "You're an African living on American soil and American law does not allow you to marry at 13 unless you have my permission. And there's no way I am condoning a marriage for you that young."

"Screw, President Bush."

"What?" I said in shock. "Watch your damn mouth. Where the hell did you learn that, Brainiac?" I asked with a wicked eye on Dajuan.

I did not promote profanity in front on my child, nor did I assault him. I have a powerful mouth that gets through to him without beatings. He was the kid. I was the parent. We're not pals in the school-yard sense.

"CNN," Brandon confessed. "The Venezuela president called Bush and America devils. I thought that was mean, but Bush is being a devil if I can't marry at 13, Dad."

He was very calm and oblivious to the depth of his ideology.

"CNN is your work," Dajuan told me, pointing a bite size square of bacon and cheese omelet on his fork at me.

He had that one-of-a-kind stupid grin on his face.

"I'm smart, Dad. I remember everything that I hear," Brandon confirmed.

Thanks for the heads up, I thought.

"But how did you remember, Venezuela?" I asked and totally wanted to know.

Brandon replied, "My Spanish teacher's name is Victory. Venezuela begins with V, so I remember it as if Victor said it."

"Ooooo-K!" Dajuan said. "I guess he's going to Harvard like his dad."

"I have two daddies," Brandon said smiling. "May I be excused?"

"Yup, but can you tell me six times six?" Dajuan asked.

That was their little game, which I was not invited to. Before Dajuan discovered that he had a voice, he wanted to teach math. It was his favorite subject and Brandon was his favorite student.

"Thirty-six, Daddy D," he replied and dropped his dish into the dishwasher. "Believe me, I think I know the whole times table chart," he said with the analytical flair of Pythagoras.

His tiny feet slapped the marble floor as he left the kitchen.

I heard the telephone ringing and snatched it up in the living room and greeted the caller.

A smooth, husky, unidentifiable voice asked, "Are you watching the noon news, Ravonne?"

"No," I said and then asked, "Who is this?"

"You ought to be! Channel Six Action News," the female said.

The line then went dead.

I immediately picked up the TV remote and the projector displayed the news on the very white wall above the love seat. Newscaster Calvin Bridgeford and his brown toupee were showcased with the Dave and Buster's entertainment mecca as a back drop. I only caught the tail end of his report:

"...Police are currently searching for Destiny Fernandez of the North Philadelphia Bad Lands area for questioning about the robbed Dave and Busters. She went missing, either voluntarily, or at the hands of bandits who have made off with an undisclosed amount of cash late last night at the gaming establishment. Anyone with clues should contact Crime Stoppers at..."

The anchor moved on to a story about the murderer, Mr. 357 being back in Philadelphia for seconds and already responsible for the death of Dorothy Kincade. I would've bet dollars to donuts that Mr. 357 was responsible for the shipment of her body to the FBI office and the robbery, as well. I was in a state of confusion.

For starters, I needed to know who had just called my home and advised me to catch the broadcast, and, why? I dialed *69 to activate the call-back feature. The caller was out of the area. I then consulted the caller ID, which proved useless.

Belatedly, I wondered could I, or my family, be in danger. I typically did not panic, but my life had been threatened on occasion. Although, I may have been acting prematurely, I activated Operation Disappearance.

CHAPTER 19

He was built like a V-12 engine and tested his legs horse power in downtown Philadelphia, totally having forgotten the slaying of Dorothy Kincade. She had done salacious sexual acts utilizing an aerobics Swiss ball in her law office. She performed the same acts for the senior partner of her department and received a bonus. Mr. 357 rewarded her with a sliced throat, decapitating her prior to tearing her body into parts and FED-EXing her to the local FBI office.

He would have enjoyed having an odometer showcase the kilometers that he had walked in search of gainful employment. Mr. 357 had covered the radius from Front Street up to 22nd and from Vine to South Streets. That far, he had been sans good luck.

The winter air was biting, and justified his husky jacket. He waltzed down Chestnut Street and weaved in and out of weekend shoppers, watching everything around him. He wore a faux set of teeth and a faux groomed goatee. His tan was painted on. Onlookers spotted his lanky gait a block away. He was methodical and confident, so why was his pursuit of gainful employment an upstream expedition. Probably because the moment he signed the W-2 tax form, he would robotically put in a plan to effectively rob the joint.

Everything else in life would be secondary. He wouldn't taste food. He'd ignore sleep. And sex would not be pleasurable. He would be consumed with the business at hand: finding the company's weak links.

He walked into the Lord and Taylor department store and strolled steadily, smiled, and nodded professionally: a Brazilian gentleman out looking for a job, or a bargain. He passed carousels of perfume and make-up before he arrived at the women footwear department.

Mr. 357 eye-fucked a sexy pair of legs on a woman. Her hair looked naturally long and was pulled into to ponytail, which allowed her face to glow.

He knew that he was to approach her. She was his target. He did a general assessment. She didn't look wealthy, but successful. No engagement ring, but she was undoubtedly married. *A former cheerleader and easy bed mate*, he thought. But he had instructions not to fuck her or even attempt to. Her normal boobs exuded confidence, considering a tit raise was quite cheap. She glided across the department and wore a whiff of authority and power.

The woman tried on a pair of navy pumps that were dull for the suit she wore. She caught him looking and he made his move.

"Are you shoe shopping as a hobby, or looking to compliment your suit?" he asked in a heavy South American accent.

She raised a shoe with a broken heel.

"Broke it trying to jump over a puddle of water from the melted snow."

"Where's a gentleman when you need one?" he asked, charmingly. "The shoes you have selected are well...cute...but these," he held out a pair of crimson pumps, "would definitely do your suit justice."

She looked deep into his eyes and became enveloped by his sexy baritone voice beneath the chit-chat surrounding them. It seemed for a moment that they were all alone.

Intimately, he said, "Just try it."

She sat and tried on the display. When the salesman returned with the mate, Mr. 357 grabbed the box, kneeled in front of her and slipped the shoe onto her feet like a seasoned salesman. When he looked up, he caught her admiring him. That was what she was supposed to do. She knew he'd be coming. That was the way it was supposed to be. Both of them pretending to be oblivious to this meeting.

"This works better," she said and sashayed to the mirror. "Your interruption was smooth and inviting," she said and complimented him as she was instructed to do. "How long have you..."

She froze in front of the full length mirror. She was speechless. A seductive twist and twirl, very mode-lesque, before she walked back toward Mr. 357, but he had vanished. She searched for him when he tapped her shoulder with a matching bag.

By the way that she tucked the bag under her arm, a photographer should have been there to snap a Vogue cover. Her eyes gleamed as if he was a gift from the fashion God--a gambit that could label her a fashionista. Mr. 357 had a look in his eyes that a vampire had when it wrapped it's fangs into the throat of some unsuspecting dame. She trusted him, he thought. She knew that he was full of authority, business and power--all of the things that her husband lacked. That was their common interest; her husband had wronged both of them.

She dug into her purse and he spied a flask. She retrieved a gold plated business card holder and proffered her claim to fame.

"You must be new to this city," she said and waved a flamboyant hand in the air. "Men like you were not made in this tired town."

Just like that, she was off to the register to purchase her shoes.

Neither of them knew that they were participating in a game to destroy her husband. With his duty done, Mr. 357 made his way to the Market Street exit of the store. He looked at the business card, knowing that Ariel Greenland believed that he was a transplant from another city and he made no attempt to correct her. He would also take her up on her offer to give her a call. Why else would she have passed along her business card--written in a cute script with a black and white photo of her on the back? He would get with her and she would believe that he was new to the city. Problem was, the masterful Mr. 357 had no idea that he would be believing all of her lies, as well.

CHAPTER 20

The Jones-Lemmelle family had gone to the Egyptian exhibit at the Philadelphia Museum of Art, despite my protests. We followed that up at the Please Touch Museum, where Dajuan and I had to chase Brandon around in tyke fashion. We had a mock Boston Tea Party with the cast of Alice in Wonderland, and, we played supermarket clerks in the museum's mock grocery store. Afterward, we had brick oven pizza at Bertucci's and by 8 p.m, I was sprawled out on my luxuriant bed with Brandon curled under me drifting to Lala Land. Usually, I would have sent him to his room, but with that morning's phone call flashing before my eyes all day, I was very protective of mine. The only reason I detailed my Saturday was to assure you that I did not chase crime every minute of the day. I did have a life outside of my *ami de cour*.

For the life of me, I could not fathom a solid ground for the call. Could it have been a wrong number? No, the caller said my name. Hadn't mentioned anything else to identify me. I was taking no chances, though. Earlier I had Clinton Armond, security chieftan for all of the Prudential Building, install tracer and recording devices in my home. I had also left several messages for agent Quadir Gibson to contact me. I grabbed my cordless and decided to give him another try.

"Gibson." He came on the line as if I had interrupted a meal consisting of carbs, protein, and creatine. He was a man as stiff as a Rodin bust who wore slim suits to showcase a steroid-induced physique. Word around was that he was a terrible ladies man who needed to be spaded.

"Ravonne Lemmelle, here--"

"What the hell do you want?" he said, recognizing that I was that new barrister in town that reduced him to squash the only time that I had the honor of battling him during a mock trial at Germantown High School.

I was a freshman and he was a junior and that made it all the more devastating.

"I tried reaching you a few times. Left a couple of messages, to no avail."

"I am on a big case. What you want?"

"I know. The Dave and Buster robbery."

"If you're thinking of defending that case, I will bury you alive, Lemmelle, I swear."

"I love being threatened, Quadir--"

"Agent Gibson. I have earned that."

That guy was a study in egoism, but I let him relish in his glory without rebuttal.

"Agent Gibson at exactly 12:09 this afternoon, I received an anonymous call informing me that I should tune in to the midday news."

He did not reply for what seemed like an eon.

"Funny how you could nail down the exact minute of the call. Would you happen to have the seconds, too?"

I didn't tell the asshole that as an attorney I paid attention to small things like that.

"Listen, the time was displayed on the goddamn screen during the news along with the temperature. It was 32-degrees. I was a little concerned that I'd received a crank call on my home number, which is unlisted."

"You have resources. Find out. I do not handle pranks."

"You're the resource and despite us being on different sides of the fence, don't ever forget that. If I receive any other calls telling me to tune into a broadcast of a crime like I did for the Dave and Buster's caper, I'll be sure to use the media as a resource and start a whole shit storm over there. I'm sure SAC Lemeux will love that. Chow, China!"

I hung up and was pissed. I know he hated being called China in those days, having left the hood and all that jazz.

Dajuan stood in the bedroom doorway.

"Let me guess. No one cares about the call because you're a defense attorney, as if you're not a citizen."

"This is very crazy," I said. "Take him to his room."

Dajuan tossed Brandon over his shoulder, and took him to his room. He quickly returned.

He said, "Tomorrow we are getting guns." Dajuan sat next to me. He turned on the TV to Sports Center as if what he said was logical and normal conversation.

"What the hell are you talking about?"

"We need precaution protection, PP," he said and smiled.

He made a gun with his hand.

"No guns in the house. So Brandon can play with it. Hell no!"

"Man, Brandon is not going to play with a gun. Carry it when you're out. Keep it in the trunk when you park in the garage here and at work."

"I can defend myself, Dajuan."

"Dawg, Judo black belts and boxing do not stop bullets."

"You're jumping the gun," I said and chuckled. "This may all be a mistake," I said and leaned on his shoulder.

"Aiight. You're right. Maybe. But. Okay, not yet. One more incident of any kind and we're handling business. I'm itching to bust a clown's ass for playing on my phone. Yup, that small."

"Yeah!"

"And you better tell me. In fact, promise."

"Why?"

"Promise."

He then stacked on top of that, "I know you'd try to save the day on your own not to worry about me. You have priors."

"Okay, I promise, dammit!"

"Why didn't I get a prank call?" he asked and huffed.

"You could get one," I said and rolled on top of him. I lay between his legs.

"Really!"

"They'll be obscene," I said kissing down his chest.

When I reached his belly button, he asked, "When do I get the first call?"

I licked along the waistline of his boxers and used my teeth to pull them down his legs and over his feet. They landed on the floor, and I then said, "Right now," and began to place my call.

CHAPTER 21

Anyone who missed that party would go mad. One-hundred-seven of Philadelphia's finest converged center stage, dressed to impress. Quite a few were stoned out of their minds like any party goer who had been drinking, smoking, and snorting at that hour of a Saturday night. The crowd was busy eating, laughing, two-stepping, and spitting game to get themselves into someone's bed.

The guests had many things in common. They were all mutual acquaintances and professionals of the same trade. The party could have been happening in Chicago, New York, or St. Louis. It happened that that ghetto-fabulous event took place in Shannon McKeithan's pad in a Chestnut Hill expansive tudor. Chestnut Hill was an area next to Germantown and the northernmost point in Philadelphia before entering Montgomery County.

Suspect--Shannon's street moniker, given to him for his brushes with the law--had only one reason to host this highly anticipated mansion party. Like many street pharmacists, Suspect liked to pack his pad with men of the same cloth to verify the distinct difference between them and his self. At that moment he was glad. He had chilled in the kitchen with Low-Down and a voluptuous vixen at that fortunate moment. Both men wanted to awake to her in the afternoon.

Lawrence Miller--better known as Low Down--had his undivided attention on the slender, expertly built, Dominique Dorsey. Otherwise, he might have noticed the suspicious activity happening around his homey's pad. Of all the drug dealers gathered in the home, Low Down was most qualified to get a handle on the conundrum before it commenced. But, Dr. Lawrence Miller, too, had had as much fun as the other men chasing the cat.

Standing in the kitchen with an unmolested bottle of Courvoisier, Suspect grinned at the string that the tasty Dominique dangled in his comrade's face. Her tawny-yellowish complexion and ample tits must have been enhanced in his drunken state, that illusion of playboyism which got him through Germantown High School and catapulted him through UCLA undergrad, Georgetown Law and U of Penn Law School to his corrupt post as chief legal advisor for the thriving Philadelphia illegal narcotics circle. If Low Down did get the pussy, at least it would be kept in the family. Suspect and Low Down were cousins. Suspect was by no means jealous of Low Down for having Dominique's attention. When she first stepped into the pad, very fashionably late and noticeable, like most of the blood hounds had tried his game. He must have acquired his game from Milt & Bradley. It looked like the attorney was about to interrogate the woman in the bedroom.

The hip-hop blasted from the stereo speakers and drowned all of the chatter. Holding bottle and glass up in the air, Suspect glided into the living room and sank into an armchair, which was snuggly perched in the alcove by the bay window. The bevy of youngsters was amazingly animated. Suspect admired his work. He gestured at the bottle and one of the kids happily helped himself. Unselfishly, he poured rounds about the room until the bottle was empty. Ideas of his next business endeavor was more intoxicating than the booze, it seemed. Astonishingly, Suspect uncapped a bottle of Dom Perignon.

The "kids" weren't young, they were seven or eight years short of Suspect's 30. At 30 he couldn't count the miles he had traveled pushing his product. He had many experiences through his life and was wholly dedicated to his current status. On the contrary, as time progressed, he became more and more aware of the truth of the king-pin credo that the game was to be played thoroughly until the end, and it must end. It consoled him that, however dull his love life, there would always be new business to invest, new stocks to buy low and sell high, and crack houses where street pharmacists and their brothers grind to eat. He had vastly set himself aside from the masses. He was regarded as a High Priest in the game, despite some rivals' suspicion that he had to be a rat, to keep getting off. But professional paranoia did not affect his drive to conquer poverty.

"Suspect, lil buddy," Low Down said, smiling. "Just what the fuck do you want now?"

"Don of the Century."

"You have the conceit, Shannon, but you don't have the looks."

That was not a lie. He was not as handsome as Low Down. Thirty years of occupying his lanky body, and carrying his drop-dead ugly face was no longer one of his concerns. Money had introduced him to more vaginas close up than a life-long gynecologist.

Suspect took the Dom P. to the head, and relaxed to get a bar of the dialogue probing between the young ballers. The street dealers were talking about where cooking the product, running game on women and managing a corner met, that road of "ghetto significance."

Suspect slumped lower in his recliner, stretched out his legs, and sipped Don Perignon appreciatively.

* * *

Across the street from the party sat another large home. It too was set back from the sidewalk. Many windows faced the street side of the house. From the second story balcony overlooking the circular driveway, Suspect's party was clearly visible.

The man sat in a porch chair, peering across the street at the assholes partying. It was too cold for anyone to be roaming about outside. That was excellent. He had had plenty of time setting up. The home owners of the balcony were not at home. He lighted a Newport and then crossed the balcony and retrieved the rifle against the wall.

The rifle was a target rifle, which he had sawed off. It was crafted to exceed all requirements for long range, high power target shooting at miniature game. He had shaved off a few inches to reduce the weight and size. It had a large butt, but he had large hands. A telescopic eye was mounted to the gun. He focused the sight on Suspect's party, so that the crosshairs were on the alcove which gave a beautiful view of the party goers. Some of them would be going someplace, but not another party.

* * *

The party had been hot as usual. Everyone had a hunger for networking and intimacy and lively appetites. The best of the southern buffet was gone. Weed induced hunger pangs had already cleaned two bowls of jerk chicken that a local Jamaican caterer provided. Chocolate, creamy cupcakes--food for chocolate, creamy babes--had been destroyed, too. Regiments of empty champagne bottles, wine bottles, and beer bottles were lined militarily along the bar table. The sharpened aroma of drugs seeped in the air. No doubt, the bedrooms were being occupied by some young buck rocking some diva's boots. Now that Suspect had slung the door wide open to all, he was cured of his need to be sociable and drifted smoothly into chill mood in hopes that they would start to leave.

At that instant, the bullet of a rifle split the arm chair an inch from Suspect's brain and chopped deep into the upholstery. The next bullet did not miss Suspect's occipital.

Low Down reached out for Dominique. Astonishment froze on the face of a boy next to Low Down as the bullet sliced through his chest. Blood spurted from Pooh onto Dominique and she grabbed Low Down tightly. Two down, one to go. That happened quickly. Low Down received a shot in the back of his head and regurgitated blood onto Dominique's silky hair. Now that was low down.

Amazingly, the hip hop was silenced by terrified screams.

Sunday, January 7, 2007

CHAPTER 22

The annoying ring pelted me like being stoned to death in Times Square by the New Year's Eve crowd. I emoted, turned over and decided to ignore the caller. Then I had an epiphany. I heard Brandon's electric toothbrush whirling and I knew he would answer the phone. What if the caller was... *Fuck*! I groaned and angrily snatched up the phone from the cradle.

"What?" I asked the caller, groggily.

"Ravonne Lemmelle!"

Oh shit! I was suddenly alive and clear headed. "Granny?"

"Who you whatting? I know you have caller ID." I imagined her in her Sunday's best on her way to Sunday school at New Inspirational Baptist Church.

"Nobody. It's seven-thirty, though, Granny."

"I know morning is not a good time for you, which amazes me how you manage to be in an office at seven some mornings and deal with Brandon."

"I lock myself in my office and sleep until I can cope with people. If I have court, I feel sorry for the DA. Brandon inherited my sense of time."

She laughed lightly and then quickly changed her tone. "I'm sorry, but this is an emergency. Wydell, Odella James' boy was arrested for a triple murder."

"When?" I asked and furrowed my brow and scratched my balls.

Wydell was just at the hospital yesterday with his mother to visit his brother who was shot when he called me to thank me for visiting his brother on Friday after the Mark Artis acquittal. Now he was arrested, and I was willing to bet money that this involved revenge.

"They kicked Odella's door in about four a.m. I was up praying and then I heard the police radios outside. Guns everywhere, and they drug him naked out of the bed with some gal. They found a gun."

"Sounds like more than an emergency."

"They need your help."

"Constance, you told them I'd help didn't you?"

"Well..."

"Granny, my firm will never go for a *pro bono* case right now."

"How 'bout *gratis* then," she said and chuckled. I was not laughing, though. "Just go and talk to them. Please."

"Okay, but no promises. You better pray for them. After the Mark Artis mess, a murder is not exactly on my menu right now."

"Thank you."

"Love ya."

"I love you, too."

Dajuan had eyeballed me as I talked. Ms. Pearl jumped on his side of the bed. I tried to pick her up and she wiggled out of my arms, licked her leg and wiped her face to cleanse herself of my touch, and yawned. She was obviously still perturbed that I ignored her on Friday. Nerve, right? I'd make it up to her at Jacque Cuisine. The 4-star restaurant had a posh patio where leashed pets could feast on delights from the pet menu. I bet she'd circle my feet like Jack the Ripper outside of the home of a co-ed if I pulled out her leash.

"Get up," I mumbled to Dajuan and nudged him.

Outside it was raining fiercely and I was absolutely over that. For one, Granny wanted me to go to the James' on my rest day. More importantly, the Eagles would play the Giants in the playoffs. I had intended to watch the game with my two homeboys: Brandon and Dajuan. I knew that once I made an appearance at the James', I'd find myself at a precinct obtaining Wydell's story, and later at a bail hearing at the bare minimum. Then I'll be conferencing with my contacts at the Public Defenders Association to see that he gets special care.

Dajuan found his boxers on the floor and went into our private bathroom for his perfunctory wake-up piss. He gargled some mouthwash, brushed his teeth and returned with a mint mask on his face. I turned to the doorway and there was Brandon also in a mint mask and boxers, which were as big as a sheet of paper.

"So, this is what it's like not to have jobs?" I joked.

"It's Sunday," Dajuan told me. "We do this weekly, but you're usually sleeping."

"Yeah!" Brandon said, hopping on the bed. "It's the Eagles color green."

"How sweet?" I said and slipped on my boxers under the covers before going into the bathroom. I did a quick bathroom tour and met them in the kitchen.

"Listen, I have to take care of something for my grand mom, so I need you to TIVO the game."

"Aiight," Brandon replied.

"No one was talking to you, brainiac," I said and tickled him. "Tickle monster...tickle monster," I said tickling him more.

"That was her talking to you?" Dajuan asked. "I knew it had to be because you did not go postal," he told me.

He turned and asked Brandon, "What kind of cereal, King B?"

"My favorite."

"Honey Combs coming right up."

"Not no more," Brandon said, playing with a Leap Frog electronic spelling game. He mimicked the computerized voice, "Spell house. H-O-U-S-E."

"What kind, Brandon?"

"Cap'n Crunch."

"Hey, that's my favorite," Dajuan said, playfully.

"I know," Brandon confirmed, kicking his feet into the air.

I poured my breakfast into a glass: a protein shake. Then I watched the scene with these two unfold. Sometimes I wished Dajuan had a biological kid. I still hadn't brought up the Ariel visit. I wanted to get to that later. I knew that her return would scare Dajuan. He would believe that she could win me back for the sake of Brandon. Not! There was nothing in the world that would make me make that backwards step.

I stumbled into the bathroom, tossed my boxers in a wicker hamper, and turned on the shower. I let it run while I slapped Noxzema on my face. I stepped into the marble, double head shower stall, which doubled as a steam room. The water was freezing. Don't tell me that the pipes are frozen, I said under my breath. I jumped beneath the water and dithered as the ice-cold water rivulets ran down my body. I washed quickly, rinsed, and was drying myself with the blow dryer when Dajuan waltzed into the bathroom.

"What kinda kinky shit are you doing? And without me?" he asked with a sinister grin on his face.

"No hot water. I'm heating myself up."

"I don't get it, but I can heat you up."

"Pipes are frozen. I paid the water bill, if that's what you thought, fool."

He shut the bathroom door and wrapped his arms around me. "What I tell you about calling me names? he asked and kissed my neck.

"What are you going to do about that?"

"Put you on bird punishment," he said, exiting the bathroom. I followed. We had dubbed the penis, bird for Brandon's sake. "And booty punishment, too."

"Please! You do that and you'll punish yourself," I said and tapped his bubble butt.

I threw on a baby-blue button down shirt, jeans, and Timberland boots. No tie. Then I picked up my trench coat and briefcase and headed for the door. Gave both of my boys a hug and told Dajuan,"I need your keys."

"They're on the counter."

"Gotta be incognito. I do not feel like getting caught up in Germantown all damn day."

"Incognito in a Range Rover?"

"It's not mine, so they won't know that it's me."

"You're nothing but a corner boy. I know all your colleagues see you as a thug with a degree."

"Probably, but have you seen me in a courtroom? They know that I am the Kobe Bryant of legal eagles."

"Whatever. Get out."

"Bye dad, Brandon said."

CHAPTER 23

Wydell James and his mother--no father--lived in a broken down duplex up the street from where his younger brother had been shot earlier in the week. Now his mother's oldest boy was in jail on a triple homicide rap. Her life had to be in shambles.

I pushed the Range Rover through the rain along I-76, which meandered along the Schuykill River and exited at the Germantown Avenue exit. At the first light, I made a left onto Wayne Avenue, and then at Seymour Street, I made a right. I parked in the Fitler School yard, hopped out of the truck and snatched my briefcase off the seat. I then said a silent prayer. I walked up the block and was mobbed by a few childhood friends. I know that they were glad to see me there. They had been unable to escape the ghetto. Or, didn't have the parental encouragement to do so. It was a sad thing. They had correctly assumed that I was there to see Wydell's mom. I shook their hands, as they gave me the ghetto gospel, but I was uninterested. I wanted facts. Not rumors and speculation.

I approached Odella's crib, and blankets were up to the living room window posing as curtains. I knocked on the door and it swung open. What a shame, I thought as I looked at the living room. I was almost scared to enter and a stench eddied through my nostrils. I nearly choked. I did not recall it being that bad. There wasn't a sofa. Just a few folding chairs and a host of dingy pillows thrown about. From the upstairs came Odella James.

"Who the fuck? Oh! Little Ray-Ray," she said. "Come in. You're still handsome."

"Thanks, Ms. James," I said.

Had she forgot that she had seen me two days earlier?

Odella was tall and perhaps younger than my mom's 48-years. She wore jeans and a tattered sweater with a cigarette in her hand. Her wrists were bony. She watched me staring at her home with disgust and I caught myself, but my nose was on fire.

"It's a mess in here, I know. But shit has been hard."

"Don't trip. I've been here. Remember I used to spend the night here."

"But now you're a fancy lawyer. Saw you on TV, too," she said and took a long drag of her fag.

"Let's go have breakfast." I suggested.

"Really?" she asked. "You wanna take me to breakfast."

"Yes, let's go up to John's on Chelten Avenue and have some panny cakes."

She cracked up. "You haven't learned that it's pancakes, yet?"

"Nope."

CHAPTER 24

Where had I been? John's had an entirely new staff. I guessed the Korean owners rotated the slaves. Johns? It should have been called, Wong's. We sat at the counter and

I let Odella fill her tummy before I began to drill her with the preliminaries.

Without preamble, I asked, "Did Wydell say anything to the police?"

"He had some story about basketball at some school gym and then going to a campus party."

"Did he mention anything about a gun being found?"

She thought a moment and looked perplexed. "Well..."

"Ms. James?"

She corrected me. "Della."

What the hell was with people correcting me about their names?

"Della, you have to be honest with me, if I am to have any chance to help Wydell. Besides, my grandmother already told me."

"We have no money to pay you, so why should I tell you squat?"

What the fuck? That was so left field, but this was about Wydell and not her, so I pressed on.

"Della, I am trying to help and I need you to cooperate in order to do that effectively," I said. "Now, what's with the gun?"

"I'm not going to rat out my boy. He's a good boy. Sell a little dope, but Wydell ain't a killer."

She's not going to rat out her son, but she confessed that he sells drugs. Interesting. I did not feel like this obstinate crap.

"Okay, there was a gun."

"I never said that," she yelled, drawing attention like an Etch-a-Sketch.

"Conjecture."

"Don't sass talk me."

I chuckled. "That means to guess."

"Big words either." She warned me, and then ordered another coffee.

There she was giving me the business and running up my tab. Had we been in her home, she may have kicked me out. I knew there was a gun. The question was whether the Philadelphia Police Department (PPD) had a warrant to search and seize the gun. And, if so, did the warrant arise with probable cause? Somehow, I didn't think Ms. James, pardon me, Della, could tell me the answer to that, so I switched gears.

"Has Wydell been arrested before today?" I asked as her coffee arrived.

She slurped her coffee without manners and said, "Kid shit. Nothing major."

I'll be the judge of that, Missy! "Like vandelism? Boosting?" I threw out a few minor infractions.

"A little more."

"Was a gun involved?"

"Huh?"

"You heard me, Della."

I was getting bored with her dumbness.

"Stuck up the pizza delivery man," she said. "But no conviction from that."

"With a gun?" *Here we go*, I thought.

"How else?" Sarcastic. Wicked glance over the coffee cup.

"Do you have any idea why they came to arrest your son?"

"From what I heard on the streets, dat boy,"--she snapped her finger trying to complete her thought--"the big drug dealer, Ray Ray."

"Uh!" Shit there were a lot of them. I named a few.

"That's it," she said, excitedly. "Suspect, had some baller party up there in Chestnut Hill. Has one every year.

You gotta wear all white like it's a P. Diddy party in that place...Uh..."

"St. Tropez." I helped her along.

"There. They were partying and then bang, bang, bang. Three people dead and on the news."

"So, where does your son come in?"

"He was arguing with Suspect. Wydell thought that he was responsible for my baby being shot."

"Did the police read him his rights?"

"Yup." A coffee slurp. Loudly. Other patrons' necks whipped in our direction. I was embarrassed.

"Did he talk after they did that?"

"Nope, my boy didn't confess to shit." He's smart like his mama."

Oh, really. I wouldn't testify to that under oath. "Let's get you home. I will see what I can do."

"Could you take me to visit Quincy?"

"Yes, and I'll visit, too."

We stood and I slapped a twenty-dollar-bill on the table, as Della asked if I could get her son released. The answer was that I doubted that, but I kept that to myself.

* * *

When I pulled out of the hospital parking space, I gripped up my cell phone and called Aramis.

He picked up on the third ring. "What's good?" he asked.

"Where you at?"

"In the crib, chillen. Why?"

"I'm leaving Germantown Hospital. I am about to come through."

"Not right now, little buddy."

"Company?"

"Yeah."

"Harlot number six for the morning, you whore."
"No 26."
"Man whore."
We chuckled and hung up.

CHAPTER 25

All of the courtroom actors were on the stage by the time I arrived back downtown at the Criminal Justice Center. The fifteen story structure was where all of the adult criminal wheeling and dealing took place in Philadelphia. In the middle of the well, in front of the jury box, a 36-inch television monitor displayed a suspect on the screen at one of the precincts throughout the city. With the criminal docket busting at the seams, criminals were seen on television monitors for bail hearings. They spoke using a telephone attached to a wall at the precinct where they were arrested. So impersonal. They called Wydell's name and I walked toward the well. It paid to have associates in high places, which was the way that I knew when his hearing was being held. Bail hearings ran every four hours and the pre-trial detainees had one-hour to post bail before they were shipped to CFCF.

"Theo Baxter, Public Defenders Office for the defense, Mr. Commissioner."

I pushed the swinging door and kindly bumped Baxter to the side, and went on the record as, "Ravonne Lemmelle, for the defense, Mr. Commissioner. Baxter is excused."

All of the official attendees, the clerk, the bailiff, and the Commissioner Salvatore Diego, looked at me with raised eyebrows. No one was as flabbergasted as Cynthia Thomas, the assistant district attorney. They all probably wondered how could the poor suspect of theirs afford Martir, Savino and Associates representation. I wondered that myself.

Cynthia looked at me as if I had crashed a plane on her front lawn during a birthday party. She was an adroit barrister, with ten years experience, and was firmly under the wing of Lindsay Abraham, Philadelphia's District Attorney. She was Lindsay's pet and maybe her bed mate, too, according to rumors. Wydell James' life had become a real stew of drama, disaster, and nightmare, because of all the deputy prosecutors, Cynthia detested me.

It was only two years ago that the sassy Cynthia Thomas tried to seduce me. She made a determined effort to get me on top of her ample breasts and slim body. I declined and cited the Code of Ethics. She continued to pursue me. I confessed that I was gay. She didn't believe me. I had sex with her. Thrice. Later, she saw Dajuan and me taking a stroll down the eccentric South Street holding hands. She wanted revenge and the courtroom was her venue.

"In re Wydell James," Commissioner Diego said.

Diego was a refined South Philadelphia Italian ruffian with profound legal credentials.

"We're here to discuss bail. Ms. Thomas?"

"Remand without bail, Commissioner. The defendant is accused of a double homicide."

"Mr. Lemmelle?"

"For the record, Commissioner, I need Ms. Thomas to read the criminal complaint." Usually, the complaint was not read, but she had made an error on the record.

"That's absurd," Cynthia said and stood.

"Not absurd, Commissioner, but necessary. I specifically wanted madam Thomas to clarify how many bodies were at the morgue allegedly at the hands of Mr. James."

"Three," she said.

"Well then let the record reflect, Mr. James has been charged with triple homicide, and not double as Ms. Thomas had previously stated."

"What the hell are you doing?" Wydell said, loudly. Every eye in the courtroom darted to the monitor.

"You will not interrupt my proceeding, Mr. James," the Commissioner said to my client. He then asked me, "Mr. Lemmelle, do you have a response to Ms. Thomas' demand for remand?"

"Yes, I'd like to have Mr. James moved to the back of this bail listing to allow me to confer with the client via telephone."

"You have not spoken to your client, Mr. Lemmelle?" the Commissioner asked and removed his glasses. He was in shocked.

And so the hell was I.

"No, Commissioner, I was just asked to make an appearance by the defendant's mother."

"So, he has no idea who you are?"

"Unbelievable," Cynthia mumbled.

I had heard her and would eat her alive for that snide remark.

"He knows who I am, Commissioner. He has just not formally hired me for the instant offense."

"Do you object to Mr. Lemmelle's representation, Mr. James?"

"No, sir."

"Well then. We'll hold this for a moment. Call the next case," the Commissioner said, and on top of that he added, "Mr. Lemmelle approach." He told me, "I will have none of your suspenseful, entertaining, chicanery in my courtroom when you return. Especially without a twelve member jury for you to perform for. I like you kid and suspect that we will meet up here often. Let's start and end this gracefully."

I accepted my chide and caveat with pride. "Yes, Commissioner."

"As you were," he told me and moved on to the next case.

CHAPTER 26

Just before the 1 p.m. Eagles vs. Giants tipoff, I was on I-76 going back up to North Philadelphia. I was headed to the 35th Police District. That was after I had accepted the no bail remand for my client. I exited the expressway at the Broad Street exit and drove northbound to Champlost Street. Disbelievingly, I found a metered parking space in front of the madhouse. Dajuan did not have a dime in the damn truck. I found a few coins in my briefcase, and then I read the posted sign in front of the car. Sunday, I could park free. I was never that lucky.

I entered the brick structure and walked on ugly oatmeal-colored tile. I approached the duty officer and stated my name and business. She got up off her huge behind and walked to her colleagues. They all were probably calling me gay, faggot, butt buddy, rump wrangler, or one of the other terms associated with homosexuality's family tree. But it was I, Ravonne Lemmelle, who planned to return the favor when I had them on the witness stand.

I was ushered pass a few standard government desks. On a television, I had seen the game. The Eagles were down 6-0 with Jeff Garcia and his offense trucking down the field. I was offered a rancid interview room. I knew there was a better one and I said so.

"Who do you think you are," the slim, big booty cop asked me.

She had a serious ring of ruby-red lipstick on her plump lips. Prettiest dick-sucking lips this side of Texas. (You could take advantage of those. I was good on that.)

"Just an attorney."

Who do I think I am? Was she kidding?

"Not in my newspaper," she said, staring me up and down.

"Then you should be reading local newspapers," I told her as my client traipsed into the room in a hospital gown. "I make the crime page every time, I take on a case."

She looked at me wickedly.

"Fag." She then added, "You actually got that man off last week?"

I chuckled. Her question was laughable and did not warrant a reply. I paid her no mind, and to Wydell, I asked, "How are you holding up?"

The dumb bitch left, and Wydell had a seat. He was six-five and the gown looked like a mini-skirt.

"Barely, my man," he said.

His braids were immaculate and his eyes were red, but usually they were deep brown.

"Good looking for coming here. I know that I talked shit about you being a homo and all, but..."

"I'm not trippen on that bullshit. And I am not here as your childhood friend. We are client and attorney."

"What about the fees?"

"I'll work on that problem," I said and pulled out a legal pad and pen from my briefcase. I wanted Cynthia.

Badly!

I planned to figure out how to deal with the fees. I had one of those pens that had blue, black, red and green ink. I always color coded my notes for quick reference.

"I can pay you," he said.

"I work at a firm, and..."

"Ray-Ray, you work for Savino. I know that. I can pay you a $30,000 retainer."

Things had started out chaotic. That was how I liked it. His face was unreadable. How could someone living in the squalor that I witnessed on Seymour Street be sitting on 30K?

"Wydell?" I said serenely.

"We are on a don't ask and don't tell policy. I have the money. Period. I'll have my girlfriend bring it to you. In cash. And for the record, I am innocent."

I took a breath. Wydell stared at me. I looked at the floor. I could not ethically accept blood money as payment. I suddenly lost that instant urge to really hear all of my client's dirty little secrets.

"Okay," I said. "So our defense is what?"

"First, will you accept my money and represent me?" he asked sternly.

He had the aura of a rough neck, but sounded confident and sure of himself.

I thought for a moment. It didn't take me long to say yes.

"Good. What we have here is an alibi defense, counselor. I have a solid, very solid, alibi. And the killer is still on the loose."

CHAPTER 27

The man who sat in front of me was not the same Wydell James that I had grown up with. He was three months older than me. Since I could remember, he and I always milled around Germantown chasing girls and playing street sports. We were in 3rd, 5th, 6th, and 8th grade classes together at John B. Kelly Elementary School and Clarence E. Pickett Middle School. We were in the Rainbow Team, which consisted of all academic plus classes in elementary school, and all advance placement classes in middle school. Bottom line, Wydell was no dummy. He was as smart as, if not, smarter than me. The problem was, he had a problem proving it, and making it known.

I asked him, "What is the alibi?"

"Brace yourself. I am about to reveal some serious shit to you."

"Don't tell me that you were robbing the pizza man again?"

"Hell no. What the fuck kinda question is that, Ray! That charge was never even filed. I was at a party."

"Suspect's party?"

"You're funny. No! LaSalle University."

LaSalle University was a quiet Catholic college in Germantown. He was minutes from where we had grown up. Funny thing, it was a university that did not welcome the locals roaming about their campus. Somehow, I thought that Wydell was about to tell me how he crashed a party. That wasn't a stretch as LaSalle was a good school trapped inside of the ghetto like USC was trapped in South Central LA and Temple U was trapped in North Philadelphia.

"Elaborate," I said.

"Was at a basketball game from five to eight. A campus bash from ten to about one. And then to my house with my girlfriend, a marketing major. Oh, and between eight to ten in my girl's dorm room fucking."

He had said a lot. A mouthful. I had to really choke back my awe. Since when did this thug attend bashes? Didn't want to offend my client, so I wrote down what he had said. I wrote the crucial times in red. The facts about his girlfriend in green.

"Can anyone besides you and your girlfriend verify the time that you left the campus?"

"Yes."

"Name and number?"

"Germantown Taxi Company. Called them from my phone, which the police have, at about 12:30 a.m. They picked us up at the corner of Belfield and Olney in front of Central High School at about one."

I jotted that in red. "Have you talked to the police?"

"No!" He barked as if I had disrespected him. "I said nothing once we were here either. You see how quickly they had me prepared for arraignment."

"I'm going to get an investigator on this ASAP. And I'll pressure the DA for early discovery and your phone. The coroner should be done with the autopsies in a day or two."

"Are you done, counselor?"

"Not quite. What's with the gun?"

"I own it. Big deal."

"Very big deal, Wydell. Where'd they find it?"

"My car."

"If you had a car, why did you call a taxi?" That was a prosecutorial question, but I always played both sides of the fence. Every good attorney knew what the prosecutor would ask in advance.

"My transmission is fucked up. Leaking transmission fluid and the gears stripped. So I took a cab to and from LaSalle."

"They test you for gun residue?"

"Yup, and none was found."

"So, they have what?" I was actually asking myself.

"Absolutely nothing, but bad tips."

CHAPTER 28

I opened the living room door and the sound was so beautiful. Dajuan was masterfully gliding his hands across the piano keys as I kicked off my boots. Hearing him play cut through the air and when he added his soft voice, it was the perfect melody. I went into the bedroom and threw on a college T-shirt and sweatpants. I then gargled mouthwash. I hadn't seen Brandon, so I went to his room to check on him. I knew he would be ecstatic that the Eagles had won. He was not there. He was in my office playing a game on his laptop. Ms. Pearl was snuggled up under him.

I walked in and Ms. Pearl leaped off the sofa and traipsed toward the door. At the doorway, she said, "Meow!" I translated it for her. "Homo." I cracked up at the bourgeois act. She was a tad conceited. Strange I know, but this cat was special in a bad way.

"What's funny, Daddy R?" Brandon asked, and didn't take his eyes off the laptop.

I sat down on the sofa next to him. "Nothing. What do you want for dinner?"

"Um...Pizza."

"We had that yesterday."

"Okay, lasagna."

"What's with the Italian dishes?"

"What, Dad?" he asked and looked at me perplexed. "Daddy R, you're crazy. We have Versace dishes."

I smiled and chuckled lightly. Brandon swore that he knew everything. Calling people crazy was his new thing. He also had an air of cockiness. I caught him bragging about my car once, and I immediately corrected that conceited behavior. It amazed me that toddlers actually compared their parent's vehicles in first grade. They actually knew that a Benz cost more than a Honda. I stood and told him that I'd figure dinner out.

"Can I help you cook?"

"Yup, I'll call you when I am ready," I said and pressed into the living room.

I found Dajuan still blowing out a new song. At least I had never heard him sing it. I sat on the sofa and listened to my in-house concert. So many women--and men--would have loved to have the sexy, sultry Dajuan sing to them in private. Too bad that they had to wait until the next tour, which was in April, starting the weekend of Easter.

"Black Face, listen to this. I only have one verse, bridge and chorus. But check it..."

He began with a hasty, powerful cord, and then slowed down the tempo. The words were:

Chorus 1
Here we are once again, I've been out late, girl

I know you're pissed as ish, and you're probably
fed up now, girl

But I had to work till ten, then I had a few drinks, girl

Bridge
Please tell me babe why you're packed at the
door

When all I do is respect your wishes, girl

You don't belong out this late in the goddamn
street

I'm out working hard for you and this is what

you put me through

Chorus
Girl be real and tell the truth
If you wanna really be through
Just be real with me right now
If you don't wanna be down
I go all day thinkin' 'bout you
And this is what you put me through
Just be real with me right now
If you're the one out playing around

"That's all I have thus far."

I sat for a moment as if in deep concentration. Somehow I believed that I played a pivotal role in the track.

For the sake of harmony--that of our relationship, not his song--I said, "It definitely tells a story. And you could edit out a few of the girls in the first verse. But I am feeling it."

"You're not just saying that are you?"

"We both know if I disliked it, you'd be the first to know. I'd give you constructive criticism the same way that you shred my opening and closing arguments."

"Yeah. Speaking of trials, do you have a new murder case?"

"Yes, but don't panic. It involves the poor, so it won't be a media monger."

"If you and Aramis don't make it one, you mean?"

"Whatever, wiseass. It may easily be dismissed."

"How?"

"Not now. I really don't want to go over the drama. I know I'm hungry as a street person."

"I don't feel like cooking, so don't go there. It's your Sunday. I am busy Black Face."

"You're a trip. What you want?"

"Sautéed boneless chicken breast. Over a bed of romaine lettuce. Thick, creamy dressing..."

"I got your thick and creamy dressing," I said and smiled. I yelled, "Brandon let's go. Time to cook."

I kissed Dajuan passionately and then went to prepare dinner.

CHAPTER 29

Twenty21 in Center City was one of the most fabulous restaurants for singles to mingle during lunch. It wasn't that way purposely, but the elegant, posh spot was frequented by the Who's Who in Philadelphia. Bumping into the same echelon of people led to many business and personal relationships being forged. The food may not have been the best, but the wide selection of alcoholic elixir made up for any shortcomings. The in-house floral design was a jewel. Very elegant. The cherrywood bar was topped with glass, and behind the bartenders, all of whom were attractive to the eye, were six shelves of the best liquors. Mr. 357 was perched at the bar nursing a shot (his forth) of Louis XIII, while whispering soothing words into the ears of Ariel Greenland.

His slick, sea-green contacts were inviting with the kind of deliciousness that could trick a devout nun into debasement. His smile was easy, and he seemed happy to be in her presence again. He was clad in a charcoal gray power suit, white button down, and a snazzy tie. Ariel had actually told him that he was to cool to be a native Philadelphian. She had no idea how right she was. His shoulder length hair was pulled into a ponytail and was salt and pepper, with more salt than pepper. He told her that it was, "killer gray," when she complimented the color.

Ariel carried a conversation covering a wide range of topics about her city, Philadelphia. She had a new tan that was obviously paid for. Her plucked brows were pinched into a frown every time she put a lot of thought into a topic. Little maroon painted lip stick stains were around the rim of her goblet filled with port. She sat very parochial at a perfect ninety degrees and had a habit of holding her glass up at eye level and peeking over it while talking. She excessively re-crossed her legs, which peeked beneath a navy wool skirt. This was no cheap wool, either. It was the good stuff, a facsimile of what the Germany military used to combat winter winds during the Cold War.

"You're on your way," he told her after she ran down a list of auditions she had been on and roles that she was cast in.

She had even bragged of having a Jaguar XJ8. He was on his fifth shot of Louis treize, so he added, "Beautiful, too."

"Yeah, I do not get out of LA much," she replied. "But, I have a score to settle in Philadelphia."

The rude heifer didn't even thank him for the compliment. He was at an Irish pub in LA dressed as a Spanish man and he had chatted with Ariel Greenland then, so he knew that she was interested in killing her husband.

"That's why I am a single lady," she added purring.

He ordered another cocktail.

"Sir, you're on your sixth. I am going to need you to take it easy," the bartender admonished him.

"Yeah! Really." Mr. 357 warbled.

He then turned to Ariel and continued his conversation as if the tender had not spoken.

"So, what's a gal like you doing single and free?"

"Well, I had a husband, but he left me for a man with a dick the size of Russia," she said, giggling.

The alcohol was beginning to betray her, or so, he thought. He had not slipped her GHB, either. Mr. 357 knew that she was going to reveal her most intimate secrets by the next round.

"I was busy working, while he was busy working on his oral skills, adding up how many men he could boink in a week."

"Boink? That was an interesting synonym."

"Would you have preferred screw?"

"No, fuck!"

She leaned in close to him and he could smell the mixture of True Star and wine drifting from her.

She whispered into his ear, "Your place or mine," she asked. "Matter of fact, mine happens to be a hotel," she claimed smiling. "I want to see your crib."

"I wanna see my crib, too," he said. "It's still being built."

"Oh, that's just too bad."

"I know," she said, gleefully.

Neither of them knew that they were flirting with death.

Monday, January 8, 2007

CHAPTER 30

Monday morning, I blew into the elevator in the garage level of the Prudential Building and rode it to the 8th floor. I exited and made my way along the red carpet--

in place to give employees that celebrity feel--and greeted Marsha. I was smiling at her as I entered my office. That was appropriate, but until I had a cappuccino, I would hang upside down in my bat cave.

Slapping my briefcase on the desk, I plopped into my burgundy, studded executive chair and rolled to the cappuccino machine. It was already brewing. Thank God for the genius who created a timer. I poured some in a mug with Brandon's face plastered on it and rolled to my floor to ceiling window. I was privileged to a very panoramic view of the sixth largest city. The buildings were mostly lined shoulder to shoulder with varying peaks and shapes; a picturesque skyline. The latest edition was the Amtrak train station office building, an expansive glass structure that I tried to convince the big wigs that we should relocate there. They looked at me as if I was crazy.

I revved my computer and checked my quotidian report for that day. I had a parole hearing at eleven, and the rest of my day was supposed to be clear. But I had taken on a new client not even 24-hours earlier, and preparation for his preliminary hearing was of the essence. I pulled out a composition book and labeled it, Wydell James. I always kept a daily account of what transpired with my new cases. I recorded everything from court appearances to phone calls and tucked news clipping inside, if there were any. I did that daily, and I wrote in it with a personal tone, not professional. It was for my eyes only. Never knew when some archaic note may have driven a case into a new direction.

I snatched up my phone and contacted the detective handling Wydell's case and informed him that I wanted the crime scene preserved for the defense. Prayerfully, he did not give me a problem, forcing me to produce a motion. I have enough paralegals at my disposal to flood the DA's office like Hurricane Katrina. I mean beastly motions that would have taken half their office to dismantle. They would respond, but the 180 days that they had to try my client would be ticking.

Tick.

Tock.

I sent Jonathan Rude, my favorite of the Savino and Martir investigators an inter-office E-mail. Marked it urgent and then buzzed Marsha.

Marsha White bounced into my office with a lovely smile on her face. She was a stout, tough woman and was very protective of her boss.

Me.

We had met under very unorthodox circumstances. She was in the 1801 Vine Street Juvenile Court with her delinquent son, having taken off work for the sixth time. All of her 120 pounds were on the courthouse steps. Her pouty lips attempted to explain to her boss that she would not be able to make it in late, as she had planned. He fired her. Yes, I was ear hustling that day. Come on, I am an attorney. We had a conversation, and I hired her.

"You came strolling into the office with a bubbly, new smile. I'm ten, I mean, three years your senior. I know that smile, buddy."

"Enchanting mother."

"So?"

"Yes. We kissed and made up."

"Thank you."

"For what?"

"Fifty bucks."

"I don't owe you any money. The Eagles won."

"Karen in the tax wing does."

"And, you're thanking me because..."

"We bet. I told her that you were a family man."

"Oh!" I was shocked by the assessment. "Thanks."

"He better not act a fool again. But on to other news. This just came from the rivals," she said and handed me the package.

I opened it and found the paperwork produced on the Wydell James case that far. Two days was a record. They must really believe that Wydell was toast. The DA's office had never produced preliminary discovery material that quickly. They had even forwarded them without filing a motion to get them. There was a body warrant, police reports, a few crime scene photos (that could not convict a pencil for stabbing a sharpener), and even a prelim autopsy report. No search warrant, though. I had just found an excuse to barge into the DA's office and shake things up a bit. And I thought I'd be bored that day.

I told Marsha what I needed, grabbed a file from my desk and stuffed it into my briefcase. I grabbed my coat and shrugged it on.

"Going so soon?"

"I'm going to the Fort, and who knows what traffic is doing. It may take me a month to make the trip. I'll read what was passed along to me today while I wait, if I am early. I am curious as to what those assholes have up their sleeves. Sending me this stuff so quickly is new and interesting."

"You seem upset about it."

"No,just shocked at the sudden proficiency."

"Wanna do lunch with your admin. assist. It's on me, considering you were the catalyst to me winning the bet."

"Suuurrrreeee. Make a reservation for about twelve thirty."

She chuckled. "McDonald's takes reservations now?"

CHAPTER 31

Rhonesia Cosby awoke in the late morning elated that she did not have a class until 11 a.m. That was the way she had planned it for the last four semesters at the LaSalle University School of Journalism. Her body refused to function before nine, and for that reason she'd become an investigative reporter. A nine to five was not an option. Suddenly, she was forced to recall a very boring night of passion with a running back from the football team. He was a NFL hopeful, and that made up for his anatomy shortcoming.

She sat up in his bed and listened to his heavy breathing. The sheets were all wrapped around him, explaining why she had been cold most of the night. *Selfish, little dick bastard,* she thought. January in Philadelphia was disastrously cold and draped in complimentary snow. The chilly air snaked through the cracked window which overlooked the busy Olney Avenue. It brought with it a message: cover your soft, *cafe au lait*-colored nakedness. She followed the directive and covered herself in a silk robe. She did not like terry cloth. Like most mornings she slipped to her dorm room in the co-ed building.

In her room, Rhonesia brewed a pot of green tea. The stove-top clock read: 9:45. She had a Survey of Current Politics class at 11. It was a class that she decided to take just in case she decided to move to Washington, DC to report White House rumors acquired stealthily. She had become a drinker, as college life required being inebriated to get through it day by day. Her two favorite drinks, mimosa and screw driver, both included orange juice. She was not being looked at by any of the major newspapers, so no job awaited her after her May graduation, although, she would graduate in the top 15% of her class. She did not attribute alcohol to her class rank, either. She was a light drinker who indulged solely to stay serene. It made her feel feminine. It also made her work out. She wanted no parts of a beer belly. Hell, no belly. She didn't plan to be pregnant until after 30 and married.

After she did her morning bathroom ritual, she nursed an unsweetened mug of tea. She sat on her twin bed and looked at her pathetic roommate, a senior probably on her way to flunking out. She flicked the remote control into her hand, and turned on the TV. There was Cathy Regal, a Fox-29 anchor. Fox carried the ghetto news that the other politically driven stations didn't. Cathy was re-capping the big stories for the hundredth time since six a.m.

"Tiffany!" Rhonesia yelled and hit her roommates headboard. The girl didn't budge. *Damn shame*, Rhonesia thought. "Tiff! Get up!" She tuned the volume up and let the TV blast. "Tiffany Koch!" Rhonesia stood in front of the TV as if she was blind.

News anchor, Cathy Regal, soprano voice and bright smile that exuded confidence. Too much for Rhonesia. Rhonesia was the school's head cheerleader for the basketball team and had the alluring face and impeccable smile to be in front of the camera. As a black woman from the ghetto, she had what it took to pull an Oprah, but she liked to write her own masterpieces and not read from a teleprompter.

"What, bitch?" Tiffany asked groggily.

After the newscaster was done with her graphic recreation of the 1935 Hope Circle murders, the street reporter stood behind a live shot of a beautiful Chestnut Hill home. A triple homicide had taken place there.

Tiffany threw her long, bottled-blonde hair from her face. Brown eyes could not believe what was on the TV. Rhonesia also stared at the screen. The reporter reported that the police was tight-lipped and that they had a suspect in custody. When they heard the name and saw the picture of the suspect they both gagged.

"I don't believe it. Not for one second," Tiffany said. Her thin, pink lips quivered.

"If I fucked him, I wouldn't either."

"Please. Who wasn't?" Tiffany shot back.

"Not me. He's 30. The NBA won't want him."

"You're such a gold digger."

"Thanks," Rhonesia said, as if she had heard the grandest compliment. "I ain't fucking for free."

Tiffany sat up. She blinked and raked her fingers through her hair.

"Wydell? A murderer? Not likely."

"I'd concur," Rhonesia said, and opened her laptop. "He played a game and was at the party Saturday night. I don't believe he did that and then got to Chestnut Hill, killed three people, and then returned home as if nothing happened."

"Chestnut Hill, where exactly is that?" Tiffany asked.

She was a Business major, with no intention of working. She would sleep her way to the rank of President of Kodak, or a comparable company.

"Heading towards Plymouth Meeting," Rhonesia told her, as she typed rapidly.

"What are you doing?"

"Typing!"

"Evidently!"

"Prepping my article on the star basketball player's case."

"You're always looking to exploit somebody. Did you report whose bed ya hot ass slept in last night, ho?"

"I do not exploit people. I gather facts and fiction and report it. Keep it up, Missy, and your hell-raising Brazilian ass job will be on the front page of the school paper. Please keep trying me, hun."

"You wouldn't. I knew I should not have told you."

"Try me!" Rhonesia said and stuffed her book bag. "If I do not come straight back, do not call 9-1-1. I'll be on assignment."

"Breaking news, bitch, you're not a damn reporter for anyone. You need to bring it down, honey. On assignment."

"Bitch, you're getting real close to my anonymous scandal sheet."

Rhonesia slammed the room door shut behind her to punctuate her point. She had threatened to blast Tiffany's ass augmentation in a scandal E-mail that she sent out anonymously to the student body that created news-worthy havoc around campus.

CHAPTER 32

After poorly gratifying his stomach, Jonathan Rude hit the Schuykill Expressway by ten-thirty. He looked over at other drivers and saw a diverse mix of calm faces. He scanned radio stations until he landed on 98.1: the oldies. Marvin Gaye's, "Let's Get it On" played. That sounded like a fabulous idea to Rude.

Jonathan Rude--Mr. Rude if you tried his patience--had the warm, trustworthy face of a kindergartner teacher. He was a steel-nosed, azure eyed man, whose religious beliefs lay with discretion, not God. Call him atheist. Call him an ingrate. Just add private eye behind it.

And he'd make it easy for you to say, too.

He had won a scholarship to San Diego State University in his home town, where he was on the San

Diego police beat. Unconfirmed rumors brought him to the East Coast and into the legal hands of Carlos Savino and ultimately, Ravonne Lemmelle.

Rude's charm was experienced and brilliant. An interviewee would be in the kitchen fixing coffee--which he wouldn't drink for fear of poisoning--as he eyeballed their pad, learning all about them. He was a man of detail. A dirt man. And if there was any dirt to find, all efforts to hide it would be futile with Rude on the case.

At the Germantown/Wissahickon exit, he took the Germantown Avenue northbound exit toward his Chestnut Hill crime scene. The slow-moving number-23 bus was in front of him, making his expedition a slow one.

Finally at Chelten Avenue amongst all of the stores aptly dubbed "The Avenue," he went around the bus and passed Germantown High School. The school was not a square or a rectangle, like most of the Philadelphia high schools. The school was in the shape of a capital G. He passed a sign that announced that he had entered Mount Airy before he reached Chestnut Hill, the northernmost point of Philadelphia before entering Montgomery County. He swung around a bus depot and after a short distance, he found 1935 Hope Circle, his mark.

The gabled mansion, tucked neatly behind birch trees, sat at the end of a driveway that opened into a circle with a fountain nucleus that could rival the water show outside of the Las Vegas Bellagio Hotel. *This is the actually crime scene*, he thought. *Very nice. Posh.* With the handsome snow covering the roof and trees, ice needles hung from the porch and snow filled fountains could grace a winter issue of Architectural Digest.

Rude saw a very serious PPD foe. Sleep with someone's wife and foe was the likely result. Of all of the officers protecting the ionic columns and balcony that extended across the entire front of the home, why did it have to be Patrick Neisinger? Adding insult to injury, Mr. Rude, living up to his last name, had callously dismissed Neisinger's wife as easily as dismissing snow off of the windshield, when she came running to him with her divorce papers.

Rude escaped his car with his tape recorder and Sony digital camera in hand. Officer Neisinger looked at him with a hint of uneasiness. He was a cop before a husband. That's why he had lost his wife. The overtime was more important than his wife. Hence, no room to complain about her infidelity.

"Pat," Rude said, flatly.

"Jon," Neisinger replied flatter.

No other words were exchanged. They both knew why Rude was there.

Rude approached the outside of the alcove window, certain not to disturb anything. There were three gaping holes in the thick window. It looked like the holes were deliberately placed there by an expert interior decorator. He began his photo shoot. First, the close-ups of the holes. The glass on the porch beneath the window was next. He then backed up for some wide angles. He slipped the camera into his coat pocket and pulled out his recorder.

"Seems three bullet holes had varying effects on the window. Two very clean entries. One spider webbed."

He went to the front door with Neisinger in tow and snapped the entryway to the lair. He then recorded, "Who is the actual homeowner? The name on the deed and taxes, that is."

The alcove--or hot spot--was a short distance from the foyer. He snapped away. Uncontrollably. Unlike a Tyra Banks top model, he had unlimited frames to capture the best pics. Anything resembling vague interest was snapped for his employer to review.

All three chalked body lines were actually touching one another. Each body labeled one, two, and three had a yellow police placard identifying them. Body One's right arm was over the leg of Body Two. It appeared that Body One had toppled over Body Three. Both of Body One's legs were over Body Three's torso. Body Three must have dove for cover, Rude surmised, because Body Three was sprawled out beneath Body One. Rude figured out more upon careful review of the overall setup of the home. Once he viewed the photos at the office, he would know much more.

Rude activated the camcorder feature on his hand-held and became a videographer.

Reluctantly, Rude asked the officer, "Any bullets recovered, sir?"

"All in the victims."

Good. Rude knew where to find those and some more info.

"Has PPD located the location of the shooter?"

"Right this way," Neisinger said, nicely.

He desired to have Rude search the property himself and earn his hourly wages, but that posed two problems. One, he would come off like a disgruntled ex-husband and not a police officer. Two, Rude may have found a piece of damaging evidence that the PPD hadn't, and the press would love that.

About ten yards from the sprawling porch, Rude found three PPD placards dug deep into the ground.

"Snow had been here, so how were the shells found?"

Rude spoke into his recorder. He then began to snap away. He raced to his car and grabbed binoculars. He returned to the sniper's position and looked at the home trying to confirm if the bullets were propelled from the ground or from a limb of the tree next to where the casings were found. From the ground, all of the victims would have to have been standing; the four feet wall beneath the window and additional two feet of the porch evidenced that. The deceased could have been lying on the floor in the very positions Rude saw from the chalk lines had the shooter been in the tree. He recorded that opinion.

Rude then began thinking about the escape. He followed the path to the street looking around very methodically. He reached the street and noted the distance. No tire tracks left on the black top. No screeching marks from a tire taking off hastily. He began his trek back toward the home and snapped along the way. In the brownish, weather beaten grass, he noticed a blue object sticking out. He and Neisinger approached it. Rude snapped away at the object, which turned out to be a key chain. He used a pen to pick up the key chain and placed it in a plastic bag.

"Be sure the DA gets notified of that. I'd hate to report you for withholding evidence, or arrest you for concealing evidence of a crime."

"You would love that, I bet."

In his car, Rude opened his laptop and downloaded the photos to Ravonne along with an E-mail.

He picked up his cellphone and called the coroner's office.

"I knew you'd be calling," Deputy Coroner Lillian Matsuda said.

"Really. Were you expecting a business call or the other kind?"

"Oh, certainly the other kind of the booty persuasion."

"Can I make both?"

"Sure."

CHAPTER 33

Donald Cooley lived in Graterford, Pennsylvania--40 miles from Philadelphia. I pulled up to his home, a labyrinth prison surrounded by a twenty foot concrete wall that prohibited prisoners from looking out into the real world. Several guard towers were posted around the structure where expert marksmen took up position to arrest some buffoon with the chutzpah to scale the wall. I parked and walked past two inmate workers--evidently close to release--who were cleaning the front of the structure. Keeping their front porch clean.

In the lobby, I was greeted by a correction officer. I identified myself, he checked my creds, and buzzed a gate that allowed me to proceed into the mouth of the beast. I sat on the slender wood bench and waited for a Security and Escort Officer to collect me.

Everything matched precisely. Brown concrete bricks; dull, eggshell-colored floor tiles, which were being buffed; and a dirty, tan ceiling. I imagined Donald in his tiny cell prepping for his appearance. I've toured the notorious State Correctional Institute at Graterford and knew that the cells were as small as a tuna can. My hands had touched both walls in the cell when I held them out horizontally. There was a separate porcelain sink and toilet (no toilet seat), bunk bed, and a radiator on the wall above the toilet (often used to assist with inmates making meals using stolen goods from the kitchen together with things bought from the commissary). It was a cramped space that I wouldn't put a pit bull in.

The only plus were the windows, which opened and closed at the inmate's discretion. There were 400 of these cells painted in a shade of cream with mint green doors. Black block-style numbers were on the outside of the doors. Four hundred cells on five blocks (A-E) had to be a lot of testosterone and frustration. I mean, two men locked in these kennels was bad. One hoped to be a lifer to get a single cell.

Finally, a CO collected me and escorted me to a small corridor that led to the new side of the jail. A parole officer who waited to negotiate a plea for my client's violations awaited me. Although it was only a violation hearing, I had brought missiles and rockets and they were ready to launch.

I was reviewing my Donald Cooley file: parole report and current violation guidelines chart from the penal code. A very calm African-American, who was a tad sloppy, introduced himself as Clyde Smith, my client's PO. The hair on his head resembled a dirt ring around a bath tub.

"I'm recommending 24-months," he said without preamble.

His voice was grave and irritating.

"That's absurd."

I really disliked PO's and Clyde had just evidence why. They always proposed some irresponsible punishment for violations not involving a new crime. I really believed they harbored jealousy of some of the men they were assigned to supervise. Convicts were rebels and thugs, so what was there to hate? Their ill-gained and oftentimes confiscated wealth? Drug dealers, like my client, spent money freely and government employees couldn't stomach it, and since they couldn't cashier bullets into the skulls of those ruffians, this was the venue for them to do it, nicely. Legally.

"Your client was arrested over 90 miles outside of the county with a stipulation not to leave the city limits. And that was because of his criminal ties to various cities throughout the US. He admitted to being in Detroit and riding home, at the time a passenger of a speeding vehicle being driven by a man wanted in North Carolina for 16 counts of forgery. In the back seat were two other thugs from New York City who admitted that your client picked them up prior to going to Detroit. That, Mr. Lemmelle, is absurd."

I sat there quietly and let him ramble on as if I had not known the facts of the case. A guy goes to a couple of cities and commits no crime and two years behind bars was the absurd recommendation.

"Do you intend to come down on the offer at all to avoid going before the panel?"

"Absolutely not! He was in possession of $7,000 in cash."

"So!"

I was hot. I then caught my anger. I never got mad about the facts. They spoke for themselves.

"See you before the panel, Mr. Smith."

I have never been a good ass kisser.

Mr. Smith walked out all high and mighty with me behind him. On a bench outside the room was a long line of parole violators. I spotted Donald and the CO allowed us to confer in the cramped interview room. I also asked the CO to move me to the top of the list. He did.

"Good morning, Mr. Cooley," I said to the sexiest client that I had ever had. "Your PO is crazy."

"You're telling me," he replied laughing.

We shook hands. I got myself together having touched a big tandem of masculinity, Greek God, and Ebony Magazine Sexiest Man Alive. His hair was wavy and he had a full beard. Smoother skin could only be found on a baby. He sat across from me, and his biceps tensed each time he moved. The dull jail was lit by his presence.

"He offered us two years and I accepted."

"What?"

His eyebrows furrowed and anger lines formed along his forehead. It was so Hollywood.

"I'm not doing two bullets. I didn't do shit."

"Joking, DC. Don't trip."

An angry smile. So seductive.

"You could be a good salesman."

"Or, an even better lawyer. I'm ready to talk to the board and try to see if I can sell them some bullshit," I said smiling.

"You're crazy. But that's why I hired you."

"Glad you had that $7,000."

"Funny."

The CO knocked and told me that they were ready.

I told my client, "Let's make magic."

He had no idea that I had sent a subliminal message. He seemed relaxed and flashed me a mesmerizing smile.

We entered a boxed room with cheap brown paneling and a cheaper brown table. I sat in a wooden chair next to my client and pulled out my Donald Cooley file and opened it to the officer's report. I put on my pince-nez and then I was in character.

"Ready, counselor?"

"The defense is ready."

CHAPTER 34

The chairman, Larry Vasquez, asked Donald to state his name and inmate number for the record. He complied and spoke slowly and methodically.

The Mexican, full mustached chairman with the forehead that never stopped spoke first. "We are here at the parole office discretion for a violation hearing of parolee, Donald Cooley. He was originally sentenced to serve not less than four years, but not more than eight years in state prison on the charge of distributing narcotics. He was released with three years, two months, nine days remaining on the 4-8 sentence and is before the board for violating said parole. Specifically, leaving the jurisdiction without permission, and fraternizing with known felons. Are those the facts?"

"Yes, Mr. Chairman," Clyde replied.

Ass Kisser. Mr. Chairman!

"Yes," I said flatly.

"Now, Mr. Cooley, my job is to determine punishment if any as a result of your alleged misconducts. And to decide that, I must consider three factors: your overall probation history, the success of your attempts to be rehabilitated, and lastly, the circumstances and gravity of the offenses."

"Mr. Smith has recommended you spend a 24-month violation term at your paroling institution, SCI-Greenburg, and that the $7,000 be confiscated from you. Mr. Lemmelle, have you and your client reviewed Mr. Smith's findings?"

"We have."

"Mr. Smith, your case."

Clyde Smith cleared his throat maniacally before he spoke.

"Mr. Cooley has a grandiose arrogance and is a serious program failure. He has not maintained gainful employment, was often tardy for appointments or a no show, his residence with his mother is dubious in addition to him going to both New York City and Detroit. He was in the company of Allen Davis, a man wanted for not one, not five, but 16 counts of forgery. He was then found in possession of seven grands neatly wrapped in an overnight bag--a Prada bag valued at $1,700. Probably a boon from fugitive Davis's forgeries. That summarizes why Mr.

Cooley is a threat to the safety of others and should spend 24-months thinking about becoming a productive American citizen."

He closed his folder, and I wanted to applaud. I did.

Clap!

Clap!

Clap!

"Mr. Lemmelle?" the chairman said.

"Sorry."

Brav-fucking-O. He had run down a litany of my client's grotesque behavior and now I would air his. The Latins called it *quid pro quo*. Christians called it an eye for an eye. I called it payback's a bitch!

"Mr. Smith, you mentioned that Mr. Cooley did not maintain gainful employment, however, Mr. Cooley reports that he was employed part-time at CVS, once upon a time. He further reports that you visited him at work where he was cashiering in the pharmacy, and you informed his boss, Mr. Lockhart, that he had a drug conviction and advised that it would not be wise for him to be working around drugs that he could steal and peddle. Mr. Lockart fired him the next day, correct?"

"Yes, that is correct. It is my duty to protect companies from third-party risks. Mr. Cooley's thirst to peddle drugs was a risk to CVS and people who may consume the stolen drugs, if such a thing was to occur."

"Thirst! He has one arrest. One conviction with very sketchy details," I said hotly.

I wanted to stand and show my ass, but I was not in court. Nevertheless, it was showtime.

I dug into my Cooley file and brought out a "Motion to Recover Confiscated Cash, for you gentleman." I handed copies to both Vasquez and Smith.

"Take note, the demand is for $7,350. That's 5% interest for the ten days that money has been out of my client's hands."

I passed along two other documents.

"The one is a sworn testimony of a MGM Grand pit manager who attests that Mr. Cooley received a house card at the Detroit gaming establishment and he acknowledges that Mr. Cooley won the cash in the casino. The second form is an itemized list of the comp incurred by Mr. Cooley."

I went into my briefcase again and pulled out a DVD.

"This is a lovely home movie of Mr. Cooley raking up cash at the Pai-gow Poker table. Would you like to take a look?"

"I would," Vasquez said. "But there's no DVD player, here."

I knew that, and the DVD was blank. Ha!

I moved on. My position was on record.

"My client was a student at Temple University for two full semesters. Of eight classes,"--I passed along 12 other documents--"he's earned five A's and three B's. He has a 3.6 GPA. There's also a letter from all eight professors. All of them contradict Mr. Smith's description of Mr. Cooley. As a full-time student, finding compatible work was no easy feat and the job he did have, Mr. Smith made him leave. Ten days have been long enough for Mr. Cooley to get the point that he cannot leave the area or be around felons. He's trying and deserves a chance to complete school and work towards being a citizen."

Vasquez nodded and asked was I done.

I was.

Vasquez asked us to step out of the room. I hoped that he was badgering Mr. Smith for not responsibly presenting the facts. So many men were railroaded during parole hearings. Simply locking a man up for the slightest violation created a feeling of hopelessness and despair within men who had refrained from committing new crimes. A little road trip was hardly sufficient to lose all hopes on a man, and if he did commit a crime, he was innocent until proven guilty. Besides this created prison overcrowding, which wasted taxpayer's money and caused CO's to get overtime to babysit men. Did taxpayers really want to feed, clothe, house and offer medical and dental benefits to Mr. Cooley for leaving the damn area? I doubted it. And so did, Mr. Vasquez.

Vasquez ordered Donald Cooley to spend the next six months on house arrest, only to be allowed out for classes and work. The chairman reaffirmed that Mr. Cooley was not to leave the area or socialize with known felons.

Vasquez then gave the notorious warning, which began, "If you come before me again..."

Mr. Cooley thanked me and shook my hand with his right hand and hugged me with his left in that masculine way that men did. I nearly melted into a puddle of chocolate.

CHAPTER 35

Inside the Philadelphia County District Attorney's office, the drab style of old furnishings almost forced me to regurgitate my palatable manicotti and a glass of red wine, which I consumed at Restaurante di Mario with Marsha. Everything was standard government issue gray and needed to be replaced. The assistant DA's needed to be replaced, as well, along with Lindsay Abraham's philosophy.

Cynthia Thomas' life was such an open newspaper. She made a play to be in the face of a half-dozen microphones--probably imaging that they were penises--every chance she got. It was only a matter of time before the media wanted the official skinny on the Wydell James case, and Cynthia would work relentlessly to pollute the potential juror's minds. She was more actress--C movie Sci-Fi--than a very skilled solicitor. She was the protégé of Lindsay Abraham, who knew expertly how to drive a trial to the last stop: Felony Conviction.

After having me wait over 20 minutes, Cynthia came over her secretary's intercom and I was told that she was ready for me. (I promise that she wasn't.) I entered her office and found her behind her desk. She had glasses on her oval face,, her hair was pulled back, and she had a big nose. She wore a timeless red Donna Karan two-piece suit with a white blouse. I couldn't see the feet, but I bet they were cheap flat shoes.

"I thought that we should chat," I said. "Considering we were partners and all. One looking for everything wrong, You. One looking for everything right, *Moi*."

"I'm always open for conversation, Mr. Lemmelle. By the way, I'm looking for all of the right things to convict your client," she told me.

"Ow. Touché," I said smiling.

She called me Mr. Lemmelle when I salaciously dazzled her in that hotel room. I knew that she hated me, and I was not fooled one bit by her politeness.

"I'm not here to make a deal. That's not a part of my *modus operandi*. But if I get desperate, I'll give you a call."

"Do not flatter yourself, Mr. Lemmelle. I am so over you."

"Beautiful. I was referring to the case. You must know that. I don't expect to become desperate with this flawed case."

She looked at me crazily, and before she could try to manipulate me to ravish her right then, I said, "There seems to be a gun, specifically missing from my client's vehicle. Albeit, there was a body warrant, I assume you could provide me with reasoning for your officer's thievery?"

"Oh, that's an easy one, counselor. Plain view. As the officers were taking up position outside the home, guns drawn and prepped to annihilate your client, one of them spotted the ass of the gun poking out from under the driver's seat. And for the safety of the area children, who may have found it and committed an accidental triple homicide, like your client, the officers seized it."

"And it just so happened to be the smoking gun in my client's car?" I asked. Flashed a smile. "Your men did not obtain a warrant before they took it. And your men did not get me a charming photo. All of this seems genuinely convenient. In your favor, of course."

"Not as convenient as your client murdering three people and then returning home for a celebratory romp. An interracial one."

Interracial? That was discovery.

Who he bangs is not on trial."

"Oh, surely that gun going bang is on trial, counselor."

"Cute, but stop referring to me as counselor. We've touched on to many levels."

"Why are you here? He killed three men. One was an attorney. One of us."

"One of us. Surely he was not in my camp, maybe yours, though. He was a corrupt attorney, that is the appropriate description. My client is not an ordinary thug. There's no extensive rap sheet, and I happen to believe he would not murder."

"I'm sure you believe that all of your clients are innocent," she told me, tapping keys on her computer.

A few seconds passed and she said, "Retail theft, *nolle prosequi.* The Gap Store was a complaint and a no show. Forgery, also *nolle prosequi*, complaintant resided in Connecticut and wouldn't make the trip to testify considering his credit card balance was not affected. Two crimes. No justice. Now this. Graduated at the end of his class."

"No dope sales, which may present competitive motive. Not a matrix of violence on your little computer screen. You have the wrong guy."

I wondered whether she knew about the pizza-man robbery.

"Look, why don't you let the court decide guilty or innocent. That what it's made for."

She had really just tried it. Usher's record, *That's What It's Made For* was the song that played as I came during our escapade.

"You're really playing like whoever committed this murder did not do the city a favor."

"So sad a defense. Do you plan to present that to a jury? The lost lives were unworthy of life, so your client should be adulated for his heinous, barbaric, malicious murder? You're losing your touch, and so soon. Only four years deep. I'm sure your firm will be proud."

"My career is fine."

What I did not add was "unlike your sex life!"

"It's just that my client has an alibi."

"It better be solid as the Constitution. Have you been keeping track of the media lately with all of the violence prevention campaigns? The people do not want gun violence, vigilantism, or not. They want blood. Suppose your client had shot an innocent. Oh! He did!"

"This is going nowhere fast."

My cellphone rang. I saw Rude's name and was glad that he had rescued me from that train wreck.

"I presume that you can leave my office faster."

I rose out of her beggarly chair and made my way to her office door.

As I opened it, I heard her chuckling as she said, "See you at the preliminary hearing, counselor."

I had a lot of comebacks, but I would get my laugh in court.

CHAPTER 36

The Philadelphia morgue was sandwiched between the VA Hospital and Children's Hospital. How convenient? I exited my car and was met in the lobby by Rude.

Rude said, "Welcome to Hell's Kitchen. Today's soup of the day is human brains, a delicacy more favorable than monkey brains."

He ushered me to Lillian Matsuda's office as if the trek was as routine as a teeth brushing.

"Did you get a chance to peruse the CS photos?"

"I didn't. Anything interesting?"

"Depends," he replied. "Hopefully, Lillian can answer some of my questions."

"Her news typically states the facts. Not help decide guilt or innocence. What she explains I'll need a CIA operative to decipher all of the abbreviations and acronyms," I said.

Dr. Lillian Matsuda approached us and even captivated me with her allure. Rude looked at her as if she was the highlight of a dessert buffet. Strangely, she returned the gaze as if she'd like the chance to autopsy my anatomy. Dr. Matsuda, a forensic physician had a solid reputation and connections to various scientific fields. She ran her fingers through her long black hair before shaking my hand. She had on all black that day. A creepy beauty.

"May as well get right to it," she said, and led the way to the body refrigerator where the victims were stored.

Dr. Matsuda gave the facts succinctly and very legibly. The cause of death was undisputable. The murderer's weapon of choice was a firearm. She used murderer because she had ruled out suicide and accident. Two of the vics caught bullets in the cranium. One in the left parietal. The other in the occipital. The third vic was shot in the chest cavity, stopping all heart features needed to sustain life. The time of death was between midnight and two a.m.

"You look like there's a surprise on the tip of your tongue," Rude said to her.

I added, "Hopefully, it is not a devastating one. For the defense anyway."

"Let's take a look at the bodies," Dr. Matsuda said.

There was nothing like the features of a cold, dead body. Victim 1's toe tag identified him as Lawrence Miller, the lawyer. His yellowish complexion was pale and the area of his scalp which had been shaved was wrinkled. There was a bright orange one-inch, earplug type foam planted on the spot where the bullet entered. It was slanted.

"The bullet penetrated the back of Mr. Miller's head from a downward angle and became lodged in his throat," the doctor said.

"Which means that the shooter had to have been in the tree where the casings were found," Rude said.

I just listened to the details. Avariciously, analyzing everything I saw and heard. I'd get both of their written reports and sink my teeth into them, wholeheartedly. I was not a scientist, yet, but I would be though.

"Mr. McKeithan was shot head on. I surmised that he was in motion. And, Mr. Daniels, the last vic, was lying down based on the direction that the bullet traveled through his cranium."

Rude watched her lips say every word. He was really in investigator mode. Dr. Matsuda walked us from the ice box of bodies to her office, which was equally cold. She went into a file and handed it to Rude. Not me, as if I wasn't lead counsel.

She said, "Everything in the report is as I've stated, but take a look at page six."

Rude turned to page six, and I looked over his shoulders. We both looked at each other and smiled.

Dr. Matsuda confirmed my thoughts.

"One of our guys did the prelim report, but it'll return from the specialist very conclusive that Mr. McKeithan was shot with a different weapon than the other two."

"This was not in the initial preliminary autopsy report sent over to me this morning." I barked, angrily.

Cynthia had nerve. No wonder the report was so timely.

"I know," Dr. Matsuda said. "They intended to keep the finding and then spring it on you just before the prelim. But I always keep the defense abreast of these sorts of findings when a man's life is on the line. I become quite hostile when upset defense attorneys growl at me when I am on the witness stand, as if I am the one that shot a hole in their case."

"Lil, you're a godsend," Rude said.

"Thanks, doctor. We will be in touch," I told her.

My first time in a morgue went rather good considering I had two gunmen.

Outside, I asked Rude, "You fucked, Dr. Lillian Matsuda?"

"Maybe."

"You sly bastard. I can find out if you did. You're not the only investigator."

"Anything is possible."

"For me, probable."

"Try!"

CHAPTER 37

I walked into my office and the crime scene photos awaited me. The 8x10 color glossies were in a three-ring binder. I looked at the LaSalle keychain because it was the most damaging photo that Rude had taken. If Wydell's prints were on that keychain, I would need a BC era miracle to keep him off death row. I wished for a moment that Rude had not found it. I was worrying prematurely. If there were no latent prints, then cool, but if Wydell's prints were all over it, he couldn't get out of being at the scene. That didn't make him a murderer, though.

Next, I looked at the photos marked: shooter position. Wydell was tall enough to climb that tree and agile enough. I doubted that he could shoot through the window, jump in the tree, and then shoot two other men with a different weapon. Anyone there would be crawling away from the alcove. Even if it took five seconds, especially with the shooter's proposed shooting location.

Jonathan Rude entered my office and began going through his slides. He seemed impressed with his work. Maybe Rude had found a hobby?

"There's no picture to tell us who was shot first?" he informed me. "It'll be nice to know."

He opened the binder of photos to the picture of the tree where the shell casings were found.

He said, "If McKeithan was shot first, that means the shooter shot him, climbed into the tree, and then shot Miller and Daniels with an entirely different weapon."

"Not hardly," I replied. "We have a second shooter, Jon. I wonder what Cynthia has to say about that."

"Probably nothing. That just means he had help. Or her and her imbecile team will come up with some foolishness to explain how agile Wydell is."

"No, Jon. They're not that dumb," I said and chuckled. "They'll give him an accomplice and lean on him with a plea to rat his accomplice out of hiding. That'll never fly."

"So you believe that he did it?"

"Not sure yet. But I am leaning towards no."

"We need witnesses from that party."

"Let me handle that. Believe it or not, I used to run with a few of the hoodlums at this party. These were no ordinary corner boys. The attendees were the crème de la crème of the drug dealers."

"So we're looking for a rival drug dealer, maybe?"

"Maybe. We need to get the prints on that keychain."

"Already being taken care of."

"Let me guess. Dr. Lillian Matsuda put a rush on it for ya?"

"You're so jealous," he said and flashed a smile.

I chuckled.

"Any prints other than Wydell's on the weapon?"

"Only a preliminary finding, but there were none."

"We need that to be conclusive. We need to find out whether the bullets were fired from Wydell's gun and what type of gun was the other one. Also, could you go back to the crime scene and recreate the murderer's movements. Did he jump from the tree, or onto the tree? I've spoken with the girlfriend via telephone and she's on her way down. She's really adamant that Wydell is innocent."

"The forensics are out of my hands. I'll drive back up to the crime scene and get you that re-creation."

"Also, could you poke around the campus and find out who will, and can, testify that Wydell was at a victory party. I need the times nailed down precisely. I'm going to go up to the cab company and to the hood to get some information to reconstruct this charade."

"Good. I'll hold out on getting the recreation. Be sure to find out how much time separated the killings."

Rude got up to leave and suddenly, I had one last question. "Did you get the owner's name of the home?"

He pulled a printout from a folder and passed it to me. I thanked him and he left to do what he did best. I sat for a moment and then walked to the window and pondered. A few things bothered me that needed to be addressed.

One, my client seemed to have a concrete alibi, but the deaths were given estimated times of death between midnight and two. Wydell claimed to have called a taxi at 12:30 and was in a cab by one. I made a note to get the exact number of minutes it would take a cab to get from LaSalle to the 100 west block of Seymour Street. No more than seven I'd say. Before that was solid, I needed to know what time the shootings occurred. If they happened when the first of ten police calls came in, that would be 1:35 a.m. Certainly, Wydell could have made the Chestnut Hill trip, but wouldn't he encounter people coming and going from the home? He needed time to set up, right?

Two, Wydell offered me 30K without explanation. Who lived on Seymour Street with that much money to burn? I thought and realized that quite a few did. I had seen dope dealers own Benz's and live in housing projects with their baby mamas. I had also seen them drive the same type of vehicles and live in their moms' run down homes. But they had fancy wardrobes and TVs in the headrests of their cars. If something damaging came out about my client and his money, he would be off to Graterford's death row, and I would face disbarment.

Three, I wondered should I be looking for an alternative killer? That was the PPD's job, but I could find him and use him to set my client free. That would have been nice--to be applauded in the media for withdrawing a college athlete from the throngs of a flawed criminal justice system and depositing him into death row.

I usually did not need to rely on shady tactics to garner an acquittal, but I couldn't see Wydell James railroaded. Cynthia actually hit me first by withholding exculpatory evidence. I am a non-violent person, but it was time to practice what I had preached to Brandon. I told him that if someone hit him, he had better hit their ass back! Cynthia was about to be hit, and I didn't care that she was a girl. She had a punch like Laila Ali.

CHAPTER 38

Wydell's girlfriend, Shannon, met me at Sole Food, a seafood restaurant in the lobby of the Lowes Hotel. I ate there religiously, and had a running tab that didn't seem to quit. I had many lunch dates there to impress clients, but today was different. I was on very serious business, as a man's life was on the line. It had only been fifteen minutes of chit chat about nothing. I had already forgotten, Wydell's girlfriend's name. Despite that, I asked her to tell me about Wydell.

She grinned, a pretty look, full lips, painted a shade of red.

"Well, let's see. We're both marketing majors."

"Both!" I interrupted her half choking off lobster meat. "Pardon my rudeness."

"You didn't know that?"

"Of course not," I said and pulled out a tape recorder. "I'd like to record all of this."

"Sure. Fine. We are in our last semester. Graduate in May. He was already accepted into the Wharton School of Business at U of Penn."

I couldn't suppress the grin, or my awe. I was a little embarrassed not to know this information.

She continued. She spoke very carefully and coyly.

"He'd have to be extremely pissed off to kill."

"I'd say that is a given, wouldn't you agree?"

I sipped my Sprite.

Shannon shifted in her seat. "You once wrote that there are two types of murder. One is premeditated and the other stemming from passion. This was deliberate triple homicide, and Wydell was not there, so that rules out both for him. He was playing a school game from six to ten, and then attended a victory party."

"He was on the basketball team?"

That was a stupid question, but my Wydell updates continued to get better. Some people said that there were no stupid questions. I totally disagree.

"He was the team, Mr. Lemmelle."

All righty then.

"Do you know about an argument he had with one of the deceased?"

"No, but I know that he hated them. Always talking about becoming that man to reform his neighborhood. Get rid of the punks that were destroying people's lives with drugs."

Motive. Legally, I couldn't tell her to never repeat that to Cynthia. Cynthia could spin that line like a DJ.

I then asked, "Have you read my article where I proposed potential defense character witnesses should be barred from speaking to the prosecution?"

"I did. I have no intentions of speaking with the DA. After what they've done to Wydell. Ruining his last semester. He was going to move him and his family to a better area. I am a white African, Mr. Lemmelle. Born in Lesotho, South Africa. Trust me, I understand the plight. So, no offense."

"None taken. You seem passionate about Wydell."

Shannon batted thick eye lashes.

"Wydell is a very charming man. I adore him, Mr. Lemmelle. He worships me and does not hesitate to be romantic. A real gentleman. Beneath his braids is a beautiful mind. Upon graduation he intended to lose the braids for a conventional business look," she huffed and looked into the ceiling as if holding back tears. "Mr. Lemmelle, I once caught him reading an etiquette book."

"Wydell, the thug?"

"No, Wydell, the intellect," Shannon said and went into a shopping bag that she had brought along.

She pulled out an expertly wrapped gift.

"Here's your retainer. I know you'd like to know where this cash came from, but I'm sworn to secrecy. I will tell you that it's so legal, Condi Rice would spend it in the White House commissary."

I gave her a cynical smile and took the gift. "Thanks, Ms. Oscar. Is there anyone else on campus who can attest to Wydell's impeccable character?"

"Sure, but don't get me wrong he's not flawless."

"Meaning what?"

"A little arrogant temper."

"I know it," I said quickly. "Was it public or private?"

"Don't-complain-about-the-small-stuff temper. Being from the ghetto, he hated complainers. Epitome of excellent judgment, charismatic, a leader. No nonsense, though."

"So, the showcase of temper came when?" I needed to know of any adverse behavior. (I do not do surprises.)

"Only when a..." she hesitated.

"Strictly confidential."

"When a racial slur about our relationship was thrown at us. A few football jocks had things to say."

"Like who?"

"Lewis Barclay and his pals. Footballs lie between their ears, not brains. Wydell stole their newspaper thunder and according to them, one of theirs."

"You?"

"Precisely."

She sipped her water.

"They bad-mouthed me how some blacks badger Tiger Woods when he acknowledges his Asian descent. I acknowledge my African descent, and they can't take it."

"Where do I find this Barclay clown?"

"Don't bother, Mr. Lemmelle. He can't offer anything to help, Wydell."

"Just a little chat," I said with a sinister stare in my eyes.

"Lemmelle, he'd make trouble for me and there'd be no Wydell to protect me from their middle school-like horror."

"I won't bother for now," I told her.

"If I thought he could offer anything favorable by talking to you I'd be up for it, but he's a bad seed. The truth about what happened, and who did it, will come out. I hope so, so Wydell can come home."

What's done in the dark. You know the cliché. "We'll see," I told her. "Glad to have met you." I waved for the check. Albeit, I wouldn't pay it then, I'd be billed, but the check needed my John Hancock.

"It's been a pleasure, Mr. Lemmelle. Thanks for the late lunch," she told me and left. All of her curves went with her.

However, all of Ariel's curves stepped in accompanied by a male companion.

CHAPTER 39

Mrs. Ravonne Lemmelle had had a lot of nerve to bring that gentleman to my digs. My stomping grounds.

In a very casual fashion, I said to Ariel's back, "Good afternoon, Mrs. Lemmelle."

She turned and looked at me like a viper. I wholeheartedly desired to chuckle, but I suppressed that thought to remain within the behavioral standard that a man should be in line with men watching their wife in the hands of another man.

"That's the former, Mrs. Lemmelle. My husband is dead," she snapped back. "Haven't you seen the obituary?"

"Who's prince charming?" I asked, ignoring her comment. I was having a moment of jealousy, and praying that it did not turn into rage.

"Prince Charming?" the man asked, gruffly.

He then asked Ariel, "This must be the great orator that you told me about?"

He pushed his tongue into his cheek indicating a long sharp object was piercing his mouth.

I held marginal feelings for Ariel. I also adored my freedom, so rather than defending myself in a trial for murder, I reduced my ass-kicking to: "I can permanently force your cheek to swell like that, but..."

The bitch cut me off.

"No need for that, Ravonne Lemmelle," she said to me. Turning to her date, she said, "Excuse me."

"Yeah, before we have a..."

"A nothing," I said cutting off her boy toy's threat.

That little pretty South American, green-eyed bandit was about to get fucked up over a bitch that I didn't even want.

"I'll meet you at the bar," the man told Ariel.

"Good thing, or you'd be sipping out a straw for a few months." I told him.

I had to get the last word in. For this occasion, that was a must.

When the prince left, I asked, "So this is who you wanna spend half my dough with?"

"Not hardly. He's new to Philly. I don't need to explain myself to you, hun."

"To hell you don't," I said hotly and emotionally. I recanted that emotional outburst, and told her, "You should find a better place to entertain your flings. This will be desirable testimony during our divorce proceedings."

She stepped closer to me and rested her hand on my chest.

Lovingly, she told me, "You will not be having a divorce proceeding, silly." She smiled wickedly. "My lawyer will contact your lawyer and you'll sign what I propose."

"Really. That's a lie."

"You can pretend to be tough, Ray-Ray, but this is not a boxing match. Play pussy and get fucked if you wanna. I have a very long dildo for ya."

She then snickered at her joke, as I watched her walk to join another man at the bar.

She could stay as firm as she wanted in the belief, but I would not be beaten by any one. Not even my wife.

CHAPTER 40

Rude parked on Olney Avenue and walked a few steps to the front of the LaSalle University two-story dorm. It had been sometime since he had been on a college campus. He lusted over two sexy co-eds exiting the dorm. Behind them a geeky male exited. *Why wasn't the co-ed idea thought of when I was in college*? he thought. He entered the building and slipped pass security. On the second floor, his eyes widened as two toweled females, bursting out of their towels with busts duly exposed, skipped past him gossiping.

"Excuse me," he said to a girl with a LaSalle sweatshirt on and jeans.

She had a luxuriant, spiky hair do.

"Look cop. I was not smoking weed. Leave me alone, pal," she said and brushed by him.

"Ex-cop," Rude countered.

"Ex-con," she snapped back. "We have the ex part in common."

"I'm investigating for one of your classmates, Wydell James."

That caught her attention. "Who are you?"

"You know him."

"The entire campus knows him. Haven't looked at a conference championship until he arrived."

"How'd he do at the game Saturday?" Rude asked.

It was a leading question designed to get the student to confirm that Wydell was in fact at the game.

"Thirty-four points, thirteen boards. He's thirty and plays like he's twenty. Do you work for his attorney?"

"You must be a fan?"

"Nope. Campus reporter. The name is, Rhonesia Cosby."

Great catch, Rude thought. "Got any footage?"

"Every game, but Coach Patillo could be better to assist you there."

"Anybody dislike Wydell?"

"Dislike may be the wrong choice of words. Jealous would be more fitting. He owned the sports section of the paper, even on Saturdays when the football team played. They always attempted to pressure the paper to be more partial to them."

"Them as in?"

"The football team. I'm sure they're glad that he's in county jail."

"But Wydell didn't write the paper. How'd Wydell respond to them?"

"He once pulled a gun on Barclay, the school QB. Barclay recently relocated from LA to King of Prussia and is perversely discriminatory. He's a racist pig, but all mouth and no bite. And I am being nice with my words because you're also white."

"What room does this pig live in?"

"Check with student services," she replied.

She knew the room, but there was a limit to what she would disclose.

"Look I have a class, so I have to go."

"Okay," Rude said, shoving a card into her hand.

"If anything surfaces, even rumors, contact me. Where can I find the coach?"

Rhonesia checked her watch. "The gym. Practice is going on."

"One last thing, sweetie."

"Rhonesia is fine."

She did not like that.

"Was Wydell at a party after the game last weekend?"

"He is the life of the parties."

* * *

Rude was escorted to the school gym by another female who shared the same sentiment for Wydell as Rhonesia. She dropped him off at the gym and he all of a sudden ran out of business cards, so that he could take her number. He was such a slick bastard.

Rude forgot all about the gym when he saw a sweet thing. She had on jeans, T-shirt, and a wind breaker, like it was fall. But her long hair and breast caught his eye. He stepped to her.

"I'm Jonathan Rude, an investigator working for a classmate of yours, Wydell James. You know him?"

"I do," she said, without breaking her stride. "We can chat, but in the school cafe, as you can see I'm not dressed to talk out here."

Rude wondered what it would be like to see her not dressed at all. In the cafe, they ordered lattes, he paid and they took seats in the window.

“Calculus,” he said. “Don’t miss that. Sorry to interrupt your studying time I know how valuable that is.”

“That’s okay,” she said, and batted her eyes at Rude.

He thought that she was flirting, but she was being normal, though.

“What you wanna know about Wydell? I still can’t believe it. Unimaginable.”

“Wish you were a juror. You sound convinced.”

“No, I’m still registered in Virginia, but Wydell was...well...sweet.”

A southern belle, Rude thought.

“What you mean?”

“Well not in a gay way, but in a gentleman way. Ladies first. Thank you. Excuse me. That sort of thing. Shannon is lucky.”

“Wow! Sounds like Prince Charming.”

"All except the time that he pulled a gun on the QB."

"Yeah, I heard about that. Guess everyone explodes."

"But everyone does not carry loaded guns."

"How can you be so sure that it was loaded or even worked?"

"He shot it on New Year's Eve right over there," she said, pointing to an area which looked like it was a summertime hangout full of scantily clad females and in-heat males.

"But do you think he'd kill anyone?"

"Only under extraordinary circumstances."

Rude gave her a smile of understanding. "Happen to see him at the victory party?"

"Who Wydell?"

She gave a shrug. "Yeah, he was there."

She's hiding something, Rude thought. "What's the matter..."

"Caitlin. Nothing." Very nonchalant. A shrug.

"Listen, I'm on his side. I work for a law firm," he told her and gave her his business card. "If you're in possession of something good or bad, Caitlin, I need to know."

"What time did they claim he was at the scene of the crime?"

"Now you're asking me questions?"

"What time?"

"Unsure. Coroner says the victims were killed between midnight and two am. The first police call came in at 1:35 a.m."

"I saw him and Shannon arguing at about 12:20 walking away from the dorms."

"Happen to hear what they were arguing about, Caitlin?"

"Well, he had been caught in the bathroom fooling around, and Shannon became pissed and wanted to leave the party."

"He's sort of ladies man on campus?"

"Well, there's a rumor about, you know. How black guys and..."

"What rumor, Caitlin?" Rude said, rudely.

"Okay. Word around campus is that Wydell has a big..."

"Come on, Caitlin. A man's life hangs in the balance, here."

"Okay...Dammit...It is said that Wydell has a big cock and a lot of girls want to find out about it," she said and looked around guiltily.

"Even you, Caitlin?" Rude asked. She nodded. "You were having sex with Wydell and were caught by Shannon during the night in question?"

She hesitated and twirled her fingers.

"Yes."

Rude thanked her for her time and stood to leave. "Was anyone else shooting on campus on New Year's Eve?"

"No."

CHAPTER 41

I opened the front door and Brandon jumped off the sofa and ran into my arms. I picked him up and spun in a circle. I never stepped off the tile in front of the door there solely for shoe removal. Take that, Ms. Pearl. He had a wave cap on his tiny head that made him look weird. I could only imagine what prompted that. I kicked off my wing tips and scooted into my moccasins.

"Where's Dajaun?"

"In the bedroom," he told me.

He jumped from my arms, grabbed my hand and pulled me toward the master bedroom where I found Dajuan writing in his music notebook.

"Can I have some ice cream?" Brandon asked.

"Nope."

"You're early," Dajuan said. "Five-thirty. That's a record. We ordered cheesesteaks."

"Shut up," I replied and took off my suit.

Dajuan asked Brandon, "Did you tell that you played hooky from school today?"

I stopped.

"Uh...Dajuan, five-year-olds do not play hooky. Their parents do not take them to school." I was polite, but in no way happy. "Did he manipulate you?" I asked and smiled.

"No, Daddy R. I did not manip...whatever...him. I told him that I had to make you something nice, cause my teacher, Ms. Denise, told me that I should be a nice son."

He skipped out of the bedroom.

"There's more," Dajuan said.

Brandon came running back with a wrapped gift larger than him. He handed it to me. I had received more than the allowable gifts this day.

"Open it," he encouraged me.

He then hopped onto the bed and curled under Dajuan.

He whispered to Dajuan, "What's manip...? You know. The word that Daddy R said?"

"Ma-nip-u-late. Four syllables. Say it," Dajuan whispered back.

"Ma...mip...pa...late," Brandon said and used four tiny fingers to count out the syllables as directed.

"No," Dajuan said.

They rehearsed it a bit, before Dajuan said, "It's when you lie to get something."

"I do not lie. Daddy R is crazy," Brandon whispered conspiratorially as if I couldn't hear him."

"I heard that," I said and we all chuckled.

I had the gift fully opened. It was a painting. Nothing that I identified, but my son had written on the bottom like Picasso. "This is nice, King B. What is it?" I asked carefully. Didn't want to offend the little fella.

"Dad!" he said excitedly.

He stretched the word out.

"It's you in court," he confirmed and then pointed me out in the painting.

I was painted as a collage of colors. A rainbow. Was my son sending me a subliminal message?

"I knew that," I said, and picked him up.

I gave him a tight hug.

He rested his head on my shoulder and told me, "I love you."

"I love you, too, King B," I replied and he jumped down.

"Can I get a big bowl of ice cream?" Brandon asked again.

He was a real manipulator, and I am a sucker. I took him to the kitchen and gave him the ice cream. I returned to the bedroom and took a quick hot shower.

Out of the shower, I emerged into the bedroom in boxer-briefs and a tank top.

I asked Dajuan, "Who is playing tonight?" We always watched basketball games together.

"Don't know. Did you miss me? I thought about you all day."

"I always miss you," I told him and leaned in for a serious kiss.

"I really appreciate you, Black Face."

He pulled me to the bed and rolled on top of me.

"I know you do. I appreciate you, too. I especially love what you do with Brandon."

"That's my little buddy. To leave you would be leaving him and I can't do that."

"Don't..."

"No, listen," he warned me. "This whole weekend you did not show any sign that you were mad about what I did. You're a remarkable person, and I love you for that."

"Thanks, Dajuan. Things happen, I can handle a lot, but I do not want to be alone. You're my world, my first and only lover."

"Good," he said and smiled. "Because, while me and King B were out getting that painting framed, we stopped at Tiffany's, and I bought these"--he pulled out a baby-blue box from his pocket and handed it to me. "Open it."

Another gift. I was really on a roll. I followed his order and found five round diamonds embedded in platinum wedding bands. I looked at him dreamy eyed. I was really stunned, but masked it well. I knew we could not legally marry in Pennsylvania.

He said, "I know I've been an asshole, but Black Face, I realized you're the one for me. I know legally marriage is not possible, but will you wear this ring as a symbol of our devotion to one another?"

"Everyday, babe," I said and hugged him tightly.

I heard Brandon drop his bowl in the dishwasher and the dishwasher door slammed shut.

"Get off me before King B gets here," I said, but I wanted to be conjoined to Dajuan Jones.

Brandon walked in, and I asked, "What did you do besides my painting?"

I wanted to be into Dajuan, but my child came first.

"Victor came over and I learned the Spanish numbers again. Test me."

"How old are you?"

"I'm five," he said and chuckled. "Ask me a Spanish number?" he demanded.

"You were supposed to answer in Spanish."

"Oh, *cinco*," he said. He then said, "*Yo soy cinco*." I am five.

"And, on your birthday, you will be?"

"Seis."

"How old am I?"

"He only knows 1-15," Dajaun said.

"Old." Brandon blurted and laughed.

"Here's a hard one, funny guy. Say fifteen."

"Quince," Brandon said and danced.

"Alright, Latin lover. Let's watch the Sixers get blown out once again."

Old? I'm 30. Could I really be old to a five-year-old? Does he see me as an invalid?

TUESDAY, JANUARY 9, 2007

CHAPTER 42

I rolled across Dajuan and staggered into the bathroom. It was 5:34 a.m. on the ninth. I perched on the toilet.

Upset.

Afraid.

Heart racing to break Olympic records.

The nightmare was terrorizing. Someone had stolen Brandon and Dajuan was found bolted to City Hall like Jesus. His wedding ring was glued to his forehead. With that vision I wanted no parts of sleep.

I walked down the hallway to Brandon's room. I peered around that powder-blue room with navy carpet and cloud decals on the ceiling. I thought about heaven. My baby looked angelic. He was sprawled in the bed with a leg loosely hanging in the air. He was as handsome as me, just a lighter hue. Our baby pictures could claim us as twins. He was a gloriously unique child who loved every book on the shelves around his room. He could create a new story for every picture book. One day, he'll yarn blockbusters for Hollywood. Having him was joyous and kept me responsible.

I checked the windows to be sure they were locked and that the bolts were still conspicuously in place to avoid them from being raised from the outside, but an inch.

At 6:10, I walked out the front door. I went to the gym in the four-star Bellevue Hotel. I did a serious circuit routine and then watched CNN morning news as I conquered a half-an-hour on the treadmill. I showered, dressed for success, and then strolled into my office at 7:45.

My first thought was acknowledging that one week of this routine--including the nightmare--would be a serious prob-lemmo. There were a myriad number of reasons why; chiefly, no breakfast with my son. I was away from him enough. I didn't want him to grow up and call me a bad dad and blame his crack addiction on me chasing my dream of heading the largest Philadelphia law firm.

I had a cappuccino and peered out of my office window to the streets below. So routine. The people below walked briskly with hats, scarves, and coats on snuggly. It was freezing outside. Gloved hands were wrapped around briefcases. Employees were bustling to offices to fatten the coffers of their employers.

I checked my quotidian report That was always up-to-date, thanks to Marsha, certainly not, *moi*. I had a thought: *Was I, too, a robot*? A martyr of habit and gainful employment? Absolutely! I profited, too.

401K.

College savings.

Two country club memberships.

NAACP membership.

ACLU membership.

The law had been my life, considering dear old Dad was in politics before I was born. I always wanted to be in law. I never wanted to be a DA, though. Everyone screamed for a better, prosperous America. That began with an educated minority. Becoming a criminal defense lawyer, my motive was to encourage all minorities to find a way out of poverty, not through crime. I took on ugly cases that no one wanted, not because of the attention they promised--my sexuality handled that--but, because beneath that drug dealer was a sound business mind.

A drug dealer knew product and demand, marketing, the art of negotiating, security, when to inflate, and how to turn a profit without paying taxes. It was well documented that drug addicts needed treatment and not a jail cell. I once defended a HIV-positive client who confided in me that his only reason for violating PA Crimes Code 4101 (Forgery) was to fly the skies and dine off stolen credit cards, wearing designer labels, all thanks to someone else. Simply put, he feared death and not having fulfilled a life. He had no time to climb the ladder of success and earn his fancy lifestyle. In his eyes he may have died before he reached the top rung. That was a serious psychological issue, one that should have been addressed in counseling, not prison.

My reflection time was over at 8. Marsha was on the scene to kick my day off, but I felt like being stingy with my time that day. I began to meticulously plan my day. I had no court appearances. I wanted no phone calls until further notice, unless they were from Brandon's school, where he had better been and not conning Dajuan out of another day at home.

By 8:30, I was in my coat prepared to leave my office when Marsha's sexiness entered. She waved a greasy homemade pork chop on an English muffin sandwich in her hand. I snatched it up and devoured it greedily.

I told her, "Do not text my cell phone, unless Osama bin Laden needs a lawyer. And I am not taking any clients today."

"Where are you off, too?"

"To see the wonderful Wizard of Oz."

CHAPTER 43

It had been my fourth courtroom visit of that day at the Criminal Justice Center. I had no cases, but touring railroad central was always my favorite past time. My laptop and I had not been bored. I was building a legal career and what better way to spend part of my day than watching my opponents try their cases.

I walked into a courtroom and became excited. So many dirty secrets, embellishments, half-truths, and flat out lies were revealed in court. It took a fine lawyer to reconstruct the facts through exhibits and testimony and unearth the truth. For a good legal drama, forget about what Hollywood had to offer. A trip to the local courthouse did justice.

A courtroom spectator watched a horrible trial be put on and heard all of the hallway gossip as a bonus. That was more intriguing than what happened inside the courtroom, at times. The delicious behind-the-scenes myths and scandals were tasty. Beware of the graphic crime-scene photos, though. I had seen a few races to the bathroom from some gut-wrenching photos. Don't have a pity party for the vics, either, as they are on the witness stand letting beautiful tears fall from their eyes, as the DA asked, "Are you okay? Do you need time?" until you have heard both sides. I promise unparalleled let-down when the defense exposed that the true victim was not as pitifully distraught as they let on.

By 10:35, I was in the Honorable Francis Willis's courtroom, and my only purpose there was to build my dossier on Assistant District Attorney, Guy Dietz. I had a file on all of them at the DA's office. I knew their weaknesses, strengths, and conviction records. I studied them with vigor. I may have known the legal them better than they did. My file on them contained character flaws, attitude problems, and mood swings. Did they whine about being overruled? Did they offer abusive objections? Did they speak clearly? Eloquently? Were they sartorial and exuded confidence? What did they drive? Where did they reside? Married? Single? Kids? Clubs? Memberships? Affairs? Thanks to Rude, I knew it all.

Take Guy Dietz. He donned a navy suit more than enough. I knew it was the same one because it had a miniscule cigarette burn on the bottom right side of the jacket. He adored clip-on bow ties. He was an absolute slob without table manners. We lunched--once, and trust that was enough--to discuss a plea. He raised his spoon to his mouth ninety going south. He kept his mouth packed. Never did he stop shifting his food in his mouth creating that abominable smacking sound that cattle were notorious for. He was a vile and viscous viper toward defense witnesses and the presiding judges. And his mother gave him a sexy name like, Guy. He was no Guy. Not even a

Bartholomew. I had heard him punctuate a question to a witness with a curse. Now there he was before the Court to hear all motions *in limine* of a robbery case that was tried shortly after the *limine* hearings. This was what unfolded before the Court:

"What other motions do you intend to file?" Judge Willis asked David Tom, the defense attorney.

David Tom was a veteran attorney who spent 17 years at the DA's office prior to private practice. No doubt he had the DA's number. He knew their strategies, how they selected a case to try, prep witnesses, select experts, and gather case law. He had a fairly solid image. Nothing to scantily clad in his legal closet.

"Honorable Willis, the defense will file a motion to dismiss based on the prosecution not bringing my client to trial within the 180-days as set forth in the Penal Code..."

Good ol' Guy Dietz, interruptive-attorney-at-law cut his colleague off.

"Undoubtedly, the Commonwealth will oppose that motion," Dietz said, loudly and rose to his feet. "We..."

"Mr. Dietz, please have a seat," Judge Willis chided.

He had his glasses, which were tinted, looking directly in Dietz's direction. As far as I knew, he could have been looking at a Playboy Magazine behind those glasses. They were shades.

"I will not be yelled at as long as I wear the black robe."

That was a pompous statement, and one to be noted in my Judge Willis file.

That far, my Willis file reflected that he was 61. I was at his 60th birthday bash, as Wydell called them. He had been on the bench for 19-years and made a play for General Attorney. He had his political path paved until scandal brought him down. He was accused of taking a bribe. I digress.

"Undoubtedly," he continued sarcastically, and I wanted to hoot, "You'll oppose. I would think that when you walked into this courtroom you were aware that today is the day that I'd hear motions *in limine*, and you would be doing a lot of opposing. Now do your job and please allow me to do mine without the grandiose interruptions. There's no media here, but if you'd like some, maybe you can have Abraham re-assign you to the Torres cannibal circus on 10."

Dietz bowed down in his seat. I had never seen that, or Willis being so calloused. The pressure was now on the defense, too. Tom knew he had better not become a victim of that harshness, especially when a jury was involved. But, I'd bet that Willis would not pull that in front of a jury.

I received a text message from Rude, and was rescued from this train wreck.

CHAPTER 44

Aramis looked forward to going to the LaSalle University campus. At precisely 11:35, he stumbled into the bathroom. He showered, trimmed his goatee and dressed. He looked like a Harvard student all over again. He donned jeans and a college sweatshirt, sipped coffee and sat at his desk reviewing his notes from Ravonne. His home telephone rang. He glanced at the caller ID and gripped it up.

"Yes, Mr. Lemmelle," he said, chuckling.

"Good boy," Ravonne said and laughed. "Listen, you've got to get over to that campus. I need a story on my client, Wydell James. Nothing negative."

"You've told me this."

"Miz, this is tricky, man. I need some sympathy."

"And you're going to get it by the late edition. Stop sweating me man."

"But it's already noon. You know all of the campus will be drunk by two. I know this reporting thing is fun for you. Just another day in Vegas, but a man's life is on the line. The stakes are high. You have to get back to the newsroom to type this bad boy up and have ninety-nine editors review it. With all that, won't you miss a deadline?"

"Come on, Ray-Ray. Step into the millennium. I'll E-mail the article. I'm only doing color and background. Besides, I already have the shell of the article written. I'll E-mail it to you before I leave out the door."

"Okay. Could you add a name to your list? Shannon Oscar is my client's girlfriend. She tossed me a $30,000 retainer. See if you can find anywhere the money came from. Don't ask right out; just suggest that I am so expensive. If Wydell was into anything crooked, especially selling drugs, I need to be prepared."

"Why doesn't he just tell you that?"

"Clients usually have no knowledge of the law. They believe they can't be represented by me if I know the truth. I can and would. It's just ethically I could never claim that they're innocent, only that the prosecutor can't prove it."

"That's why I report the law, and not defend it. And you call what I do Vegas. I am going to the campus no. Bye!"

Life without a woman was bad enough, but Ravonne wanted him to run around college campuses and be surrounded by well-favored females with brains and retentive knowledge. He had been driving for ten minutes before he thought about how much fun that may be. Maybe this investigative escapade would take his mind off sex for a moment.

Not hardly.

He would run down his list of students he needed to interview, write up his piece, be back home by eight to catch *24*. As he watched *24*, he would have the phone chat line on hold.

He parked his car on Olney Avenue in front of a building that mirrored an Italian cathedral. He found the registrar's office there. He did not want to be on campus long, so he handed the student clerk a list of basketball players that he wanted to interview. He also gave her a lie that he was writing a piece on college hoop stars. The student looked at his press credentials suspiciously, but she handed over the class schedules of three students. It was against school policy, but how could she deny those students the possibility of receiving coverage that could put them on the NBA's radar. *It'll be a little trickier to get Shannon Oscar's, though*, he thought.

"Thank you," Aramis told her very nicely. "Would you happen to know, Shannon Oscar?" he asked coolly with a smile on his face.

It was warm like she was an old friend.

"The runner? Yeah. What about her?"

"Happen to have her schedule? I hear her boyfriend is the star of the team? I'd like to get her take on him."

"I don't know, Mr. Reed. I could be in trouble for the schedules that I have already passed to you. I better talk to the Dean first."

No deans, he thought. He may get kicked off campus and not get to the boys if the dean was called. He thanked her and flashed from the hallway before she felt guilty and confessed her crime to the dean and security. *I'd report that, too*, he thought and laughed out loud.

CHAPTER 45

Aramis studied the Spring 2007 listing of classes, professors and classrooms on a bulletin board in the school cafe. The board reminded him of Harvard's advertisements for old text book sales, tutors, roommates, off-campus rooms/apartments, party announcements, intramural games, and club meetings. A pretty little woman skated past him on roller blades. He smiled at her and signaled for her to stop.

"Sorry to bother you," he said as she removed her earphones from her ear. "Could you point out these three buildings for me? I'm new and haven't learned the campus, yet."

"Sure."

She began to point out the buildings.

"Thanks," he told her and locked in the building locations. Before she skated off, he asked, "Do you happen to know Shannon Oscar?"

"I do."

"I need to talk to her. I wanted to check on Wydell."

"Wydell?" she asked. "What happened to him?"

"You haven't heard?"

"No."

"He's in jail for murder."

"No way," she raved with her mouth ajar. "He's no murderer."

"Cops say so," Aramis replied like a college punk.

He recalled that coy tactic working excellently to get Harvard co-eds into bed.

"That's why I wanna talk to Shannon to be sure that he is holding on."

"From what I know, she stays in a rooming house on 20th Avenue. I don't know the address, but the house has a lot of lights and Christmas ornaments on the lawn, which eight days after New Year's the girls continue to light."

"Thanks a lot. What's your name?"

"Dora."

"Antonio."

"Nice to meet you, Antonio. I'll see you around."

Aramis watched her cute little butt skate away and he made his way to Jared Vetter's Art History class. The class should have been ending, and he hoped that the professor did not release early. He entered the hallway and four classes rushed into the hall. He eyed the students coming out of classroom 107B. It was not hard to spot Vetter. He was 6'5", lanky and boisterous. Jared was no doubt a jock.

"Excuse me? Jared? You're Jared Vetter, right?"

Cocky stare. "Who's asking?"

Here came the lie. That was the part that Aramis loved.

"I'm Kevin James, Wydell James' brother. He was arrested and I'm trying to find out some information about him. He told me that you were on his team and would help him with an alibi."

"I heard about that. I thought it was a rumor. What kinda help does he need?"

"Solid alibi help."

"I like Wydell. Great guy and all, but I won't lie for him."

"Just confirm that he was not at a party on Saturday and that's all he needs."

"Sure, he was there! He's the Main Attraction. He comes to every party."

"Main Attraction?"

"You know like, Allen Iverson, The Answer. Wydell James, the Main Attraction. Your parents must be proud?"

"You have no idea."

"He pushed out of the ghetto at 26 to go to college. He proves that anything is possible."

"Yeah, that's my lil' bro."

Five minutes later, Aramis found Michael Rains' Ethics class and peeked into the door. The professor had the students working in groups, which made it easy for him to slip into the class and approach the professor.

"Sorry to bother you professor, but I have an urgent message for a student named Michael Rains. He has a family emergency."

"Who are you?"

"John. I'm the part-time student clerk at the academic advisor's office."

"Well, Mr. Rains is not here. He cut my class and be sure that the advisor gets that," the professor said.

"I'll be sure to."

Amongst a row of duplexes on 20th Avenue, Aramis found the only home with enough ornaments to be in the Christmas Day parade. He approached the walkway leading to the front door and accidentally bumped into an alluring, dressed down co-ed. He excused himself and picked up her cell phone. He handed it to her. Her touch was soft. Very feminine.

"You're quite excused," she told him and brushed pass him.

"If my phone is broken, I'll track you around this campus for payment." She wanted to add: "With ya fine self."

Feisty, he thought. He handed her a business card. "If it's broken, I'll take care of it."

She scanned the card.

"Why are you here?" Plenty of attitude.

"Looking to talk about Wydell James. I hear his girlfriend lives here. Do you know Wydell?"

"Of course I do, and I'm investigating his arrest. This campus is my turf," she then tossed him a card of her own, and said, "Rhonesia Cosby, LSU campus reporter."

"How coincidental?"

"Very. Now be gone before I have campus security escort you out of here."

She had no idea if that was possible, but the threat was cute.

"To late," he said as security pulled up.

Two youthful, gunless, security guards hopped out a Chevy Cavalier. They exited their car as Shannon Oscar appeared in a second story window.

She yelled, "Both of you, get off my property. None of the girls that live here want to speak to you. So leave."

She slammed the window shut and closed the blinds.

"You heard her," fake cop number one said.

The other one told Aramis, "Sir, you need to leave the campus. All interviews must be cleared through the deans. Do not come back here asking for student rosters, or you will be arrested."

He then told Rhonesia, "You have enough enemies."

"None in the security office," she snapped, "but I could create a couple."

Aramis got the point and strolled nonchalantly to his car. He was mad that he had to leave that soon. Not because he had one more student to talk to; he wanted to be in the company of Rhonesia Cosby.

CHAPTER 46

Rhonesia had spent four hours trying to convince the executive editor of the school paper that they should allow her to effectively pursue the Wydell James case. He only agreed after she agreed to be partial to no one and report what she found without bias. That would force her to print up a scandal sheet of all the things that she found which ordinarily provoked a libel law suit. She had convinced Shannon Oscar to meet with her after showing genuine concern via E-mail. They did not meet on campus. They met at a McDonald's at Broad and Olney, four blocks from the campus.

"Hey, Shan," Rhonesia said as she slipped into the very last booth in the back of the fast-food joint.

"Hello, Neesha," Shan replied.

Her tone was low and extremely timid.

"I'm glad you changed your mind about meeting me. I am definitely on your side. Well, Wydell's."

"Thanks. I'll tell him. Sorry about my rudeness earlier, it's just so many people pestering me," she said and sipped her coffee.

She was in mourning.

"I can't go anywhere without feeling like I am being stalked by reporters."

"I am sorry if I upset you. I am new at talking to real victims," Rhonesia smiled.

Shannon smiled, too.

"He was so protective. No one would be bothering me if he was here. These idiots be playing on my house phone and sending me crazy E-mails."

"I bet every boy next door has you on their to-do list. They're like high schoolers. We're so lucky," Rhonesia said, chuckling. She was warming up to being an investigator. "How's Wydell?"

"He's fine. He called me once. I can't even see him until he's out of quarantine. He's so healthy. He said he's sleeping in a closet full of bunk beds. It's him, a drug dealer, a robber, and three drug addicts. Two of them are dope sick, vomiting and defecating everywhere. It's terrible."

"That sounds horrible. What if he gets sick with TB, Hep-C, or a staph infection in there?"

"They don't care. It's insane. I can't wait to see him."

"I'd like to see him myself," Rhonesia said. "Could you ask him for me?"

"Sure."

"I can't imagine having to go through this."

"It's surreal. Believe me, you want no parts of this loneliness. Just alone. Everything hurts. I'm still in shock. It's right up there with a funeral."

"Do you have any idea why he was thrown into this mess?"

"Don't print this. He had an argument with one of the guys that was shot. I guess that's the motive."

"Does his lawyer know that he has an alibi? I have been trying to get the tapes from the gym, but to no avail."

"That's crazy, Neesha."

"I know. I am going to flash his picture around the area of the shooting. He had to be around there setting up. I'm also gonna get all snazzy and go to the bar where he lived to get some information."

"I would go with you, but..." Her voice trailed off and she sipped her coffee again.

"No, I can do this. This is my job."

"I'm sure he'll appreciate your help."

"Have the police searched his room?"

"Yup," she replied, quickly. She had a conspiratorial smirk on her face.

"You cleaned his room?" Rhonesia asked earnestly.

"Left the furniture." Shannon giggled, finally.

"Was there something to hide?"

"Not exactly."

"Meaning?"

"Meaning, I can't tell you what he is doing in his spare time."

"Must've been nice to pay for Ravonne Lemmelle?"

"He must really have a reputation?"

"Shan, he is the newest attorney on the rise. He represented the Bezels. And he's gay. That's newsworthy in itself. Usually the two do not go hand and hand, but he produces acquittals like plastic surgeons produce youth."

"Lemmelle is gay?" Shannon asked perplexed. "He didn't seem gay."

"You've met him?"

"Yes, and he's not a gay man."

"Dear, he is gay and makes no attempt to hide it."

"To hell he don't."

"Shan, baby, gay does not mean leather and flamboyance. Step into 2007."

"He's so..."

"Delicious. I know, but wouldn't touch either of us."

"A wasted dick." She smiled and laughed.

Rhonesia laughed.

"Anybody hate Wydell?" Rhonesia asked trying to stay on track.

"Barclay, of course. Everyone knows that."

"Anybody outside of school. Did he tell you about anyone in this hood?"

"No. I only spent the night there a few times."

"So, maybe he was hiding something."

"No, Neesh. He always went home during the week. I don't know."

"Must be love."

"It was. Well...is."

"Okay. I'm going to do a colorful article on him and add a bit about you. Got a photo?"

"In the dorm."

"Let's get that. I need to get to the press room."

CHAPTER 47

Aramis was a freelance reporter assigned to the police beat at the *Philadelphia Inquirer*. He had been there four years now and had yet to move in the communications world. If he kept working in tandem with Ravonne, he would get that one case that would take his career off like a space shuttle. He wanted to crack a big case, write it up for the paper, have the Associated Press pick it up, and then have literary agents beating his door down with advance checks for him to write all about the details of the case in a hardback.

He hopped into his car, drove, and twenty minutes later, he found himself in Chestnut Hill. Island Reality was an executive rental company who catered to wealthy clients.

"Aramis Reed, *Philadelphia Inquirer*. I'd like to speak with someone in charge. I'd like to know about the three murders that occurred at 1935 Hope Circle this past Saturday," he said, introducing himself and stating his business.

The blonde receptionist was taken aback.

"Oh, I'm sorry, only the manager can release that type of information."

"Release? Sounds like the real deal."

She sucked her teeth and took an irritated deep breath.

"Ms. Percy is in a meeting with a client, and..."

"And I'll wait," he told her and had a seat.

"Her entire afternoon is booked."

"But she is here now. I'll only be a minute. Just a few questions."

"Yes, I heard you, but..."

"There is no but, sweetie, I will wait."

"It would be wise to make an appointment. To see you means," she checked her calendar, "delaying her appointment with the Scotts due in twenty minutes."

"She'll be delaying more than that if she doesn't see me."

"Like."

"Her next sale."

Aramis looked around the walls at the photos of many homes. Some were rentals for parties and vacations. Others were for sale. Each photo had the skinny on the property printed on index cards neatly tucked in the corner of the picture frame. He spent the next fifteen minutes looking at pictures in an issue of *Architectural Digest*.

The door to Ms. Percy's office opened and a neatly trimmed brunette stepped out. Her business suit was a tweed Chanel. Behind her were a man and a woman.

"...the property is beautiful close up," Percy said to her clients. "You'll have plenty of space to build that green house, Judy."

The couple left and Percy said to Aramis, "You must be Mr. Scott?"

"No, Mr. Reed. *Philadelphia Inquirer*," Aramis replied. Ms. Percy turned crimson. "Sorry to disappoint."

She gave him a toothy, faux smile.

"Oh, how can I help you?"

"I'm working the case about the murders that happened on your property at 1935 Hope Circle. I specifically want to know who rented the property and how they paid."

"Oh! That's easy," she said slyly. "That's confidential."

She nodded her head cockily and rubbed her palms together.

"To bad Island Reality won't be confidential after my article hits the stands."

"We adore publicity, Mr. Reed," she snapped, unbothered by the clandestine threat.

"Not this kind. Three men that were very deep into the drug game with not a single job listed on two of their social security reports rented a home from you to throw a party. The attorney who happened to have assisted both vics beat multiple drug, assault, racketeering, and murder-for-hire charges was on the property at a drug dealer's event on par with the Democratic National Convention. This hardly sounds like the press that you want. Who'll buy a home haunted by three drug dealers?"

"Give me a day or two to think about this."

"Sure, that sounds fair," he lied.

He watched the Scotts come in the door. With their attention on him he switched gears and barked, "I am going to sue you for discrimination, ma'am. You took my money and now because I am black, you're telling me that the neighbors do not want me renting from you because of the three drug dealers killed on your rental property."

"Mr. Reed, I..."

"Name and method of payment." He hissed.

Ms. Percy collected the Scotts and as she entered her office, she told the receptionist, "Give him what he needs."

Aramis collected the data from the receptionist and then left the office. He walked to his car and dialed the 35th Police District. He had a contact with every police district in his cell phone .

"Callaghan. Aramis Reed."

"Look! I've been avoiding the media for the past hour. How'd you get through?"

Aramis ignored the query. "I've got the basics. What's new?"

"Nothing."

"How 'bout the autopsy? Has it been released yet?" Aramis asked.

He knew the answer, too. Aramis had started law school at Harvard with Ravonne, but he decided to report crime rather than defend it. He was lucky to get into the Journalism master's program without being a journalism undergrad. He was in law school long enough to learn the questions to ask, and not to believe any of the answers.

"No, Reed. Now if you don't mind, I am working on a big case."

"Liar. I hear two different types of bullets were found. Care to explain where the other perp is? I've spoken to several party-goers and there's no way there was one suspect."

"That's privileged information, and if you air it, I'll have you arrested."

"How do I know if it's privileged. You're right, though. The autopsy is privileged to me and every citizen in the nation. Now be a nice sport and give me some background and I'll lay off that you guys need to be pursuing another shooter."

"You are a real Class A asshole."

"Can I buy you a drink?"

"Maybe."

"Tonight. Eagles Bar on Broad and Erie."

"They'd kill me in there. That's the worse area in the district."

Aramis chuckled.

"Just checking and I was right. You are a wuss. I'm only going to cover the perp's background tonight and their relationship to the suspect in custody. I'll look forward to a call from you for lunch by 10 a.m. tomorrow, or I'll have my pals at 3, 6, 10, 17, 29, and 57 air the autopsy findings at noon and my article will follow in the late edition. Have a blessed day, Detective Callaghan."

He hung up and then drove to the Metro Room of the Inquirer, just in time to pollute the jury *voir dire*.

WEDNESDAY, JANUARY 10, 2007

CHAPTER 48

After a hot shower, I dressed and left the Bellevue Hotel's gym. I loved hump day. I had a steady appointment with a handsome masseuse Wednesdays at three. Dajuan joined me, usually, while Brandon enjoyed Drama Class. Ordinarily, I drove back to my office, but that morning I parked at the Prudential Building and jogged back as a warm-down. At 7:25 a.m., I found myself showered and having breakfast in my office.

Having forgotten the newspaper, I ran out to get it. When I returned to the building, the front was cluttered with reporters. Two television vans from local media affiliates were half parked on the pavement and partially in the street, obstructing a free flow of traffic. Unbelievable! The nerve of those ingrates. I did not like that at all. At the courthouse, I was fair game. That was private property and I had no idea what brought those media meshugas to the law offices of Martir and Savino.

"There he is!" yelled a reporter.

"Can we get a statement?" screamed another.

"You can. Have them move the vans," I replied as eloquently as I knew how.

"What do you know about the Chestnut Hill murders?"

"Three dead drug dealers. Move the vans, or I disappear."

The vans were rolling away, but the cameras and microphones were moving in for the kill. I walked slowly to the corner and stood in front of the T-Mobile store. They were closed. I held my briefcase in front of me with two hands and rocked slowly with a smirk on my face that would annoy any mother if it came from a misbehaved child.

"What happened up there?"

"Unfortunately, I was not invited to the soiree. Glad I wasn't."

I was being sarcastic and for good reason.

"Who is Wydell James?"

"School paper says he was framed. Or, had an accomplice. Any truth to that?"

I knew that voice and planned to curse his ass out for filth. I had to get a handle on those mongers.

I flashed the camera a smile, and said, "At present I am preparing to defend Wydell James, a 30-year-old, black male, and a basketball star of the LaSalle University team. It's highly unlikely that Mr. James would participate in or perpetuate a crime of any sort, and there's no tangible evidence linking Mr. James to a charge of murder. As a crime reporter, you're fully aware that I cannot divulge much more and I'd appreciate if you respect the defense, prosecution, and Mr. James' family. That is all."

I simply walked away, ignoring their queries like I was the President of the United States. I entered the Prudential Building and instructed the security to request that the media vanish, and if they didn't, he could call the police.

Entering the elevator, I looked at my cell phone. No reception. I rode in solitude to my floor and strolled into my office. It was 8:46 a.m., and there was no sign of Marsha. She was due in at 8:30 that day. She was becoming a thorn in my ass with her excessive lateness, but she was the best when at work. I needed to get a handle on her, though, before her-royal-lateness became unemployed.

Cappuccino was what I needed, but I had a bone to pick. I commanded my cell phone to dial my best friend. I looked out of my window and watched the crowd of reporters beginning to evaporate. A few lingered doing intro's and/or outro's to their news bites, scheduled for the noon news.

"Get your ass up here to my office. Now!" I told Aramis when he answered.

As if Aramis was in the elevator when I called him, he walked in as soon as I hung up the phone. I immediately went in.

"Why did you invite that imbecility to my office?"

"I needed to," he replied matter-of-factly.

"Needed to?" I barked.

"I'm going to find the true killer and I needed to get something about the alibi out of you."

"You got some way of getting an alibi," I said hotly. "Since when do you need to orchestrate a circus to report crime?"

"Since I decided to earn a Pulitzer."

"Miz, I am not joking. You need to confer with me when you want to do things like that."

"Alright, Ray. Damn. You do not need to get all butt hurt."

"I do not get butt hurt. That shit was uncalled for. No one learned anything not available to them through public records, and besides, you could have requested an exclusive."

"I know. That's why I am here. I just thought that it made sense to do that so that I didn't look like I was being fed info. I was looking out for you. At least, I thought I was."

"You're a journalist. You report crimes."

"That's just it, I report. But, I want to solve them like an amateur sleuth. No rules like the police."

"You're off the hook," I said with a light chuckle.

"What?"

"How in the hell are you going to solve this? I hope by not promoting nonsense in the school paper just because you can get away with it without a libel law suit. You think you're slick."

"I didn't print anything in that paper, and there are ways."

"I've got methods to get the goodies to get Wydell acquitted."

"Good for you, but I am going to hand over the killer on a silver platter as soon as Wydell walks," he told me confidently. "If you want in, you're in, but, you got to let me do my thing without you knowing much."

"And that means?"

"Look, Ray-Ray, you know that the police love accessories before the fact, so don't worry. Whatever I find, you and the public will know."

"And the DA and cops, too," I said and smirked sarcastically.

"Good. Let's keep them honest."

"You're my best friend, Aramis, and an excellent reporter. At both capacities, I am relying on you to be ethical and not do anything to get me hung."

"Come on, Ray-Ray. I would never do anything to ruin our friendship. You know that."

"Technically, you could not jeopardize that because even after disbarment, I'll be your best friend because I knew you meant well. I know you want to solve this case, and you may feel the need to withhold intelligence from me. That is what reporters do and I respect that as long as it does not interfere with my case. I do not need my credibility shot to hell. I have enough enemies in the DA's office, and judges hate me, too. I do not want to become legitimately tainted."

"Roger that. Loud and clear."

"Now, I planned a press conference, but why don't I leak a little to the media. And I know the perfect media outlet."

"We both win. I'll have found things that the police haven't to make my name soar, and Wydell innocent appearing. A win-win for us."

"Who says that I was talking about you?"

We both chuckled and, oh my, I let something slip to the media.

"Be careful out there," I told him as he prepared to leave. "Let me know when you are going into a hostile environment, so that I can track your ass down."

"Alright. Now, can I write this scathing report?"

"Yup. And don't misquote me!"

"I'll be sure to."

"Aramis, I will sue you..."

He walked out on me. I laughed and said out loud, "My buddy, Aramis Terrell Reed."

CHAPTER 49

"All rise for the court," the bailiff yelled.

"Please be seated," the Honorable Joseph Defaria said as he dropped lazily into the tall, ebony, leather chair behind the bench.

His voice was serene beneath his thin lips. He had the kind of blanched complexion and rosy cheeks that could make Santa envious. Defaria had slipped into the black robe for the past 22-years, and at 70, he was on his way out the door. Easy cases were all he was assigned to. He surmised--and it was delusional--that he was privileged not to have to deal with high profile cases. Truth was, he couldn't be trusted in his old age to effectively oversee one.

Prosecutor, Carmen Gonzalez sat on the right side of the courtroom poised next to her partner, Deborah Craig. Carmen's suit was being selfish to her skin. It choked certain areas and exposed too much cleavage for a courtroom. Deborah, on the other hand, was a hefty black woman, who looked more appropriate for nursery school. I was not fooled. She knew how to exhume a suspect's crime and neatly lay it all out for the courts. She would do it without malice, too, with a smile on her chubby face the entire time. The two of them were swamped with about 50 cases that day. It would be a long day for them, starting with me.

The bailiff said, "Mark Fields, come forward."

I threw on my pince-nez and got into character as I walked toward the well. As I lay my briefcase on the defense table, Mark joined me. He wore a brown suit with a designer tie and expensive shoes. With teeth capped in gold and braids in his hair, my client looked like a pimp. I recalled the day that he came to my office. I had labeled him a masterful story teller. He could've made the men hard at work in Hollywood miserable. The same fantastic storytelling was the catalyst in him waltzing out of a PNC Bank with nearly six grand without ID. I could not wait to hear the one and only, Deborah Craig explain that.

Both Deborah and I introduced ourselves and I sat.

"Very well, Ms. Craig. This is a preliminary hearing for Mark Fields. He is not willing to plea?"

"That is correct, Your Honor."

"Good. Call your first witness."

"The Commonwealth calls Lacey McKinney."

* * *

On the morning in question Lacey McKinney was performing her teller duties at the PNC Bank at 2000 Market Street. She had been fine tuning her performance for three years. That morning she was approached by a gentleman dressed in a college sweatsuit and Polo ball cap. She recognized the suit because she was also a Temple student.

"Good morning, Lacey," the man told her.

He was a man who paid attention to the details.

"Good morning to you, sir," she replied.

"Sir? That was polite, but I am Elmer H. Booz," he informed her with a confident smile on his face.

She volleyed a braced-tooth smile, and said, "Okay, Elmer. What can I do for you today?"

Elmer handed her a withdrawal slip which was already filled out. It was not one of the generic in-house withdrawal slips, either. This slip was actually pulled from the back of Elmer's checkbook. The request was for $2,933.00.

"I'd like to make a withdrawal," he informed her.

She punched a few keys on her keypad and brought up Elmer's account. He had a balance of $5,975.22 in his checking account and over $22,000 in his savings.

She said, "I can do that for you. Can I have your ID?"

Elmer fiddled around in his pockets and did not produce a wallet. He did produce an excuse for the *faux pas*.

"I came all the way downtown from the school to do some Christmas shopping, and I have inadvertently overlooked my wallet rushing out of the door."

"I need an ID, Elmer," she said skeptically.

"I forgot it, but I can verify my social and birthdate," he confessed. "And you can also check my signature."

"I guess I could," she confessed.

She looked at the monitor as he said his social security number and birthdate.

"What year were you born again?" she asked. What he had said did not match her records."

"1984," he told her. "They must still have my grandpa's year down there as 1944. That is an error that I have vehemently told them to correct, to no avail. I'll go over there after I leave here with you."

She looked at him puzzled.

"I am sorry for the drama, Lacey," he said, affectionately. "I just want to get my shopping over before finals start."

"Yeah. I go to Temple, too," she said, beginning to count the cash. "What year are you in?"

She had not even verified his signature.

* * *

Deborah threw her hands on his hips flamboyantly. She asked Lacey, "Did you have any more contact with Elmer, Ms. Kinney?"

"Yes."

"When was that?"

"The very next day."

"Where?"

"He was back to make another withdrawal from his account."

"He did, in fact, withdraw another $2,930.00. Is that correct?"

"Objection."

"I'll rephrase," Deborah said, throwing me a crazy grin. "Did he withdraw more money the next day?"

"Yes."

"What amount was that?"

Lacey consulted her notes before, she said, "$2,930.00."

"Is there a policy at the bank regarding withdrawals under $3,000.00?"

"Yes. They do not need to be approved by the head teller."

"Let the record reflect through exhibits A1-A5 that all of the defendant's withdrawals were under $3,000," the DA said to the Court.

To Lacey, she said, "Do you see Elmer Boozer in the courtroom?"

"Yes, he's the defendant."

"Nothing further."

"Cross, Mr. Lemmelle?" the Judge asked.

CHAPTER 50

Lacey was such an innocent appearing witness. I was prepared to tarnish that visual. She looked like she was ashamed of her stupidity. Wait until she gets a whiff of me. Everything that she had testified showcased how apprehensive she was about my client's authenticity, but she had augmented his craving for fraudulence. Mark Fields awoke everyday to con. He jokingly referred to himself as the Confidence Man.

"I'll make this hasty, Your Honor," I said as a promise, as I walked toward the witness box.

I wanted to get all up into the face of "Bimbo" McKinney.

"Ms. McKinney, is it true that you were arrested for stealing your father's car and selling marijuana in high school? For you that was three years ago, right?"

“Objection!” Deborah catapulted to her feet. “The defense is testifying, and McKinney’s priors are irrelevant and inadmissible. That’s if they exist.”

“Oh, sure they do,” I said before the Judge could reply.

I passed along her arrest record. I was more pissed at this bimbo because I banked with her bank and she could have easily given away my money.

“Sustained!”

“I appreciate that, Your Honor,” I said in agreement, as if he had patted me on the back.

Lacey’s lips quivered. I was not done. I wanted tears. Blood too. And I’d at least get tears.

“You’ve been a banker for three years, right?”

“A teller.” Defiant.

Was she coming at me sideways? She attempted to correct me, Ravonne Lemelle. I walked to the court clerk and borrowed a dictionary. I adored courtroom theatrics. She had written a withdrawal slip and I planned to cash it.

“Ms. McKinney, could you read for His Honor the definition of banker.”

She grabbed the dictionary, and I thought she had read the definition to herself, before she read aloud. “One that engages in the business of banking. The player...”

“That’s good right there. Note for the record that the witness read from the Merriam Webster’s 10th edition collegiate dictionary. Ms. McKinney would you regard yourself as someone who engages in the business of banking?”

“Yes.”

“I thought so,” I said. “Now, as a banker, how many men have you allowed to molest your customer’s hard-earned money?”

"Objection! Objection!" Deborah Craig's voice boomed across the courtroom and she threw her arms in every direction begging Judge Defaria to say...

..."Sustained. Sustained. Mr. Lemmelle you're completely out of order."

"I most certainly am not, sir," I replied and walked to my table.

All of this caused McKinney to allow tears to escape her eyes. The gallery began to whisper. The bailiff beat me to hand McKinney a tissue.

"He should be admonished, Your Honor," Deborah suggested.

I ignored her stupidity. I shut her up, too. I handed her a document and a copy to the defendant, I mean, witness, and Judge.

I asked, "Ms. Mckinney, do you recognize this report?"

"Yes," she whined.

I then asked the court reporter, "Could you please reread for the Court the last erroneous objection by the prosecution?"

The reporter repeated it, and I replied, "Music to my ears." Oops.

"Mr. Lemmelle!"

"Sorry, could you ask the witness to answer my query: "As a banker, how many men have you allowed to molest your customer's hard-earned money?"

"The witness will answer the question," the judge said.

"Once," she replied after a brief hesitation.

What the DA neglected to report was that Ms. Kinney had pulled this stunt with her brother and the bank forgave her.

"Ms. Craig should be admonished, Your Honor," I requested. I then asked, "Your Honor, I'd move to have the witness impeached."

"I object, Your Honor. As far as the Court knows they were in cahoots."

That was such a foul statement. Good thing this was not a jury trial.

"Even if impeached, I have a corroborating witness, Your Honor."

"Great. Nothing further. I will preserve my right to raise this motion later, Your Honor."

"Ok, perfect," Judge Defaria said. "Any redirect?"

Deborah said no, and the judge asked her to call her next witness.

CHAPTER 51

"The Commonwealth calls Detective Fletcher."

Detective Fletcher was a ten-year officer with the PPD. He had responded to the PNC Bank at the request of the branch manager, Amelia Pechmann. She had received a complaint from Elmer H. Booz that he was missing $6,000. Upon investigation, Amelia determined that Elmer had been robbed considering she had a black man on camera withdrawing the money.

The detective testified under direct examination that he had taken the surveillance from the bank. At his office, he reviewed the surveillance and printed a hard copy of the suspect. He subsequently matched the photo to a man in the crime book. He then filed for an arrest warrant.

The DA asked, "Detective Fletcher, is the man in the surveillance in the courtroom today?"

"Yes," he said and pointed.

"Let the record reflect that the detective pointed out the defendant, Mark Fields. The Commonwealth tenders the witness, Your Honor."

"Mr. Lemmelle."

CHAPTER 52

"Just a coupla questions, detective. Let's start with, can you be 100 percent certain that Mr. Fields is the man in the video?"

"Yes."

A one word slick answer. I was pissed that fast.

"The photo appears grainy and is in profile. You're sure that you can unequivocally identify him?"

"Asked and answered," Deborah said and smiled.

I looked for him to bite and lower the percentage just a little. That left room for reasonable doubt. No such luck with the pit bull sitting to my left.

"Nothing further, Your Honor," I said and headed to my throne.

"Counselors approach," Defaria said.

My opponent and I approached the bench. Deborah stood far away from me as if I had a caution sign pasted on my forehead.

The judge asked, "Who else do you intend to call, Ms. Craig?"

"I have a forensic handwriting specialist and Mr. Booz, the victim," she said.

"I have heard enough, Mr. Lemmelle to hold this over for trial. Calling them would add overkill. Do me a favor and advise your client to plea. Craig, can you rest your case."

I had no objection. The old man was right.

* * *

I left the courtroom at 10:45 with mistake number two under my belt. My client was on my heels.

"What just happened in there? I paid you $4,500 to get me off." Mark had claimed.

I pressed the down elevator button. "You're going to be paying a lot more to represent you in trial."

"More money! I ain't rich."

"Then you need a new attorney."

"What!"

"Mr. Fields, I have done my job. I warned you that you had zero chance to beat this at a preliminary hearing." I was whispering. "Surveillance put you on the scene of the crime, visually. Little whirls on your finger tips put you at the crime scene, too. Let's not forget the finger print analysis that solidifies you as the writer of the slips. And Lacy, despite her stupidity, recalled your charming award winning production to get the cash quite vividly. Must've made a good impression."

"You're an asshole. So you want more money? What happened when the Judge called you to the bench?"

"Doesn't matter," I said as the elevator door opened. We rode in silence to the lobby.

We exited in the lobby, and he said, "You have to get me out of this, Ravonne. I can't go back to jail, man."

"You should have been thinking about that before you did the crime."

"Who said that I did?"

"Right," I said and frowned. "You better come up with a grand scheme to get yourself out of this. You're in a tough situation."

"I hired you to come up with a scheme."

"Here's the scheme. Let's try this," I said as we crossed 13th Street.

He followed me. Stayed close. "Bring me the exact amount that you stole in cash and I'll play footsies with Amelia Pechmann to see if she'll drop the charges for the cash. Throw in $500 for her troubles."

I walked along Juniper Street and walked into the Juniper Street entrance to the Marriott Hotel. The bell hops and valet nodded at me. That was my normal routine as I headed back to the office from CJC. The valet knew me as an attorney.

"And when should I have the money?"

"That doesn't matter if I don't get a new G4 from Apple along with the cash."

I was not above bribing a client.

"What!" he yelled.

His voice echoed in the hotel lobby and all eyes were on us. He caught himself, and then whispered, "You're trying to strong-arm rob me?"

"The laptop costs about $1,200. I'm sure you can get your hands on one." I winked. "It's that or pay me a retainer to prepare for trial. And my magic tricks are costly, sir. Very!"

"You're a cold-blooded piece of work."

I exited the hotel on the Market Street side, and then said, "Look, you're not getting off. Raise Johnny Cochran from the dead and you would not get off. You can fire me and go with a PD to save you money, as no one can save you. Get me the money that you stole, an incentive for Amelia, and the laptop. This case can disappear. You get the last laugh. Everyone wins, and I keep my acquittal record."

At the corner of 12th and Market Streets, I crossed the street and walked pass Sole Food (my hangout), and 50 yards away stood the Prudential building. I had stopped walking to let what I had told him sink in.

"So what's it going to be," I asked and rocked on the heels of my Ferragamo's with a dumb smile on my face that would have pissed me off had I received it.

I was in power, and planned to keep his cash, and give Amelia some money to not show up in court. He (and probably you, too) believed that I just tried to extort my client. I didn't. I didn't encourage him to break the law either. As far as I knew: see no evil and hear none.

"I'll call you when I get the shit man," he said as if it pained him.

Could what I asked him have been that noxious? He was a penny-ante yegg who needed to pay his taxes to the street.

I collected.

CHAPTER 53

Explorer's Den was an Uptown takeout spot with superstar popularity and a menu that surrounded the famous Philly cheesesteak sandwich. The shop also sold hoagies and pizza to the students of LaSalle University.

Aramis sat in a booth awaiting his pizza steak when he was approached by Rhonesia Cosby, reporter for the LaSalle U newspaper.

"We meet again, Mr. Reed," Rhonesia said, and held her hand out to shake his.

She wanted to feel his manicured hands.

"That is I," he confirmed. "And call me Aramis."

"Why'd you invite me here? We are competitors. In fact, I want your job. Besides look around, no one eats in."

"Right," Aramis said sarcastically. "Very investigative. Hope you like pizza steak and cheese fries."

"I do, Mr. Reed, but I am not hungry. Thanks, though."

"Have it wrapped to go. It's even better after it has sat for a moment. Aramis, for the second time."

"Right," Rhonesia chuckled. "So what's up? It's kind of strange meeting a real journalist."

"How come?"

"Well the journalism industry allows in a handful of newbies. The competition is like the NBA, but there's no real bench."

"Sure there is. Freelancers like me."

"Aramis, I pulled a few of your articles from the Internet. They are better than the staff writers."

"But a paper can only use a certain number of staff writers. I have done good work, but I've yet to take the media by storm. You pulled my articles. Must've been interested," he said and smiled.

"Don't flatter yourself. Just wanted to see if your work reflected your character."

"I'm okay, but enough about me. You've got to get some real credits under your belt and I am here to help you get credit number one."

Rhonesia was an independent woman who was not impressed by the promises of a man. She had no idea what Aramis spoke of. "I need an ear for the campus scuttlebutt and thought you'd be willing to lend your ear," he said as lunch arrived. He took a large bite out of the steak sandwich, stuffed a handful of cheesy fries into his mouth. He sipped a soft drink, and dabbed the cracks of his mouth with a napkin.

"Excuse me. I'm famished."

"Uh, Aramis. I am going to be very straight forward."

She looked him in the eyes and used him eating as her chance to do all the talking.

"I can't dig up dirt on Wydell. He's getting stiffed, man."

Aramis sipped his Pepsi.

"Good, because that's not what I want. See there was a keychain found at the scene of the crime, a LaSalle U key chain to be exact. Prints pulled from the keychain are not Wydell's. I'm looking for information on anyone at school with an interest to frame Mr. James or a motive to kill three people."

"Oh, Rhonesia can do that easily. As a reporter around here, students are careful around me. But a few of the girls around, you know, the party chicks, they may prove to be worth more than a blow job."

"Do they still claim to be virgins?"

"Yup."

The two reporters chuckled. Aramis used the moment to alter his sandwich again.

"Mr. Reed, how do I get a credit for that? Why should I trust you?"

"Did I say credit? I meant byline. This is off the record. I have a leak in the defense. You don't. Good enough?"

"Byline in the *Philadelphia Inquirer*?" she asked and shook her head.

"Yes, I will share the byline with you. Your name in the Philly lights."

"Just what I need. My name listed with yours. You better not be kidding," she said and snatched one of his fries.

"Is this a date?" he asked.

"No!" Fire in her eyes.

"Then keep your feet off my fries." He chuckled.

"I've been many things. I stopped kidding at ten. I studied journalism, got a masters at Harvard, but not even that prestigious U taught me how to dig up the real dirt. Do you..."

"I can handle this, Aramis."

She held up a hand.

"I've been hustling around this campus. I know how to get things shook up."

"My kinda girl." Aramis confirmed. "Here's my card. Call me anytime, day or night if you get anything hot. I have night vision goggles and all."

"I like the way you think," she said.

Rhonesia snatched up his business card and looked at it before stuffing it into her pocket. She stood and gripped up her sandwich.

"Thanks for lunch, Aramis. I won't let you down."

Aramis watched Rhonesia walk out into Chew Avenue. She headed toward the heart of the campus. Hopefully Rhonesia obtained what was required to help elevate them both to stardom. Aramis had no idea if his witch hunt would lead anywhere, but until things were going somewhere, he would not tell Ravonne about his little meeting with the novice reporter. Besides Aramis would love to crack this case and so would the *Philadelphia Inquirer*. He planned to get into Rhonesia's bed. He adored chasing stories, as well as, independent, demanding, feisty women like, Rhonesia Cosby.

CHAPTER 54

I had walked into my condo with Brandon at 4:30. Dajuan was startled. He looked at the clock and then back at me. He turned back to the piano and continued making a song as if I had not been there. Brandon waved and went to his room. At age five, he knew not to disturb Dajuan while he made a number one Billboard hit. Hopefully, he learned that hard work paid off handsomely.

I tossed my blazer onto the piano keys.

"Wedding rings one day. No acknowledgement the next."

"It's 4:30. You're home and you picked up Brandon from Drama class. Two days of anything seems habitual, but I do not want to be deceived by you spoiling me coming home early. I am pretending that you are not home."

He tossed the blazer and went back to the piano keys.

I straddled him and slipped my tongue into his mouth and we kissed passionately.

"Still don't see me?" I asked softly into his ear.

"Nope."

I slipped my hands down his pants and massaged his erection.

"Still not here, I presume?"

"You're in the garage," he said with his eyes closed. "You're going to have to do a little more to be in the condo."

"Too bad," I said and laughed. "I came home early because I'm going to the bar tonight," I informed him walking into the kitchen. "I gotta go mingle with the ghetto folks to get a little info."

"Sounds like fun. I hope you come home drunk. At least a little," he said and smiled. "You like to get rough when you're drunk a little. I want you drunk, so that we can flip and flop all over the place."

"I'll be sure to have a club soda all night just for you," I joked.

I had every intention of getting drunk. Just kidding. I planned to be working, so no liquor. I would return home and pretend to be drunk for my lover, though.

"You're such a loser. I would go with you, but some idiot may have the news waiting outside for me. I don't feel like being mobbed."

"It could be a good diversion, but I'll pass. All of them hoes all over you would turn my stomach. Speaking of stomach. What's for dinner?"

"Don't know, but I have the dessert just for you."

"We still have the turkey, veal and pork burgers and wedges."

"Yeah, but I don't want burgers tonight."

"I'm not doing any gourmet cooking tonight, so do not ask. That's the only reason you dragged me to those cooking classes."

"No. I drug you there because your spoiled ass could only cook basic meals, and Brandon needed well balanced meals. Fried chicken and hot dogs wasn't cutting it. How about we have breakfast foods?"

"Yes, I can go for that. Belgian waffles, Canadian bacon, eggs scrambled, and raisin bagels," I offered and went into the kitchen when my cell phone rang.

I wanted to ignore it, but it was the ringtone assigned to my family. I checked the caller ID, and answered, "Aunt Diana, what's up?"

My Aunt Diana was a recovering drug addict, but also a damn good dental hygienist. I had encouraged her to go to rehab in the small town of Williamsport, Pennsylvania where the Little League World Series was held each year. She took my advice, and 12 years later she had no desire to move back to Philadelphia, the rotten city that I love. She sprinkled a visit here and there, but "The Port" was hers and her second husband, Kyle's. Her son

Karon and her three adopted kids lived there, too. What a bunch.

"This is Kyle," he said and corrected me. "We have a problem."

"What's up?" I asked with some hesitation.

"Your aunt is in jail. They locked her up."

"What?"

Now that was a comment worthy of the front page. In jail. That was the most insane thing that I had ever heard in my life as it related to Aunt Diana. I put the phone on speaker, so that I would be able to dress as he spoke.

"Remember our wedding?" he asked.

Of course, I did. Dajuan and I were groomsmen, and Dajuan sang.

"Your cousin Kareem paid for our wedding flowers and our honeymoon. He ordered us a roundtrip Amtrak sleep car to Myrtle Beach, South Carolina, and a limo service the entire time that we were there."

"Stop, Kyle. I know all of the details. What you're really saying is that Kareem ordered all of this with a stolen credit card, and they arrested my aunt for this."

"Man, he told Diana that he had a friend do it as a favor. I gotta get her out of there."

"I'm on my way. Chill out."

"Well you don't have to come all the way here. They want the money to release her."

"How much?"

"I have..."

"Kyle! How much?" I growled.

Brandon ran over to me and hugged me. I picked him up and saw him as a baby all over again. Dajuan was up from the piano bench, probably in the bedroom getting dressed.

"Sorry for yelling, man," I said. "But you know how I feel about my aunt. Whatever they want they can have tonight."

"They want $4,278.19."

"Can we Western Union that much?" I asked Dajuan.

"The banks are closed," Kyle said.

"Kyle, go to the Giant Supermarket. They have a Western Union station there. I'll send you $4000 and you can add the change."

"We will pay you back."

"Goodbye, Kyle. You can't get to the market on the phone with me." I hung up and asked Dajuan, "Do we have that much in the safe?"

"Ravonne, calm down," Dajuan suggested. "Yes, we do."

"I am calm, dammit. She's too damn fragile to be in there. I can imagine her shaking and crying. Damn, Kareem. That fool is paying every dollar back for this. I might not get him out of jail for this."

"Can't we use my credit card?"

"Yeah, even better idea."

"No, let's go with the cash because the verification process takes too long with credit cards over the phone. I don't want the court to close and she can't get out. I'll go count the cash while you call the courthouse and work your lawyerly magic."

I picked up the phone and acted. Dajuan was serene and seemed to have everything under control. I usually held my composure, but this could not be thought out as methodically as one of my clients. This was something totally different. I would not sleep knowing she was being strip-searched and made to sleep in a cell. I knew that she was sitting trying to be patient, relying on her faith in God that Kyle would contact me and I would run to her rescue.

She was absolutely correct, because she had always been there for me.

"South Williamsport PD."

"Hi," I said into the phone cordially.

I sat on the sofa and tried to relax. Brandon was right under me. He rubbed my leg as if he was trying to calm a tiger.

"You have a Diana Bezel-Sampson in custody and I wanted to know what time you closed and the latest time that the money could be brought in to have her released?"

"Who is asking?" a gruffy male voice asked.

"This is Ravonne Lemmelle, her attorney. I'm in Philadelphia and am en route to wire the money to your town for her release. I was wondering if I faxed you the receipt from Western Union could you hold off forwarding her to jail?"

"You do not sound like an attorney. You sound like a parent."

"I am a lawyer, and her nephew, sir, and I am very concerned. My aunt is no criminal."

"I know that. She's here because she refused to tell us who the male was who ordered the flowers from our local florist. See the local florist remembers the call and the transaction, because it was her biggest sale ever. Your aunt was on the line with the male and pretended that it was her father. She claims to have no idea where her father is."

"Wait, how do you know that she pretended?" I thought a moment and then said, "Ignore that. That's testimony and we're not there, yet. I will say that it was a shock for her dad to be at the wedding. He is very estranged. With whom am I speaking with?" I was absolutely lying through my teeth. That creep wasn't there.

"Deputy Tomlinson."

"Okay, Deputy, I am going to wire the money. It's 4:50. The money should be in Williamsport by 5:20. It's going to the Giant, and I am unsure how far that is from the station, but..."

"Five minutes."

"Then her husband will be there just in time."

"I'll start the paperwork now for her release, but she's going to the prison at six, Mr. Lemmelle."

"Thank you, sir," I said and hung up. "Thanks Dajuan," I said to him as he entered the living room with the cash in hand and ready to leave.

CHAPTER 55

After we sent the cash, I was relieved. My part was done. I had fulfilled my duty. Dajuan was driving us back to our home. I was no longer in the mood to be in the hood gathering data for my client, but that was also my duty. I knew that when I accepted my law degree and license to practice. I had to multi-task anger, grief, sadness, happiness, depression, family, and work. No matter the emotion, I was the ultimate actor. Bottom line, I was going to Charlie B's and I'd love doing my job. I also planned to cook for my family, because I was a strong black man.

Dajuan interrupted my thoughts. For the most part, he had been quiet in the wake of this drama with my aunt. It paid to have a mate who knew me inside and out.

"What do you want for dinner? We can eat out," he said and then added, "I can't believe, Kareem."

"Me either, but she was in on it. With his encouragement, I'm sure. She's a woman and a fancy wedding is a dream from being a young lady."

"So glad that we don't have to worry about a fancy wedding."

"What does that mean?" I had a little more bass in my voice than normal.

"Don't start Ray-Ray. You know how I feel about same sex marriage."

Dajuan looked at me weirdly at a red light. His glare penetrated me. I knew what he meant, but deep down I knew that he would marry me. I let it go, and switched gears.

"I'll cook dinner."

"Don't play superman, Black Face. Fo' real. We can eat out and get the same meal that you planned to cook," Dajuan told me.

He had a point. This was not the time to be obstinate.

"Let's go to the Midtown Diner on 11th and Samson."

Midtown was a cozy 24-hour diner where the gay children flocked after the club and hanging out of Philadelphia's notorious gay strip: 13th Street.

"They have good breakfast."

"And hopefully my girl Gladys is there," Brandon said and smiled at me.

"You're too darn much," I said to Brandon as Dajuan laughed.

"Ladies, man," Dajuan said to Brandon, and then to me, he said, "What time do you plan to go to the bar?"

"Happy hour. Seven-ish. Most of the caddy girls will be there then ready to gossip, and the dudes will be there for them."

"Okay, I'll drop you off and take Brandon to Cheltenham Mall. We will grab you when you're done. You don't need to be driving. You need a driver," he told me and smiled. Such a charmer. So protective.

"Take me home to change out of this suit, and then we can go to the Broad Street Diner, since you're going Uptown with me. They have nice Belgian waffles."

"Yeah, I hope so. What are you going to do about Kareem, though? I cannot not believe that he did this."

"Alright. I will get with him the next time I talk to him, but in the meantime..." My words trailed off because I had nothing to say.

CHAPTER 56

After a relaxing fortification break at the Oak Lane Diner, Dajuan hit Broad Street going toward downtown at 6:50. There was a light touch of rush hour as workers from the Willow Grove area took Broad Street to the I-76 entrance. Slowed to a crawl, I put Nemo on for Brandon to watch in the headrest TV. He sat in the back seat whining about nothing at all, of course, aggravating the hell out of me with the gay shit.

The houses along that stretch of Broad Street were large, three story A-frames. Some houses even posed as physician, dentist, and veterinarian offices on the first level. The second and third levels were the professional homes.

I was snapped out of my day dream by Dajuan punching his hand on the horn and swerving to avoid a Camry. He chanted imprecations and gave the finger to the Camry's driver, which was quickly volleyed. He had to get off Broad Street to avoid testing the Range Rover's airbags. He flipped a right onto Olney Avenue. At the next light, we were on the corner of Olney and Belfield. On the SW corner was Central High School, and also the same corner that Wydell claimed that he picked up the taxi that had taken him home the night of the murders.

Dajuan proceeded through the light. The next light was the LaSalle U campus. Had it been earlier, I may have had the urge to stop. I need not worry, though. I was sure that Rude had done his job. At the next light, Dajuan turned left onto Wister Street and passed Germantown Hospital. Wydell's little brother was still there recuperating. We meandered along Wister Street until we reached Germantown Avenue and Dajuan made a left.

"I wanna go to Nana's, Daddy B?" Brandon said with imperious niceness.

He obviously recognized the landmarks and knew that we were in the vicinity.

I looked over to Dajuan who simply shrugged as if nothing mattered to him. There was something on his mind. I could tell. I often wondered if he missed being in New York. I had the luxury of being close to my family, while his entire life was still there. We did visit occasionally, but I wondered if that was enough. He barely received calls other than the begging type. That would break my heart, partly because I valued my family and made every effort to show it.

I called my grandmother, and she answered on the second ring.

"What are you doing, Granny?" I asked without any intro.

"Nothing, baby. Doing this here puzzle that you bought me for Christmas."

"I am a block away. So don't be alarmed when I come in," I said as Dajuan made a right onto Seymour Street. We hung up.

"I'm going to Nana's. I'm going to Nana's." Brandon was singing that like a Broadway show tune.

* * *

Dajuan parked in front of Constance Lemmelle's and we hopped out into the cold. Nana--who was fortunate enough to have a lawn and outside porch--stood in the storm door sporting a new wig. That one was a short do with a duck tail. During the spring and summer, Nana planted flowers at the head of her lawn. The flowers complimented the tree that she had planted years earlier to use as shade against the deadly summer sun.

Her light hue glowed on the porch. She had all of her stoutness expertly packaged in a floral print dress.

Brandon raced up the block to her and hugged her legs tightly. She bent down and hugged him. He was too big for her to lift. Even though she was strong with a set of powerful arms from 40 years as a nursing aide, she was not picking him up.

We entered the home where I lived during my college breaks, considering my father--Nana's son--didn't want a gay trader in his then Mount Airy home. Nana had an olive green sofa with cream *fleur-de-lys* embroidered throughout, which matched her cream carpet. The walls were eggshell white, and she had a serious entertainment center. She loved movies, and I often heard her scream "Kill him" at a dizzy bimbo in a movie reluctantly pointing a gun at some man. Just a strong fearless woman.

"Where's Ralph?" I asked her.

He was her veteran postal worker, live-in boyfriend, and a gospel guitarist in a band. My natural grandfather was a mystery that I had not been able to unravel. I wasn't all that interested in it anyway, since he abandoned Nana.

"He's at practice," she told me from her Boston rocker.

Brandon stood at her side, resting on her leg like a bodyguard.

"I was just sitting here having tea and toast, listening to Jeopardy and doing my little puzzle."

"Tea and toast? You swear you're a rich white woman." That was our joke.

"You do, too," she said.

"Runs in the family," Dajuan said and glared at me. We all laughed, even Brandon."

"What are you laughing at?" I asked Brandon, and we all laughed more looking at his blank stare.

"You're telling me that a gal cannot have a little green tea and lightly-buttered pumpernickel to cap the night. You use to love jeopardy and pumpernickel."

"Still do," I said and purloined a slice of toast from her plate.

"Nana, can I have some cake?" Brandon asked.

"No, boy. You just ate dinner," Dajuan told him.

"No, we had breakfast." Brandon whined.

"Boy, sit down somewhere. You're not getting any cake. Go get some fruit." I growled at Brandon.

He was trying to pull one of his manipulation tactics on Nana.

Nana chuckled at the family sitcom.

"Ya'll had breakfast just a while ago? You're trying to starve my baby?" she asked with a funny smile on her face.

"No, Connie. You know we didn't starve that punk..."

"Stop the name calling," she said and gave me a wicked glare.

"Okay, don't kill me."

"You didn't like your father calling you names, especially that one. As I recall it, that forced you to learn how to box, so that you could beat him up. So don't call this here baby names."

Brandon stuck his tongue out at me. The little bastard.

"I'm going to get you when we leave. And keep your tongue in your mouth."

"Nana, he gon' beat me," Brandon said and hid behind her.

He was just a phony.

"No he's not," she said and gave him a reassuring smile and hug.

"Yes, he is. I'mma call the cops, too," Brandon said confidently. He was really showing off.

The adults in the room cracked up with laughter.

"He always gets over here and starts fronting on us," Dajuan said. "At home he be chilling and all well behaved, and as soon as he gets here, he doesn't know us and sticks out his tongue."

"No, I don't, Nana. Nana, you got grapes?"

"Have," I said correcting him. "Does she have grapes?"

"Okay," he told me. "Nana do you have grapes without seeds?" he asked and flashed her some teeth. Just a little manipulator. I wondered where he learned that from.

"Yes. Go look in the bottom of the icebox," she said, and Brandon ran off to the kitchen.

"Granny, I am about to walk around to Charlie B's to see what's happening over there."

"Not a damn thing," she said. "Why are you going around there. I can't imagine you being caught there going over well with your career."

"My career is taking me there. Crazy, I know. I am going about Wydell. You do remember our call from Sunday, right?" I asked and then slyly added, "Of course you do. I took the case."

"Oh?" Coy.

"What time are you leaving for the mall?" I asked Dajuan.

"Ooh, can I go?" Nana asked like a school girl. "Value City is having a sale and I want to buy some kitchen things."

"Yup, Nana, you can go," Brandon said coming from the kitchen with a handful of grapes.

"You're too much," Dajuan told him. "Yes, Granny, you can go. We will have a ball."

"Cool, I am leaving. Call me when you're driving back from the mall and I'll wrap up at the bar."

CHAPTER 57

Back on familiar turf, I walked down Seymour Street toward Wayne Avenue. Taking this late-night stroll had forced me to recall memories that I packed in brain cells that now had dust and cobwebs. It had been a while since I had actually made the trek on foot. So many things that made up my character were given birth on Seymour Street. The one thing that stood out was my sexuality. I often wondered what sparked that characteristic to become a monster inside of me that it has.

I distinctly recalled fondling with boys as far back as kindergarten. I couldn't remember if I was the catalyst to those boyhood experiments, but I do know that I began to like them. What started out as accidental grew into deliberate acts of sex with quite a few of the thugs around the way. They may not remember, but I did. The feelings were mutual, too, and most all the way up to high school. My special buddies and I called each other when our homes were free and we engaged in sexual acts. We also had sex with girls and as soon as they left, we had sex with each other. If family were home and we had a desire to play, we used parks, school play grounds, and alleys. Hell, any where it was dark and secluded.

I was often around a lot of boys who liked to pull trains on girls. Most enjoyed the company of another man to secretly lust off them. I mean some guys were eager to announce that they had a chick to flip, so that their homey's could get on board to have sex with the girl, strictly so that they could watch.

I once had a special buddy who confessed that he liked watching me have sex with girls. What he really liked was watching my ass in the air and my penis going in and out of a young lady, and I was sure to give him a great show. Amazingly, none of these guys were out of the closet like your scribe; but, I'd bet my 401K that they enjoyed gay sex.

I approached a small barbershop on the corner of Seymour and Keyser Streets. I was one block from Wayne Avenue. The barbershop constantly changed ownership. It was often an illegal drug flagship, which the police probably raided twice a month. I stepped through the door and examined the place. The known local players were present and sat on folding chairs. I recognized one of the barbers, but not the other one. In the back, two buffoons played PS3 on a TV. Normally, they'd be outside drinking from a brown paper bag and playing craps, but it was too cold for that.

I was greeted with a gay joke. Stretch, the barber, usually had jokes. It was a part of the black barbershop experience.

Hastily, I replied, "Want to know the best position to make ugly children?" After a brief pause, I said, "Ask DJ's mom."

The shop burst into laughter. My knack for jokes had not dulled since I had become an attorney. I was the king of "Yo Mama" jokes in high school.

The laughter died down and I gave one of my childhood buddies a conspicuous head nod.

I said to the barber, “I was just in the neighborhood, so I figured I’d swing through to see if you were still renting.”

DJ confirmed, “I ain’t going nowhere. What’s up with my boy, Wydell? You gon’ get that fool out, right?”

“I’ll be back, yo,” Kensan announced before I could reply.

He had noticed my head nod and probably thought that we were in for ephemeral pleasure in the darkened back of Fitler Elementary. Just like the old days.

“I am trying my best to get him out,” I replied.

“Trying! You get them white folks off all the time, Mr. Big Shot Lawyer. Now when it comes to one of ours, it’s a problem.”

Smoov had said all that.

“That’s a damn shame.” Someone echoed.

“You’re on some other shit. I am trying to get him out, but I need, no, he needs your help. Starting with some witnesses who saw the shootings.”

“I wasn’t there,” Smoov said quickly.

I bet he lied. Everybody else looked crazily as if I had spoken a foreign language.

“I am not looking for snitches. I really need to know who was there or anything like that because I am not trying to put him at the scene.”

My cell phone rang interrupting me.

My aunt Diana was released, but I could not talk to her at that moment. I got back to the barber shop clowns.

“I need the order of the deaths and I need to know what time the shots were fired.“

Everyone was quiet.

“You mutha fuckas were all laughter and chatter a moment ago. Smoov you were barking at me and shit, but no one wants to open up their damn mouths. Fuck all of you!”

"Yo, who the fuck are you talking to faggot?" That was one of the new kids on the block. He looked at me fiercely. He turned from the PS3 and walked towards me. Fists clinched and mean mugging me. He advanced closer. I had never met him, and he had obviously never heard of me.

"Dawg," I said having to turn on my hood charm. "I don't even know you, fam. And I really wasn't even talking to you. I doubt if you were in Suspect's company."

I was going for overkill because he had threatened me with his body language. Who the hell was he to talk to me any kind of way.

I studied him a sec, and then added, "Nappy ass hair, dirty ass jeans, scruffy ass Tims."

That was a very accurate description.

The motley chump got inches within my reach and Smoov slid between us. He warned us not to let anything pop off inside of his shop.

Tone said, "Fuck dat fag! I'll beat him the fuck up. I don't know why ya'll respect this nigga. He a faggot! A dick taker. I'll kill that nigga!"

"That's what you won't do," I confirmed.

I tried to relax, but that ugly ass man was trippin'. I wasn't even talking to him. He just wanted to beef with me because he probably desired to interact with me, and this was his only way to. No, I am not full of myself, but I know that men who claim to hate and detest homosexuals are oftentimes down low and in a closet dying to get out. This argument was an avenue for him to talk to me and possibly fight me. This situation was no different than a woman who picked an argument so that her man could punish her in the bed shortly after the fight.

There was another division of other freaks that would not be attractive to a wild bear and swear that I was lusting over them, when in reality I wouldn't touch them for an absurd amount of cash. I had preferences and Lil Tone, the man trying to fight me, was off the mark. Way off!

"Step outside, pussy!" Lil Tone said to me. "I ain't letting no pretty-boy fag disrespect me. Fuck dat!" he continued and walked out the door.

I made my way to the door, behind everyone else, and DJ stopped me.

"Ray-Ray do not beat dat dude up, man. He ain't no damn body."

"I'mma ignore that fool, but if he gets close enough for me to tap his chin..." I threw some punches in the air.

I did not verbally threaten him. I knew better than that. I told DJ that I would call him the following day for some info and he had better have it. He agreed.

CHAPTER 58

I walked outside and the one and only Lil Tone had his coat and shirt off. He stood in the middle of Seymour Street in a tank top. I continued past him toward Wayne Avenue with him talking trash to my back. Before I reached the busy Wayne Avenue, I had a quick chat with myself. Did I need this fool following me like I was a punk bitch? This was my turf. I helped build it. I helped defend it. I stopped walking and turned around.

"Bitch, you wanna fight. Let's fight."

I had problems and things going on in my life and I needed this chance to unleash them on this fool.

I traipsed along the pavement with him behind me walking in the street. I shrugged off my mink jacket and lifted my sweater over my head. I kept on my lambskin gloves, though. I needed to protect my knuckles from being evidence. I had on a ball cap that I turned backwards.

I marched to the Fitler schoolyard. I heard Smoov, DJ and a few other voices trying to stop him. Through the wrought iron gate, I walked in twenty feet and snatched off my T-shirt. I hoped my muscles scared him off.

I threw up my hands and prepared to spar. Before his hands rose, I threw a fake left which sparked him to dip right. I caught him with a quick blow to the right side of his face. He paused for a second. Dazed. I should have popped him again, but I danced lightly on my toes as my dad had taught me. He threw a wild punch that did not land. My next did. I knew his face throbbed and pulsated with pain. This was what the hood brought out of me. Buffoonery. He had asked for an ass kicking. Am I to be threatened, stalked and badgered with trash talk?

Lil Tone rushed toward me wildly, and I halted him with another punch. He wanted to wrestle.

I didn't.

"Smoov, come get this dude. He can't fuck with the faggot," I said and danced some more.

That angered him more. He charged me. I moved. He fell to the ground.

"Dawg, I am not trying to fight you. Go ahead, man. Damn!"

"Fuck dat!"

"Somebody get him, please." I begged.

I had already pummeled the man and he was not worthy of risking arrest. I was mad as hell and I could have pulverized him, embarrassed him, but I didn't. I wanted to get the hell away from Germantown.

Finally, Smoov grabbed him.

"Come on, Tone, this shit is over, man."

His face was swollen, and I felt no remorse. He asked for, and begged for that ass kicking. I wanted to taunt him, too. And I did.

"It's been over, Smoov.

Now he can tell everybody that the faggot beat his silly ass," I said as a few onlookers held him back from getting some more.

I looked around for my garments and they were in Kensan's hands. I tossed my T-shirt and sweater over my head. I was not cold at all.

I wanted no parts of that bar at this point of the night. All I wanted to do was curl up under Dajuan. What had jumped into me? Was I possessed? That was totally out of line.

CHAPTER 59

Kensan and all of his muscular jailhouse body walked with me toward Wayne Avenue. As we chatted about why the fight started, his eyes glowed incandescently. After five years in the penitentiary his skin was amazingly clear, evidencing that gossip about jail preserving one's youth.

"Whatchu been up to, double R?" he asked me. He looked deep into my eyes and I looked away. He possessed the keys to prove me monogamously challenged.

"Chillen, man. Staying out of the way. You?"

"Hanging in there. Still haven't found a job. No one wants to hire me. Not even stock at Target. It's bullshit. But I am maintaining."

He still had a cracked front tooth that added to his sex appeal. Full pink lips told me, "People are not going to give you info out in the open, no matter how close you are to this hood. You're a member of the bar, and no one knows your obligation to the courts. You're going about this all wrong."

I began to cogitate. It didn't take me long to conclude how correct he was.

"Walk me to get a soda from Nikki's."

We walked down Wayne Avenue to the soul food joint. I went into Nikki's and grabbed a Sprite for him and a Hawaiian Punch for me.

"You still drink Sprite, right?"

"You remembered that bullshit?"

"No doubt. I am a lawyer. I have a good memory," I replied as we walked down Wayne Avenue toward Charlie B's.

We walked slowly. Romantically, actually. Was I cheating?

"So, you remember how we used to get down, right? Don't think that I am coming on to you. I am not," he confirmed after noting the expression on my face. It was splashed with awe. "I ask because I was in love with a boy in jail and he crossed me."

Why the hell was he telling me that? I had no idea where he was headed, but cheating on Dajuan was absolutely out of the question. Kensan and I had not been sexually involved since I was 22. He helped me with Brandon, so I named him Brandon's godfather. He went to jail and fucked that up.

I told him, "Ken, dawg, you're going to get crossed by lovers. That was some jail shit. I am sure that a woman out here..."

"I don't want a woman."

That was the moment that I felt like I was in a horror movie and the music that introduced danger was coming had just played.

"I want a career, a house, and a real car. Hoes come a dime a dozen," he said clearing up his last statement.

Oh my. This could not be happening to me. I was lost for words. I just continued to walk, but I was speechless.

"I know you're all happily involved and shit," he said. "I want to be happy, too, Ray-Ray. I am tired of Germantown, and I want to get my life together like you and get right. I do not want to be thirty and still living in my mom and dad's basement."

"So how can I help you? How much money do you need?"

"None. I don't need you to give me anything. I'll earn mine, but I need your direction. Show me the way. You know my family situation. In jail, I took a few classes through Penn State. They had professors come to my jail. I just can't find a job. Not even cleaning dog shit at PetSmart. And I am not up on college enrollment."

He sounded sincere, and I wanted to help. I knew the road to success and I knew the road was bumpy for an ex-con. The question, "Have you ever been arrested," on an application was highly discriminatory. In fact, I thought about writing an article on the topic in the next issue of Brotherly Love. Kensan proved that all black youth were not as lurdan as the media portrayed them. Many wanted to be distinguishable, but without the guidance that Kensan asked for, how could they begin? Many were afraid to even reach out for help.

It would have been a dereliction of my duty had I not replied, "Take my card. Come to my office tomorrow morning at seven a.m. sharp and dressed appropriately."

"You want me downtown at seven? All jokes aside?"

"Yup, and bring a resume."

"I'll be there," he told me.

"We will see," I said and then called Dajuan to pick me up.

Thursday, January 11, 2007

CHAPTER 60

I awoke to the pernicious blare of an alarm clock at 6 a.m. on the dot. It was Thursday, and I had a banging headache. It was a hangover. My last hangover was in my first year of law school. I recalled that much. In addition to some little man within my head chipping away at my brain cells, my mouth needed to be invaded by a rainstorm to stop the draught. My breath was short, as if I was asthmatic, and my eyes were on fire. I had vivid memories of tackling five screwdrivers in very short fashion at Charlie B's. My cocktail had more vodka than orange juice. My body absorbed it and had become so pissed that it was teaching me an early morning lesson.

More trouble was obvious when I tried to keep my eyes open. The light blinded me. The veins at my temples throbbed. This was no headache; it was a tension migraine. The mother of them all. I could lie in bed and have Dajuan massage my temples and sleep that monkey off my back. I had to shake this off all on my own.

Why?

I am an ambitious attorney who managed to plan to get up, down some aspirin, grab a cold shower, and be out the door by six thirty, as I had planned the night before.

Quickly, I swung my legs to the floor. What was I thinking? My head began to spin dizzyingly. I was nauseated because the quick movement probably shook up my dinner. I grabbed my head and squeezed my temples to no avail. I took slow, deep breaths. I cursed my heart, because it pumped more blood than necessary, forcing the arteries in my head to swell. Unlike the penis, my brain could not expand to accommodate the blood.

Water.

I need a gallon of water.

Carefully, I stood and walked retarded to the bathroom. I looked in the mirror over the sink. I looked like dried shit. I turned on the faucet and let water run into my glass that I used to rinse after brushing my teeth. I drank slowly and did not allow a drop to run from the side of my mouth.

That was better, but I was not fully hydrated. I had three more glasses.

I stood in the shower for ten minutes. I had slapped a cucumber mask on my face and prayed it would rejuvenate me. My time was precious, and no day would be wasted because of a hangover. That was a copout. A defense of insanity.

I stepped out into the warm air and toweled. In the bathroom, I got dressed. I was finished at 6:22. Eight minutes later, I walked out the door.

Four minutes was all it took to get from my condo to the Prudential Building. I was cheerful, even hyped to meet with Kensan. Rebounding from a felony was the most difficult thing on Earth to do. Harder than becoming President. Ex-cons had to be fearless, hopeful, and optimistic. Most had the fearless bit to a science, but to be hopeful was hard to learn.

I grabbed my briefcase and exited the car. I walked a few feet, and then looked at myself from head to toe in the garage parking lot mirror. Something about a Gucci suit gave me confidence. I developed the swagger of a millionaire when I donned a suit, tie and wing tips. Powerful. Unbothered. I imagined one-million other confident men of color dressed for success as I crossed 12th.

I saw Kensan looking around aimlessly. He looked lost. I did not help him find the building. The first step to success was taking responsibility for himself. Learning to control himself. Knowing that his destiny was in his own hands and not his employers. No one held him back, but himself. It was imperative that he studied the men who came before him, and learned how they jimmied their way to where he wanted to be.

Regaining strength, I walked solidly into my office. I had a cappuccino with an additional spoonful of Folgers to give it and myself a boost. I attached an Icy Hot patch to my right shoulder blade to relieve the soreness.

Sometimes, I stood in my office window for an hour and watched the cars zip by rhythmically. It helped cure my legal block, which was like writer's block. The sun was still rising and cast an orange glow across the sky. It warmed the City of Philadelphia. Everything seemed to be in perfect working order. This was my life. I could sit and devour the law until my legal appetite was content. That never happened.

Security rang my desk phone. "*Dammit*," I screamed.

The sound was so loud. The hangover couldn't take it. Hell, neither could I. I knew what they wanted, so I didn't answer. I went down to the lobby to collect Kensan.

The elevator opened and Kensan smiled at me. His face shone in admiration for a second. He had mixed an unexpected sartorial combination. A cream colored baggy suit with six buttons enveloped his tall body. He had on cream shoes with deep brown shapes, and a matching tie. His complimentary off-white shirt was ironed, but did not have that starched crispness.

Kensan's face was chiseled out of lemons. He had a bright yellow complexion, no more than two ounces of body fat, and inviting eyes. But he was dressed inappropriately. We shook hands and proceeded to my office.

CHAPTER 61

When I closed my office door behind us, I smelled the cappuccino and offered him a cup. He took it, but wanted to know what it was. He was standing at the door, as if he was afraid to enter.

"Negro, if you don't come into this office and get comfortable," I told him.

I then handed him a Harvard mug.

"That's expresso coffee mixed with frothed hot milk, and flavored with cinnamon, and Nestle Quik."

"You said that like I should have known that. I'm not a Starbucks kinda guy," he said and had a seat on the sofa. "This is a nice office. They must pay you a lot of money?"

"They do, but I earn it. More importantly, I practice law because I like it, not for the pay. Ergo, I work hard."

He laughed and said, "Stop lying."

"Ken, I do not do any lying. Look at teachers, they aren't paid a lot, but they have a passion for their roles in America," I said, checking my E-mail.

Both Aramis and Jon Rude had forwarded reports of their findings from the James case. I printed their reports and avariciously snatched up the hard copies from the printer.

"Aiight, you have a point, but you lie."

"In court. Maybe." I laughed.

"Whatever. I brought a resume."

I kept reading my investigator's report and made notes on a yellow legal pad of what I needed done next.

"That's nice," I said.

"You don't want to see it?" he asked.

His face was twisted with confusion.

"Not yet," I said and sipped my drink. I typed a reply to Jon and simultaneously asked Kensan, "What courses did you take in jail?"

"Uh...English, College Algebra, Creative Writing, Art History and Sociology," he said. "I have 15 credits from Penn State that I can transfer to any college and Penn won't even release that I took them in jail."

"Creative Writing?" I asked and kept writing.

"I wrote a manuscript while I was down. I wanted to learn a few tricks."

"Makes sense," I said, typing a reply to Aramis. "I want to write a legal thriller."

"You type fast as hell. What's that 60 words per minute?"

"Eighty." Bragging. "But you must type fast, too to have done a novel."

"Actually, I wrote it long hand, but I type about thirty words a minute looking at the keys.," he chuckled.

"What kind of grades did you get?"

"Three B's, one A, and one C. The C was in Art History. I was not feeling the Teenage Mutant Ninja Painters."

I laughed. "Cute, but Art History is a humanities requirement in all schools I would think. It was for me at Georgetown. What kind of job do you want?"

"Telemarketing. Retail. Customer Service. That sort of thing. Something for me to pay my own rent, while I get my book published. I am already writing another one."

I snatched up my phone. It was 7:40.

"Johnson, this is Ravonne Lemmelle. My friend that I just let up will be coming down to make a run for me. You can let him back up."

I then turned to Kensan and said, "Ken, on the corner of 12th and Chestnut a few short steps from here is a Seven Eleven. Could you go grab me a *Daily News*? I need to read the article about Wydell's case."

"Come on, Ray-Ray. Don't turn me needing your help into being a flunky."

"I don't need a flunky. I need your help. I have to run to the law library to check some things for a case this morning."

"I thought you asked me here to help me. How are you going to do that in court?"

"I am going to help you. And like you told me last night, you wanted to earn your place."

"Not by being your slave. I had enough of that shit in jail. I don't want to start out as an errand boy. You haven't even looked at my resumé, Ray-Ray."

He glared at me like a piranha, prepared to bite my head off.

"I do not need errand boys, Ken," I said. It was like a warning. "In fact, I don't need the paper, either," I said and pulled the *Daily News* from my briefcase. "Let's get this straight. I do not need you for anything. I do not owe you anything. I have no intentions of using you. So the next time I ask you to do something as small as that, do not interpret that as disrespect. You're a sage man, I mean wise..."

"Sorry to interrupt you from meandering on, but I read the dictionary in jail about an hour a day. I have a vast vocabulary."

"Good," I said and could care less. "Do you have a license?"

"No."

"Permit?"

"No."

"Pen and paper?"

"Nope."

"Zero for three. Nice!" I raved and rolled to my credenza.

I grabbed a legal pad and slid it across my desk to him along with a pen.

"Take notes," I said and began to pace behind my desk. "Penn-Dot is at 11th and Market. You're going to need to get the current copy of the driving manual."

He sat there.

"You're not writing, Ken." I mentioned that and went on. "Afterward, you should walk, take the train, or get a cab over to the public library on Vine and 19th Streets. There you will find the business section, get a resume book, and write a resume that will get you a job doing whatever you want. Don't forget a sample thank you letter for after interviews, as well. When I see the resume in your hand and the one that you will do today, I should see an improvement. Do you have a library card?"

"No."

"While you're there, get one and borrow the current *Writer's Market Handbook*," I told him, slipping on my coat.

"Excuse me a moment," I said to him.

I dialed Marsha on her cell phone. She was running late.

"Marsha, please get me a reservation for two at Twenty21." I hung up and turned back to Kensan. "At one, please meet me at Twenty21. It's a restaurant. That's all," I said and headed to the door. "Let's go, Ken."

"One problem," he said. "I do not know where that place is."

"Find it!"

CHAPTER 62

Wydell James had managed the front cover of the Philadelphia Daily News, and an article in the *Philadelphia Inquirer*. That was despite his case being five days old. On the cover, he donned a LaSalle University basketball uniform. He smiled under the caption: Could This Distinguished Student Have Committed a Triple Homicide?

I sat at my desk and read Aramis's article. It was a detailed account of the past five days in Philadelphia, involving the murders of three very known street pharmacists. I wondered was it widely accepted that Wydell had done the killings by people not employed by the State. Aramis's article began speculation that there was another shooter. He highlighted that the detectives were not pressed to track them down. As far as they knew, they had the killer. I planned to disprove that.

An hour after I had been preparing a *habeas corpus*, Marsha said through the intercom that Jon Rude was there to see me.

I was ecstatic.

I had her send him in and asked her to hold all of my calls.

I straightened my tie before I shook Rude's hand.

Without preface, he said, "What's your plan for the motion to dismiss hearing? Who are you going to call?"

"Nobody," I replied. "I have not filed a MTD."

"Oh, but you will, my friend," he told me and raised his eyebrows a few times. "I have the evidentiary nourishment to support one."

"Let me be frank. You have evidence to vivify that my client could not have shot and killed anyone?"

"Maybe."

"I can't file a MTD, then. I need a clear innocence defense in order to do that."

"Sure you can. I have the goods to darken the prosecution's case until it is as blackened out as a phallus running across the screen on an episode of Seinfeld."

"And what is that?"

"The police found very good footprints in the snow going to and from the crime scene. Size nine. Saucony running shoes. That was not in the preliminary discovery."

"That's interesting, but we need the second shooter. Hell, the first one while we're at it."

"And I have one for you."

"Stop!" I said in awe.

"The shell casings found on the property around the tree belonged to a pistol, but the bullets in two of the vics belong to a rifle."

I sat at my computer and pulled up a few of the guns on our data base.

I then said to Rude, "The pistol belongs to Wydell. And I guess you have no idea who this rifle belongs to?"

"No, but I have these," he told me and pulled out a bag with spent shell casings. "These belong to the rifle."

"You found them?" I asked puzzled. "How'd the police miss them?"

"They didn't miss them. They did not look for them."

"Pretty good, but get to the crime that you committed to get these shells."

"Oh, brother, I never commit crimes. I am a sworn blah, blah, blah. Anyway." He pulled out his digital camera. "Load these photos into your computer."

I did what I was asked and before my eyes were photos of a very stately home with a massive balcony and expansive columns.

"This was the second shooter's position, huh?" I asked.

"You better believe it!"

"And you got the casings with the owner's consent?" I did not need my investigator arrested and this marvelous intelligence inadmissible. "Come on, Rude. Now I have to work magic to get this into evidence."

He pulled out a letter. "Typed on the homeowner's computer. It's a letter confirming that the maid is a resident of the home and had the authority to allow me to search the balcony for evidence of a crime."

"Good, but..."

"They are away for the winter. Paris. The retired Mr. & Mrs. Gottshalk."

"We need that Saucony, or a blabbermouth that can put someone on that balcony."

"There's more," Rude said. He smiled and rolled up his sleeves.

I was excited. "More?"

"Absolutely."

"Do tell all."

"Saucony's are worn by the winter cross country team at..."

"LaSalle."

"Yup. Guess what else?"

"Only women wear them."

"Yup. They were donated."

"Get the hell out of here, Rude."

"I gathered that from a reliable source," he said. "Very reliable," he added mischievously.

"Okay, Rude. How many of them did you screw?" I asked with a sarcastic smirk on my face.

"Two."

"Legal?"

"That's still 18?"

"Yup," I said in his voice.

"Then yes, they were legal."

"So we have two shooters. One female and one unknown. One or two from the school. So we are looking for someone looking to frame Wydell, or hurt Shannon Oscar?"

"I'd concur."

I checked my watch. "I think I better have Marsha set up a press conference and a team to get my legal research materials for this motion to dismiss."

CHAPTER 63

"Thank you, ladies and gentleman," I said to the press.

They were piled in my office, and it was such an invasion, but that was where I wanted them. I really did not like media hounds, but during times like that, they served their purpose. Seated behind my impressive desk, I looked at the cameras, microphones and tape recorders and wanted to vomit. I cleared my throat, sipped a hot tea, and commenced to pollute my potential jury with the preliminary facts.

"I have a brief description of the past few days regarding the investigation into the murders of Dr. Lawrence Miller, Shannon McKeithan, and Casey Daniel. Could you please cease with the picture taking until I am finished. Geesh. The flash is blinding me!" Stupid idiots.

* * *

Barbara tapped on her boss's door. "Cynthia, Lemmelle is holding a live press conference."

The DA hopped to her small portable TV and turned it on to watch the broadcast as she called the head DA.

* * *

When the reporters settled, I began my fairytale.

"On Monday, I was retained by Mr. Wydell James to represent him against murder charges. He has maintained his innocence. He was childhood friends of two of the victims and had no motive to kill anyone on Hope Circle. He sends his condolences to the families and hopes that the Philadelphia PD leaves no stone unturned during their investigation in pursuit of the true killer."

"What about the gun found in James's vehicle which has been linked to the deceased?" Aramis asked in cue.

"I am getting to that, Mr. Reed," I said.

I sounded like George Bush as if I knew all of the reporter's names in the room.

"Now, if I may proceed?"

The room hushed again, and I went on. "Excellent. This is what the defense has proven thus far. Late last Saturday, drug king pin Shannon McKeithan sat in an alcove chatting with Casey "Pooh" Daniels and Dr. Lawrence Miller. Suspect, also known to police as Shannon McKeithan threw the bash to host all of the who's who in the Philadelphia tri-state illicit drug business.

"Low-Down, also known on the streets as Dr. Miller, the attorney at law who has worked to keep many of the partygoers out of jail, was shot when a bullet passed through the seat which McKeithan sat in. It seems like it was a warning shot. The next three shots did not miss their marks. Mr. McKeithan and Dr. Miller both received a gunshot to the head. Mr. Daniels received a fatal shot to his back. Several partygoers summoned the police to investigate.

"An anonymous tip led the police to Mr. James's Germantown home. Police officers took up position at the home of Mr. James and just so happened to have found the smoking gun hanging out on the floor of my client's inoperable car, which brings me to alibi.

"Mr. James, my client, is the star shooting guard for the LaSalle University basketball team. On Saturday night between seven and ten p.m., Mr. James played a ball game. He scored in excess of 30 points and had 10 rebounds. It was a hard game that wore him out. Afterward, he adjourned to his girlfriend's dorm room and then a victory party from ten until half past midnight. He then took a cab to his Germantown home. He was home by ten after one.

"Investigators have proven that there are at least two shooters. Bullets removed from the victims confirmed two different weapons. Hence, multiple shooters. Mr. Wydell James offered a reward of $5,000 for any information leading the police to the identity of the perpetrator of this heinous act.

"Lastly, the defense has submitted a beautiful Motion to Dismiss the charges against Mr. Wydell James. I know because I wrote it myself."

The media hounds laughed, rather than bark questions. Someone always had to be a bad apple, though.

"If Wydell did not do it, then who did?" someone asked.

"I surely didn't," I said.

Another round of laughter.

"That's all for today. I will not be answering any more questions. Believe me, if there are any significant details, I'll be sure to ring all of you. You've been a delightful audience. I'll be glad to have you back."

They chuckled. And so did some man with cheesy bucked teeth and bifocals. The cameras were turned off, but the man who I thought was a reporter had not made an attempt to move.

"May I assist you, sir," I asked.

"One crucial last question, Mr. Lemmelle. I am not a reporter, but I saw them piling in and decided to join them," the man said, and wiped the smile off my face. "Were you as eloquent when you abused your wife, counselor?"

I remained stone faced, despite all of the reporters staring. I was on a runway and the headlights of several Boeing 747's blinded me. I said, "That would depend on what you call abuse." I was fishing.

"How 'bout grabbing her and pushing her to the bed while cursing her, Mr. Lemmelle, attorney-at-law?"

"I wouldn't know anything about that, sir." I remained calm.

Outwardly I was unmoved by the mental quandary, but I wanted to call security. Who the hell was this man?

"Sure counselor," he said and then pulled out a thick, paper-clipped set of papers from a cheap briefcase. "You've been served." I looked bizarre. "Yes, divorce papers."

"Thanks," I said. "Yay for me, because I have always wanted a set of these."

* * *

Mr. 357 walked from Rayvonne's office with a grand smirk on his face. As soon as he stepped off the elevator, he called Ariel.

"Hey, babe! You should have seen the fright on your husband's face," he said lying. "He couldn't believe that he was served, and at a press conference. It was priceless."

"How'd you do that? He has seen you with me."

"Don't worry I wore a disguise."

CHAPTER 64

I blinked at the afternoon sunshine. I was pissed that I had not closed the curtains in my office before my 45-minute power nap. Ordinarily, sleeping on the job was not a necessity, but my therapist claimed that it was as therapeutic as a bath. I had no fear of becoming caught by one of the partners, either. I had a watch dog named Marsha, who was an hour late, but I paid her and ignored her tardiness. So she watched my tail.

This was an unfair day, but who did I blame? I caused the gargantuan headache that no longer broiled, but simmered. I would bet had I slept one more hour, my headache would have been gone. I looked at my watch. 12:46. Fourteen minutes to get to my lunch date. I would have to play big brother under this stress. I never had that chance to have a sibling. I wanted to lead Kensan to the water, but he had to drink.

"Marsha, come sweetie," I said into the intercom.

"You rang, Masta," she said, barging into my office with a smile on her face. A gorgeous smile.

"Did anyone from upstairs come through?"

"All was quiet. They were at a luncheon. Besides, who cares?"

I gargled Scope and spat in a small sink in my closet. A convenient luxury for being employed by a legal conglomerate. I looked into the mirror and saw restless eyes and sagging cheeks. I needed rest. I was also getting old. Maybe Brandon was right.

"Listen, hun. I am going to lunch. I am helping a friend learn the dynamics of becoming a valuable Philadelphian."

"Take him to a firing range," she said and folded her arms.

"You're insane. I don't want you beside me in court as a defendant rather than an assistant." I laughed and walked to my office door. We both exited. "If anyone calls, I'll be taking calls after three."

"Do you need that MTD delivered?"

"Yes, ma'am," I said. "Thanks."

CHAPTER 65

Inside Twenty21, I found Kensan perched in the lounge area reading a book. He actually looked like he belonged there,with the exception of the over-sized suit, which was suitable for a grand ghetto wedding, not an interview. The shoes were more flashy and prom-esque, than suited for a boardroom.

"Ken," I said.

He snapped the book shut and went right in.

"Do you realize how much parking is. You had me do a lot of running around. I spent $40 in parking. Then you have me in this bourgeois restaurant and this salad costs $18."

He lifted a large Caesar chicken salad in the air to eye level.

"Are you done?" I asked.

He nodded.

"I specifically told you to walk, take a cab, take the train, or hitch a ride. You did not listen. Key number one to success. In court, I hear so much yak, gibberish, and chatter, and I consume every syllable. You have to listen! Lunch is on me."

"No, I got my share."

"Cut the rich shit. You don't owe me anything. I invited you here. And this is hardly bourgeois. This is a very cozy restaurant. It's more to life than Nikki's Soul Food on Wayne Avenue and the greasy Chinese food joints. Everybody is trapped in the BMW and high fashion ideology. There's more to being big time. Driving a Benz and living in squalor is something I will never get."

"Man, you can't talk down on our people. That's what we do. You're not better than anyone, Ray-Ray," he told me. He was calm, but probably angry as if I gave a damn. "Some people just wanna stay comfortable. Don't knock 'em."

"Or some people want to knock the people around them by dangling their European vehicles, which are probably in someone else name, and can be taken by the feds at any time, in the faces of poor people. People that are not competition. They're afraid to live anywhere where they wouldn't be paid any attention. They can't live without people kissing their asses."

"Look, this is a free country and people can live where they want. I do not care about them and do not want to waste time talking about them. All I can do is speak for me, and I want out of Germantown."

"Excuse me, Ray-Ray. Can I get you a drink?" the waiter asked me.

"The regular, Nate, and some chicken cordon bleu," I told him.

Kensan ordered another drink before I asked to see the resumes. Kensan handed me a manila folder. I opened it and found a generic jail house resumé. Then I scanned the resumé created on the yellow pad.

"I did three different ones. One for each position."

"Good," I said. "But..."

"I knew you'd have a but."

"Hear me out. These are great, but you forgot to add key info."

"Like?" he asked, and gave me a condescending smile.

"What happened to you attending Penn State?"

"I didn't get a degree."

"No, but you can delete the GED Test completion from the Education Section and replace it with the fact that you spent two semesters at Penn State. That confirms a diploma and college credits."

"You're such a manipulator. I'll fix it."

"I like how you describe your duties at your previous employers. It's colorful. Now all you have to do is get this bad boy typed up."

"I do not have a computer, yet. I thought about renting one, but never got around to it."

"So, what are you going to do?"

"I thought," he began.

I saw it in his eyes. "My office is off limits for that. My computer has classified info and I'd be fired if you were on it."

"What about your house?"

Good question to which I had no answer to. What should I do? He was only a friend. A close childhood friend. A friend that I had sex with. Could I have him in my home? How would Dajuan react to that? Good thing, Nate brought my black and white milk shake and cordon. I had a reason to stall. Kenan would have never understood me denying him entrance into my home.

"You could use the library computer on Chelten Avenue. You need to become familiar with the library anyway. Kinko's has executive paper in a myriad of colors. You could buy some..."

He cut that bullshit off. "That library is closed. Budget cuts and all that. Why can't I use the one at your home?"

"Tonight is not a good night. I have a Judo class with Brandon."

"Tomorrow then."

"You need this resume done by tomorrow morning."

"Then I'll go home and wait for you to return from Judo class and then I can drive to your spot myself."

"That'll be too late."

"You don't want me in your house?"

"What?"

"You're scared of me Ray-Ray. That's crazy."

"No, I'm not."

"You either think that I am going to steal from you? Or that your boyfriend is going to act like a nut?"

"I would really not trust my judgment if you stole from me."

"So it's your dude?"

"Put it this way. This is complicated because he was just in a situation where he admitted to cheating, so if I bring you home, it'll look weird like I am cheating with you."

"That's dumb as shit!"

"Come on, man. How do you think your girlfriend would respond to you bringing me home?"

"For one, she would not know that you were gay."

"What if she did?"

"She wouldn't. Do you think I'd say, hey, Marge, my friend, Ray-Ray here is gay? Guess what else, babe? We used to freak when we were younger. That's old shit, man. I am focusing on my future. I don't have a girlfriend and I am cool with that anyway."

"So you're settling for whores when you could be focusing on a strong woman," I said to him. He ignored me. "Listen, do not deny yourself what you truly want. Do not accept substitutes. You want lobster, so don't settle for tuna. You can't get the girl of your dreams, so you settle for a substitute. Wrong. Go for what you want."

"Okay, Oprah. You're digressing. I am no fool," he said like it was a warning. "What you have is beautiful. I am actually jealous. Not of Dajuan, either, but the whole love affair."

"It takes work. A lot. And you'll find it with some woman soon enough." I sucked on my milk shake straw, and then said, "True love goes hand and hand with your promise to success in life. Now, did you get the driver's manual?" I asked and switched the topic.

He caught me. "Make time for me at the crib. Lover boy doesn't have to know about us. We are grown, Ray-Ray."

"Yeah, but..."

"But we..."

"See what I mean?"

"Nix that. We're grown. That shit is in the past. We would never do that again. So let's be say...brothers. That's thicker than water."

"Alright. I am feeling that."

"Besides, I am about tired of them hoes and ready to test the waters anyway, but I want a good situation like yours."

"Stop trippin'. You're not ready for all of that. So let that go."

"I may be. I am fighting a devil inside me every day. When I see a pretty boy thug like myself, I wanna stop them like a girl, but I can't.

"Shit, in today's day and age you can."

He chuckled, and then said, "That's crazy. Listen, can we chat about that personal stuff later? We are here on business."

"You're right."

"Okay, did you get the manual?"

"Yes, and I know it. I had the book in jail."

"So you can take the test tomorrow?"

"I need a physical."

"I'll have my office set you up with one in the morning. Do you have another suit? One that fits?"

"What!" he barked.

"Look around," I said and waved my hand in the air. "None of these suits are baggy and what color are they?"

"Blue. Black. Some gray." A nonchalant shrug.

"And the shoes?"

"Brown. Black." Another shrug.

"I rest my case," I said. "When we leave here, I want you to go to the store on the corner of 18th and Chestnut Streets. Daffy's. Put a navy suit on layaway. Three dress shirts. Three ties. And a pair of shoes without designs. Maybe wingtips. Be sure to have your neck measured and try on the suit. I'll have my assistant pay the balance and pick them up."

"Okay, thanks. Anything else, boss?"

"Earlier we discussed what kind of job you wanted, but what career do you want?"

"Good question. So good that I will get back to you on it."

"You are..." My cell phone rang and interrupted me. It was Marsha's ringtone. I answered and listened carefully, before I told her that I had it. I then told Kensan, "I have to go now!"

CHAPTER 66

Let me be direct about the way I feel about losing. For me, it has no existence. I don't lose. I do not let things progress to the point that I cannot arrest losing. As a criminal defense attorney, I researched case law religiously. I always looked for answers in case law before I argued a point before a judge. Sometimes I got them, but others I didn't get.

I had a phone call from Marsha who gave me answers to a question that had bothered Rude and me. I could have had Rude get answers, but black folks tended to be stubborn when whites showed up on their door steps. So, there I was parking my car near Destiny Dorsey's home. She resided in a duplex row home in North Philly at 17th and Master Streets. Ordinarily, I avoided the area because I was an armed robbery target. But when duty called, it yelled, and I answered.

I had left Kensan in the car for my vehicle's protection and began to stroll up Bouvier Street. All of the houses had no porches. No lawns. Just a simple Philadelphia street. Between the curb and the homes, three steps or three feet, and there I was knocking on the door. I heard locks begin to clamor and the door opened.

The man gave me a once-over. He had a bald head and I put his age at 26. He had wide and deep brown eyes. He was high off something. For some reason, he did not look intelligent or generous, but rather cruel and uninviting. Like he was thinking, *Why the hell are you here?*

"Who you?" the man asked me. His voice was dark. So dark, I didn't remind him that it was *who are you.*

"Is Destiny here," I asked very cordially.

"What da fuck you want my bitch fo'?"

It was then that I was reminded that I was in Kuwait, Iraq. I had no business being there without being accompanied by General Braxton Bragg and his troops. "I am a lawyer, and..."

"You ain't no fuckin' lawyer, asshole! You be fuckin' my whore?" the man asked me, as he stepped out of the door.

Then I sized up his stocky build. He was wide, but mushy. He had a prison-built body, which was all arms and no legs and a gut. I wasn't taking any chances. I stepped back. Not cowardly, but very natural. The one thing that I knew about the ghetto was that it needed drama to survive. Millions were energized by it. Some people were so dismal and repressed that they were alive when they manufactured drama, gossip, and pain. They had no lives and causing pain to others was easier than college. The man before me was a prime example.

"I am an attorney, and your companion came up as a potential witness that could help exonerate my client. I need to speak to her."

I remained calm and was very polite. I did want to piss him off.

The man stepped down two stairs. He was a full head taller than me, and his being on that one step made him tower over me.

"You that clown that she been fucking! I'm back and that party is over."

"That's great," I said and smiled. The statement was laced with mocking excitement.

"You think it's a game?"

He threw a punch at me with the speed of a speeding train. I moved, but not fast enough to completely dodge the bullet. I instinctively grabbed his arm and snatched him off the step. I had his arm twisted behind him in a compromising position and wrenched his thumb. I should have broken it, as I was taught to do.

The man yelled miserably. Luckily, it was winter and the street was empty. He was on the ground, on his knees, and squirming like a bitch.

"I'm not fucking her. I don't want to hurt you, homey," I whispered.

"I'mma kill ya ass," he growled. "Let me go and I'll kill you."

I let the bad ass go and quickly stepped back. "What the hell is your problem?"

He stood up, and the idiot threw another punch at me. Considering his height over me his punch was downward and awkward. He had already sucker punched me, so I dipped and his punch landed somewhere in Texas. I delivered two into his soft stomach. He folded like a tortilla shell wrapped over beef and beans, and glared at me murderously. I decked him fiercely enough to put an average man to bed, but he was a bull. He reached out to grab me, but stumbled into a parked car.

"Man, I am not trying to fight you," I said. I was breathing heavily and didn't know how a witness interview turned into a fight. I was winning, but the pain in my face distracted me.

"Ah, you too late. You fighting for now. Until I get my gun," he said. His light hue was beet red, and his eye was wrapped in a Pepsi-blue color.

The imbecile jumped off the car, and raced toward me again. I had enough. I broke his nose. I felt the cartilage shift beneath my knuckles, and I was reminded why I even took Judo and boxing. This guy had proved why I needed it. He was holding his face and yelling when a sex siren charged out of the door with a duffle bag. She was strapped with a pistol and raised it into the air.

"Don't shoot me. I am a lawyer."

Not that that mattered, but I was scared to death. Was I about to die in the line of duty?

She pointed the gun at the thug I had been fighting; not me. Thank you, Jesus.

"You got a car?" she asked me with her gun and eyes trained on the man. She then told the man, "You better not fuckin' touch me and this is your last time seeing me." She spat in his face. "You fucking raped me. I should kill you, faggot!"

Hearing her say that brought a bit of fate into the mix. Here he was a rapist and I kicked his ass. Karma at its best. Served him right.

I cupped my right hand with my left, which was in serious pain. The woman was right behind me. I was in a serious quagmire. My right hand felt broken. Kensan had no license, so legally he couldn't drive. Gun girl was definitely not driving. I walked up to the passenger side of my car, and told Kensan to drive. He looked at me crazily, as the girl hopped into the back seat.

"This is an emergency," I told him, as I opened the glove compartment. "The cops will understand." I then said to gun girl, "Put the gun in here."

She looked at me through the prettiest little eyes and I could tell that she wanted to protest. Luckily, she complied.

"Hold on," I said and got out of the car. I motioned for the woman to get into the front seat. I needed to keep an eye on her from the back seat. When I shut the door, I told Kensan, "Drive!"

"Where are you taking me? Are you really a lawyer?" the woman asked, as Kensan pulled off.

"Take me to Einstein," I told my driver. "Yes, I am a lawyer. I represent Wydell James. He was accused of a triple homicide at the party Suspect had. Are you Destiny?" I asked so that she knew that I knew her name.

"I am. I do not know shit about Wydell. I was almost killed there," she said and looked back at me. "How'd you know that I was there?"

"A little bird told me. Through the grapevine. Were you talking to Low Down when he was shot? Listen, I do not want you as a courtroom witness. In fact, you can forget that we had this conversation. And vice versa. All I need to know is whether you recall the order that the bodies were killed. And if you recall how many shots were fired. Two very simple questions that I pray you can answer.'

"What do I get?" she asked like a true bargainer.

We were at Broad and Glenwood.

"Pull over," I told Kensan. I jumped out and jogged to the ATM. There was a loud mouth hood-rat at the machine pushing buttons and gossiping on a Nextel chirp phone. She was rudely blasting her conversation, as if anyone wanted to hear that her man slept with her cousin. I was pissed, and this confirmed why I hated public transportation. I finally withdrew $600 from the ATM. Back at the car, I asked Destiny to get out.

"Here's $600,"--I waved the money flamboyantly--"$300 per question."

She answered my two questions and volunteered a bit, as well.

"Thanks," I said and sat in the passenger seat. I opened the glove box and told her to grab her weapon. I was not touching it. She did, and I said, "Have a nice day."

I slammed the door shut and told Kensan to get me to the doctor for my face and hand.

CHAPTER 67

Mid-evening, I strolled into the door massaging my bruised hand. It was not broken, just sprained. I walked into the bathroom and just as I ran the water in the tub, the telephone rang. By the time I reached it, the caller had hung up. The condo was quiet. I did not need quiet. I needed Brandon running around to remind me of my existence. I needed Dajuan playing a song in G-minor. They were at Judo, but I had my lesson for that day in the streets.

I was in the kitchen with a glass of red wine in one hand and an ice tray in the other when the telephone rang again. Pulling the plug was a delightful idea, but I thought better of it and I answered.

"What the hell is up with your cell phone?" Aramis barked as if I was his woman.

"Nothing. Who the fuck are you talking to?"

I checked my cell phone and it was on silent-ring versus vibrate.

"I tried calling yo ass a thousand times."

"What's up? I had a rough ass day."

"I didn't. I'm trying to solve a case. Your case to be precise."

"Really? I'm trying to lose this case. My case to be precise," I joked.

"Don't be an ass. Listen, I went up to the realtor. The property was rented by a Mr. Donald Barclay."

"Barclay...Barclay. That name sounds familiar," I answered.

"Well, here's the deal. The property was actually leased for six months by a company called, Barclay Industries. Went by City Hall. It's a dummy corp. And your former colleague, Mr. Lawrence "Low Down" Miller was written all over the paperwork."

"Who the hell is this Barclay clown?"

"Don't know at this time, but I am on that, trust me!"

"Oh, I do."

"What's with you?"

"I had a fight with some nut today. Two this week. I am on a roll. My hand is swollen as hell. That's all. Nothing major. I'm looking forward to going to jail."

"You're taking this as a joke. Do we gotta go kill someone?"

"Nope," I said and then told him about the whole adventure.

"Now that's crazy," was Aramis's subtle response. "If he only knew that you wouldn't dare touch his woman."

"I'm telling you."

We both cracked up.

"It's awfully quiet over there. Where are Pinky and the Brain?"

"Judo class. Brandon has no desire to take over the world and he hates Bush."

"He's five, how in the hell is that. I forget, my bad. You have the boy taking enough classes to become a straight A school yard bully. Such a contradiction."

"I don't have Brandon doing anything. I just let him know what's available. That is how kids develop talents. He has to know what the world has to offer. Maybe if you had a child and stopped depositing yours into condoms or throats you'd know that."

"And if you stop depositing babies into Dajuan as if he can bring them to term..." he began to laugh before he got the full joke out.

I loved my best friend.

"You're a damn retard," I said laughing.

"Right. Let me get off here. I have a very salacious date."

"Always. Before you go. I have a friend that wrote an urban fiction tale. I'm about to review it. When I'm done, I would like you to use one of your contacts to help him get it published."

"If it's any good. Let me know."

"Sure thing."

I hung up with Aramis and grabbed a quick shower. Afterward, I sat back in my office and read the first line of Kensan's novel: "The man who had three hours to live kissed his wife goodbye." I was hooked.

CHAPTER 68

The over-weight cop stood in the doorway of the Sanchez home. He had his note pad out and took down the lady-of-the-house's complaint. She claimed that she had not experienced domestic violence and had not called 911. As she shut her front door, she heard a loud thud. Something had hit the front door. She opened the door, prepared to read the cop his rights, but he was dead. A small hole was in the back of his head. Three other officers were killed while responding to fake cries for help in other parts of the city at that precise moment.

When I was forced awake by the slam of the front door, I realized that I was having a nightmare. The details of the nightmare surrounded the plot to Kensan's manuscript. Then I heard my baby's voice.

"Dad!"

That was a joyous way to awaken. I knew that he was about to tell me all about an ass he kicked at Judo.

"What?" I said.

"You missed Judo. It was fun. And Daddy D took me to South Street after class. I got this." He held up a fluffy, snow white rabbit. "It's an Angora rabbit."

"Look at that fine wool. I can make a fur coat out of him."

Bad joke. Brandon frowned. I would not be surprised if he became a fan of PETA. "Just joking, King B."

"Okay, 'cause, I do not want you to wear him. I want to take him to Show and Tell on Friday."

"Where's the cage?"

I did not need Bugs Bunny and Ms. Pearl having a living room showdown. And I doubted Brandon could train the rabbit not to leave the gum ball droplets of excrement all over the house.

"Daddy D is setting it up in my room," he said and walked out of my room.

I lay back down and stared at the ceiling. I thought about going to see Dr. Kelvin Randolph, my therapist. Psychiatrist. No, I am not a traditional psychotic, but I do stress and it's good to talk to a stranger. Who cares what they thought? They couldn't create a rumor and render you ostracized.

Dajuan walked into the bedroom wearing a black tank top. I wondered where his shirt and coat was. We had been over him being out coatless.

"Good morning, Mr. Lemmelle-Jones," he said sarcastically. "Can I get you breakfast?" he asked and sat next to me.

He pecked my cheek.

"What time is it?" I asked sitting up.

I wasn't nude, but it appeared that way when the blanket fell to my waist.

"Ten," he said. "PM," he added with a smirk on his face.

"Get out, smart aleck."

FRIDAY, JANUARY 12, 2007

CHAPTER 69

Friday morning, it occurred to Aramis why he wasn't on staff at *the Inquirer* and why he did not have a syndicated column. He had mastered his craft by solving a crime. The chase for the Hope Circle murderer(s) was intriguing. Usually, he simply gathered the information and wrote a colorful article. Not that time.

He sat in the newsroom itemizing what he had known that far. It helped having a direct confidential line to the defense. He hadn't heard from Rhonesia, but he would develop a story based on what she said. Whatever she found was a plus. He was prepared to ruffle feathers. He planned an article full of motley innuendo and famished speculation. The only evidence he had was the key chain. He needed that other gun in his possession. Detective Callaghan did not speak to him, so he planned to report what he desired to be the outcome and prayed that he was on the right track. He decided to call Rhonesia.

"Reed, you're a hard guy to reach," she said, excitedly.

"You've been calling me. I haven't received any calls or messages from you."

"I do not leave messages. Especially this kind. Never know who's listening with the Patriot Act in effect."

"What kind?"

"The criminal kind."

"I can be at Explorer's Den in fifteen minutes," Aramis said.

"No dice. Meet me at the Broad Street Diner at 66th and Broad."

* * *

Twenty minutes later, they both emerged into the busy diner. With all of the noise and patrons ebbing about, the nefarious two sat at the counter. They ordered hot chocolates and breakfast.

"Did you have to come so far from the school? You must bear great news."

"What I bear is speculation, but definitely worth your attention."

"Perfect. What do you have?"

Rhonesia waited until the waitress left. She had dropped off frothy hot chocolates to the reporters.

"Here goes," Rhonesia began. "When you left me the other day, I wrote up a speculative article for the school paper," she said and pulled out the paper. Aramis began to read the paper, as she said, "You told me to get dirty, and I did. I praised Wydell and spoke about the lost keychain with prints that belonged to someone on campus. Hence, someone else from LSU was at the party as a guess or assassin."

"This is brilliant, Rhonesia," Aramis raved and sipped his cocoa.

He wanted to hug her, but that was inappropriate.

"That should have gotten the rumor mill turning fast enough to snap it."

"Better. The next day, a certain Calc 2 student was not in class. That struck me as odd. He's a math major and loves the class. He quickly grasps topics and loves being in front of the class, working out five minute proofs."

"Could've been sick. Late. Having sex. Anything, but..."

"He dropped out! Collected 70% of his tuition and packed up. I know because I chatted with him as he packed."

The waitress dropped waffles, bacon, and more cocoa in front of them, and Aramis gave her a flirtatious smile. He adored playing with women who admired his handsomeness. When she drifted away, he asked, "Rhonesia, where is all this going?"

"This is just a hunch, but it's like this. I can be off the mark totally, and look like a buffoon, afterward. Or, I could have solved my first murder, a knack that I never knew that I had. You brought that out. Thanks."

Aramis was grateful, but becoming impatient. "What do you have, Rhonesia?"

"I have property from the drop out."

"He gave you his things. Good for you. Now, about the case?"

"No, I received them by way of..."

"You didn't!"

"You told me to get dirty and I did."

"I never encouraged you to steal. That would make me an accessory before the fact. Are you out of your mind? You risked expulsion and more important arrest," Aramis said hotly.

He almost regretted involving her.

"Come on, Aramis. Don't be so persnickety. If the prints on the appropriately wrongfully obtained..."

"Stolen!"

"Borrowed! If the borrowed pieces match, this case is solved. By us, too," she smiled.

"Maybe. It's hardly the *coup de grace* for the prosecutor's case."

"But, it casts doubt. That'll get Wydell off."

"Where are the things?"

"In my car," Rhonesia said and then added, "sealed in a box."

"What's in the box?"

"Don't know. It's marked football stuff."

"You didn't look in the box?"

"No, I didn't want to taint the prints. They may match the key chain."

"Unbelievable!" Aramis said.

He dropped a twenty on the table and they left the restaurant.

"Where are you going?" Rhonesia asked, admiring his stroll and ass.

"To open the box."

Aramis walked to the diner parking lot with Rhonesia in tow. He asked, "Which car is yours?"

"The Accord."

"Get the box."

Rhonesia opened the trunk to her red Honda, and there was a medium box in there taped profusely.

"How you managed to take this damn box?"

"Dragged it into my room. He made a trip to his car and I lived a room away from him."

"You're a cold piece of work," Aramis said and cut the box open using a Swiss army knife.

He used the knife to shift the items around. He then used gloved hands and hoisted a blue towel from the box, which was wrapped snuggly around something. He opened the rag and was flabbergasted.

"Who's the student?" he asked putting the towel back in the box.

"That's confidential."

"What?"

"I need a byline, Aramis. If this gun is the weapon used by the shooter, I want credit for it."

"You'll get it."

"Follow me to the dorm to drop my car off. Then I will take you to the possible gun owner."

"Possible?"

"Come on, would you," she replied and hopped into her car.

CHAPTER 70

A gaunt woman answered the door at the ranch home in King of Prussia, Pennsylvania. She was in her late fifties and had no care for her appearance. She donned a crinkly, polyester dress and destroyed bunny house slippers. Her hair was gray with streaks of deep drown strewn wildly on her scalp.

"What do you want?" she asked. She glanced at Aramis Reed and Rhonesia Cosby with eyes chipped from pale-blue agate. "I ain't buying nothing!"

"We're looking for Lewis Barclay, ma'am," Rhonesia said politely. "Does he live here?"

"No. And who the hell are you?"

Slowly, Rhonesia took out her wallet from her purse and opened it to where she could flash her LSU ID.

"I'm one of his classmates. This here..."--she pointed to Aramis--"is the coach of the football team. Her first official professional lie.

The woman digested the words. "Okay, folks," the older woman said. "Why are you here?"

"Well..." Rhonesia stammered.

Aramis picked up the slack. "Ma'am, Lewis dropped out of school and we were hoping to change his mind. He's a promising young man and we'd hate to lose him."

"He lives with his father in that horrible city, with the staggering death rate. You can find him under the gun there."

"Do you have an address for him?"

"Sure do. Why should I give it to you?"

"Barclay may be suicidal, ma'am," Rhonesia said and smiled.

She was such a great liar. It was quick thinking though that pissed Aramis off. Aramis quickly cleaned up her mess.

"Yes, a girlfriend of his claimed he flashed a rifle and threatened to kill himself if she did not take him back."

Now Aramis had lied.

"Yeah. Your son," Rhonesia added unnecessarily. "We need to get him some help."

"Sure. I'll get the address," she said and left the door.

"Don't you say another word," Aramis told Rhonesia.

"Why not?"

"Please, Rhonesia. You put too much on that suicide comment."

The woman returned to the door with an old phone in her hand. She explained to the father of Barclay that his beloved son was suicidal again over some bimbo. She went on and confessed that he always pulled that number to get a girl to love him.

She said, "He thinks because he is a jock, he can have whomever he wants," to the father on the telephone. "That's your problem. You had the same attitude and now you feed that bullshit to our boy. One of these days, he is really going to off himself. And his blood will be all on you." She paused, and then said, "And my gun is missing."

She hung up and told Aramis, "Here's the address. I did not tell him that you were coming. He knows how to hide. The bastards. Here's a copy of my rifle permit.

Please have my gun returned to me because I know he stole it. Thank you," she said and closed the front door.

Aramis hopped into his car and dialed Ravonne.

"Ravonne, I have great news."

"Oh, but I have some great news myself," Ravonne said.

"Not as good as mine," Aramis said bragging.

"Wanna bet."

"Keep your money. I'll be there in a half-hour."

"You better have the smoking gun if you wanna top me."

"I do," Aramis said and hung up.

CHAPTER 71

Aramis held a 2006 LaSalle University yearbook given to him by Rhonesia. He passed it to me to look at the pages that he had placed tabs on. Photo number one was of a mathematics major standing in front of a classroom working out a geometry problem. I hated those in high school and avoided geometry in college. The second photo was of the quarterback of the football team. He wore a school jersey exposing a quarterback physique with jeans and a babe on his hip. The third photo was of the entire football team with arrows pointed at a select few of the men's faces.

"Should this QB mean something to me?" I asked.

"He does," Aramis told me with a smile plastered on his mug.

"I'm listening."

"Can I get a little back ground music?"

"I'm not in the mood for games, Miz."

"Something with a classical flare," he told me.

"Mozart?"

I cued *Don Giovanni* to play out of the surround sound and poured me a glass of white. I sat back at my desk and mixed my fingers together to show the attention I was prepared to offer this journalist/best friend.

"Okay," I began. "I saw your photo spread, so what now, Miz?"

"Listen carefully, Ravonne."

"I always..."

"You're talking. That's what you always do. I've come into possession of the missing surveillance from LaSalle U, which specifically places your client at the university at the precise times he claims to have been. A few characters, chiefly, Lewis Barclay, who you've been told by the client's girlfriend, Shannon Oscar, hated your client, has been acting suspicious along with Darren Lockman and Morgan Malone. Since I wrote that the potential killer could be roaming the campus posing as a student, Barclay withdrew from classes, collected 70% of his tuition, and is now missing in action. Got all that?"

"I do."

"Good. Me and a source located Barclay's mother in KOP. She's estranged from the boy and hates the father. Several days prior to the Hope Circle killings, she reported to the police that her home was burglarized. The only missing item was a Smith and Wesson."

"I get the strangest feeling that there is more?"

"Absolutely. I have the weapon. It's been sawed off, which is consistent with the ballistics experts."

"What! How the hell did you get that?"

"A source. A confidential source."

"Where's the rifle?"

"With ballistics."

"There's a problem. It was stolen from Barclay. Would my source be subject to the theft charge?"

"Aramis, the DA wouldn't dare prosecute your source for stealing a weapon that was responsible for at least three deaths."

"There's more to my story."

"I'd love to hear it."

"Thought so. My source went to the Hollow to do some interviewing to find out about the vics. Got some juicy info."

"He couldn't have. I couldn't even get them to talk. Who's this source? I have expert lie detectors to validate his claims."

"He, is a she, and no lie test is required. You'd be amazed at what the promise of pussy can buy these days from hoodlums in a bar."

"Right. What did she find out?"

"Barclay's father was a money launderer for the dead attorney who actually funneled the money for the two dead dope dealers. Barclay, Sr. then turns around and loans the money to other businesses fronted by Suspect."

"Sounds like motive to me. And your proof is where?" I asked. Aramis was beginning to sound like a textbook of conjecture.

"In Barclay senior's financial statements buried somewhere. Surely, you can find a tax attorney in this firm to unearth the secrets."

"I could have a secret inquiry completed."

"Not could. You have to. What if Junior killed for dear old dad and the bimbo girlfriend helped?"

"But, why frame Wydell?"

"You're not that damn smart. Because he would get rid of the man who blocks his shine and having sex with one of his kind. Duh!"

"I get it."

"Now, what do you have counselor?"

"Jon Rude tells me that the accomplice was a female."

"It's not my source, but I could ask her about that."

"The female wears a size nine, and wore Saucony's. The Cross Country team wears them."

"I'll look into it," he told me noncommittally.

I sat behind my desk, glowering at my drink. I had heard enough. "Where's the surveillance tape, sir?"

He passed it to me.

I watched it.

"You've watched it, so I'm sure that's all the proof you need to print that up. Take this to the police as well, after I copy it, of course."

I then sent an E-mail to Jon Rude. "The Barclay business does not go in the paper."

"Until you get that audit, of course."

"Yeah, I'mma have my pal, Ashton Banks, take care of it. We started together, and he'll be down to help me."

I told Aramis and hoped that I could deliver.

"The public needs to know that an industrial transplant from California and his son are being investigated for criminal ties to the Hope Circle murders. I gotta scoot."

"Catch you later."

CHAPTER 72

Rhonesia curled herself on her bed, sipped green tea and waited for a call from Aramis. She actually missed him in a romantic sense. Certainly, she was all business and was strangely comfortable around Aramis. She had her window open and let the winter breeze bump up against her body. It felt nice with the mix of heat. She hated men, and thought of the man that forced her to feel that way: her father.

She thought of his father and his abandonment. He had committed suicide after being wrongly accused of a rape/murder. By the time DNA arrived to exonerate him, he had hung himself in his Huntingdon State Prison cell in upstate Pennsylvania. He was her number one pen pal. He had written her weekly, and she enjoyed his personalized jail house cards. She kept them in a scrap book along with photos of him in his brown state uniform. She could still smell the Muslim oils that he splashed on himself when she visited him behind the glass. She thought of Wydell and did not want him to face the same doom.

Her mother had remarried a short one year after her father's conviction. Rhonesia resented her for it and though they communicated, it was often not of importance.

When her father died she was approached by a balding white man, as she exited Lincoln High School in northeast Philadelphia. He handed her a $200,000 check, which was what her father had left a pal for her.

She had a class in twenty minutes and hoped to hear from Aramis before she left for class. She had to present an English project. The assignment was for her to select the number one song of all time and analyze how music and lyrics affected listeners. She chose, Michael Jackson's *Thriller*.

As she approached her dorm room door, the room telephone rang. She snatched it up.

"Hello."

The caller was hesitant to speak. "Is this Rhonesia Cosby?"

It was a male voice and not disguised as far as she could tell.

"Yes, sir. Who is this?"

"My name is irrelevant." Arrogant.

"Don't be calling my damn..."

"Wait! Don't hang up."

"Who the hell is this? I do not play games."

He ignored the question. "I read your story about Wydell James."

"You and the entire campus. Why are you such a special reader? And I still do not know who this is."

"I know who the killer is. That makes me special, right, Rhonesia Cosby?"

She dropped her bag and raced to her answering machine and pressed record. "Come again," she said like a veteran reporter.

"You heard me, and I heard the beep. You're recording this, so let's get down to business."

"Okay."

"Do not placate me, missy. I am no cheap thrill. I have some pretty intelligence. Prettier than you. I need a commitment to ten grand and then an additional 25 once I pass along the silver platter."

"What do you know?" she asked as if she had the cash.

"Later. Not now."

"I need something to get someone to listen to me. Besides Wydell may not have access to that kind of cash."

"He does, and I already helped him once."

"How the hell is that?"

"You have probably already written a brilliant article about coming across the security surveillance. I slipped it under your door. Now get me a commitment for the cash to be wired, reporter!"

The caller hung up.

CHAPTER 73

Pacing and nerve-racked, I could not believe what was happening with the Wydell case. So many things had gone unanswered, despite all of the evidence which pointed to an acquittal. What about the true killers? The vision of them running around the streets, probably planning their next crime, was horrific. True, I loved to win cases, but I could not escape my responsibility to the public safety and ultimately my own. I did not like to see men railroaded, and I detested murderers.

I planned my weekend and made calls to confirm my events. I tried Kensan to set up a meeting to discuss his manuscript. Got no answer. I tried to line up poker with a few buddies, but to no avail. I knew I had to take Brandon to the Betsy Ross House. I had to visit Wydell James. Maybe I'd play tennis on Sunday at the Cricket Club. I entertained myself at all cause because I never knew when God would flash, The End, before my eyes. I lastly called Vergil to make an appointment to get my hair cut.

Tired of being on the telephone, I stood in my office window and looked down at the people below. I saw Aramis and a short-haired girl making dents in the snow, weaving hurriedly down 12th Street. I was looking for an armed gunman to appear. I snatched up my desk phone and called security to let them in without delay.

Definitely, a beauty entered the office with Aramis. I was impressed. Aramis shut the office door and was breathless. So was the fox.

"Ravonne Lemmelle meet Rhonsia Cosby," Aramis said, pulling two bottled waters from my small refrigerator. I shook her hand. Neat manicured nails were painted pink.

"Nice to meet you," she said looking around my office. Aramis handed her a water.

"My pleasure, Rhonesia. Now which one of you wanna tell me what's going on?"

"She is." Aramis confirmed. "Let him hear the tape."

Plugging the answering machine into the wall was easy. Listening to the recorded message was hard.

I asked, "Any idea who that is?"

"Has to be a student. Our dorm numbers are easy to get. See, the numbers are in order by dorm, so it's easy to figure out. Or perhaps that caller got the number from me or my roommate. But, no I do not recognize the voice."

"And, he called you reporter," I said. "That sounds personal."

"Only students that know me call me that."

"Why did he decide to call you and not me or the police?"

"I have been writing articles for the school paper. So I guess he felt that I was intimate to the case. And he wants money."

Ah, the source. I had a thought. I bet Aramis had banged her.

Aramis smiled at me. He knew that he had caught the biggest break. If she got the information to the killer's identity and was right, he would have benefitted tremendously. I had to grill her, though.

"Could this have been a hoax?"

"Anything is possible." Aramis informed me, answering for her. "She's scared. I doubt if it was a hoax. She believes her life could be in danger."

"Rhonesia, I hate to badger you. What I am about to say may seem grotesque and morbidly disgusting, but I must ask, are you in on this scam?"

"Are you out of your goddamn mind?" Aramis barked at me. "She's not into that. We have been working this case together. She gathered material information to acquit your client. The sawed off came from her!"

"And quite conveniently," I said. "Maybe, she was the female killer."

"This is insane, Ray-Ray."

"Maybe."

"Guys," Rhonesia interjected. "Aramis, I can handle, Mr. Lemmelle," she said and then told me, "You have lie detectors at your disposal. Get one in here. You craft the questions. Anything that you like. If I am pure, you grant me the money to negotiate with the informant, and,"--she glanced at Aramis--"us permission to print what we know this far exclusively."

"Deal," I said and gripped up my phone.

CHAPTER 74

I had found a point in which I needed to relax as the shadows of the adjacent buildings faded into darkness. My eyes had had enough of scouring legal tomes. My arms were tired of being in the typing position. My mind was tired of plotting the course to execute an effective Motion to Dismiss. I had stroked Cynthia and imagined her arching like a tiger and her back shaking like a fancy double head vibrator. I sat the legal books on a cart, and packed my briefcase with enough papers to do bicep curls.

The drive home was swift and my family was waiting for me. Dajuan was on the sofa with a notebook in his lap. Brandon was on the floor stretched out reading a book. Surprisingly, Ms. Pearl circled my feet. I assumed that she was done bitching.

Brandon immediately became bored with the book when I entered the door. It was 7:30.

"It's not six, but 7:30 is good," Dajuan joked.

"Daddy R, I saw you on TV. You made all those people laugh. I saw you," Brandon said and jumped into my arms. "It was grrreeeaattttt," he continued stretching the word like a Sugar Daddy taffy. He had obviously caught a rerun of the press conference in my office.

"Yeah. I had fun, too." I lied and Dajuan looked at me. He knew that I hated the media.

"Dad, can we make Rice Krispies treats, pleeeeaaassssseeee."

He had stretched that word out, evidencing a new fad. I hoped that it went out of style quickly.

"Come on," Dajuan said, answering for me. "We can start while dad takes a shower."

"Okay," Brandon said somberly.

I could tell that he wanted to be around me. "Just let me take off my suit and I'll be there to help. Alright?"

I didn't want to let him down, after all, he asked me to make the treats.

"Good. Let me come with you," he told me and grabbed my hand.

He ushered me into the bedroom. For five, he would not be deceived.

Dajuan followed us, and I heard him say, "So, I can wager that you're going to win?"

"Call NASA and ask if they have built a time machine that actually works," I said and hung up my blazer and slacks.

Brandon was not more than an inch from me. It was like that old Bobby Brown song, *Every Little Step I Take*.

Dajuan chuckled. "It can't be that bad. The press conference seemed fairly solid. The facts were clear and convincing. If I was a juror, I'd buy it."

"Easy for you to say," I said walking to the shower. Deputy Brandon was not taking his eyes off me. I stepped under the farthest of the two shower heads and did a once-over with my body gel. I toweled, threw on pajamas, and we were off to make the treats.

"Brandon, what is wrong with you?" I asked as we walked to the kitchen.

"Nothing," he said and smiled.

I glared at him.

"Stop telling a story."

"I'm not, dad. Just...some lady came to my school yard and said she was my mom. She said that she was going to get me from you. When I raced to my teacher, the lady ran off with some man."

CHAPTER 75

The two journalists organized the facts. Rhonesia had passed the test with flying colors. They sat in an office at the *Philadelphia Inquirer* piecing together an explosive article that would blow the jail up and free Wydell James. They had sent out for cheese steaks and Pepsi.

The article was divided into sections--small chapters--as if they were writing a novella. Chapter one was the murders. Chapter two, the arrest of Wydell James, which included the deceptive gun retrieval and the alibi--including the campus surveillance tape. Chapter three, them locating the weapon and acknowledging that there was another shooter and the shell casings found on the balcony of the property across from the crime scene. Chapter four, the LaSalle U keychain and female footprint connected to LaSalle runners.

Rhonesia was as organized as a textbook. She typed drafts, printed them, edited them on paper, and made changes in her laptop. She kept the drafts in neat piles.

Aramis, on the other hand, was a slob. His drafts were all over the floor, many of them unedited. He had changed his mind before he reviewed what he had just typed, and he would start anew.

"Why am I nervous?" she asked, looking for a little conversation.

She adored how he was so unruly, but his articles were so beautifully written. She began to appreciate him and his abilities. Not to mention that what he had taught her was gratis. He impressed her. She liked that he was an ordinary man, with pretty-boy sex appeal and the brains of a Harvard grad. He multitasked the personas of a bad boy and an intellect with ease. She occasionally found herself staring at him and hoped that she was not caught.

"You're working on a case that will be on the tip of everyone's tongue in your entire school by the morning, and you're getting your first byline on a case that will send shock waves through the DA's office and the PPD."

Aramis noted her beauty, and smiled at her. She was sexy and undoubtedly more intelligent than he had pegged her to be. He knew that some women lived on Brains Street and others on Beauty Avenue. Rhonesia lived at the intersection. Just special.

"Am I going to be safe from arrest?" she asked coyly. "I can't go to jail."

"Everything is fact-checked, so no harm no foul."

Aramis assumed that she was intentionally being adorable and needy. He wanted to hold her, but he said, "You'll be fine. Ravonne won't let you go to jail, believe me. He has favors and would use one for us."

They returned back to their work. They had a deadline. By 8:45, they had done draft three, and Aramis E-mailed what he had to his editor for review.

* * *

Aramis's managing editor and the *Philadelphia Inquirer* attorney had approved the sixth draft by 10:15. Aramis was told to call the detective in charge of the case for comments. He had also spoken to Ravonne, who had him delete the fact about the Saucony sneaker. He had the gun, so he did not need to verify anything with the police prior to going to print. He waited for the forensics to prove the bullet found in the victims matched the rifle before he handed over the weapon; and therefore, he did not need a comment, but he wanted one to authenticate the article. A comment would add to the broth of the stew that he brewed.

Aramis called the 35th police district and got the detective on the line.

"Callaghan, Aramis Reed, *Philadelphia Inquirer*. Remember me?"

"Yes, I received your package."

Aramis cut him off, "Careful, pal. I'm recording."

"For what? You can't print this," he said coarsely.

"I can. I am. Care to comment?"

"You can't be. You do not have shit."

"I am running a story in the morning paper. You should be grateful that I missed the late edition deadline. The 3,500-word piece details a conspiracy storm blowing through LaSalle University. I have painted the details as sketchy, but the fact that a missing student's mother owns the rifle used in the Hope Circle murders seems pretty solid. You found no gun powder on James. He has a concrete alibi and the PPD has not pursued a second perp considering you know for a fact that two different weapons were used."

"And James used them both. We've confirmed..."

"I'm taping, Callaghan."

"Fine. There's no proof that this weapon you've come across matches the slug found in the victims. More importantly, James could've shot the weapons."

"Not likely. See a leaky faucet dripped a little note to the press that a defense investigator found shell casings at the neighbors. Let's suppose the casings match my rifle. Then how could James kill one person and then run across the street through a house to the balcony, grab a rifle and shoot two more victims?"

Aramis already knew the answer. He knew that the weapons matched because he paid handsomely to have the ballistics tests done hastily.

"Lemmelle's a magical guy."

"He is, but there is no magic here. If the casings match, do you let James go?"

"No, we have our own intelligence."

"Okay. Tell me your side, because the defense is making a strong play with the jury pool."

"Good for them. I have no comment. Thanks. You've given me a little to relish."

Callaghan was extremely sarcastic.

"Glad to help you fight crime." Aramis hung up.

"He's pissed," Rhonesia said.

"I just have one quote out of all that to add to the article."

The room telephone rang. It was none other than...

..."Cynthia Thomas," Aramis said with mock enthusiasm. "What a pleasant surprise. Funny, I was just about to call you. What do I owe the honor of having you call me, though?"

"I do not like late calls from my detectives informing me that investigative reporters are purposing printing hogwash and threatening to pollute the jury *voir dire*. Sounds like obstruction to me. What do you think, Mr. Reed?"

"I think I have a copy of a memo from the coroner who performed the autopsies, which proves that two weapons were used. Are you pursuing two suspects? I'm recording, too, ma'am."

"No. We have Wydell James," the prosecutor said.

She did not add that, as a shooting guard, Wydell was ambidextrous and it's probable that he used both weapons.

"No, you don't."

"You're an ass," she said.

"Any other quotes?" Aramis asked and smiled at Rhonesia.

Rhonesia chuckled.

"You very casually waited until this time of night. You knew I'd have no way to stop you."

"Yes, ma'am. I did. Aren't I genius?"

"You people are..."

"I'm still recording, so be nice. Or your photo will be on the first page under the caption: ADA THOMAS SUFFERS FROM FOOT IN MOUTH DISEASE.

"Inform the editor that I'll be filing a law suit at eight sharp."

"Will do," he told her and hung up. Aramis then asked Rhonesia, "Think LaSalle will let you change majors in the middle of the senior semester?"

He was smiling.

"I wouldn't miss this drama for a trip around the world, which I really wanna do." Rhonesia smiled, showing off her perfect teeth. "So which part do we print? I really liked the 'you're an ass' part."

Aramis laughed and told her, "None of that is useful. I'll get her for that by exploiting her every chance I get. I've, well, we have ruined her night, week, and month."

"I know she despises you and when she sees my name in the byline, she'll be looking for me with a gun."

"Probably the gun used in the Hope Circle murders."

SATURDAY, JANUARY 13, 2007

CHAPTER 76

The morning light spread across Aramis and awoke him. He was on his sofa. Rhonesia was spread across the sofa, too, and her pretty feet rested on his lap. He touched her ankles intimately and moved her legs so that he could stand. Her eyes opened and blinked as she stared around the living room. They looked at each other.

"Good morning, sunshine," he said and stood up.

"Good morning, blue skies," she replied softly.

Her mind raced, trying to figure out how she looked at that moment. She had planned to wake up before him and sneak off to the bathroom to freshen up her breath and such, but he had foiled that plan. Aramis had a mirror over his sofa. She used it to cleanse the little cold from her eyes, smoothed out her hair and popped Dentyne into her mouth. When she heard the bathroom door open, she quickly lay back down.

"Rhonesia," Aramis called out delicately. "The bathroom is down the hall to the right. I put some things on the side of the sink for you."

"Thanks," she said and drifted to the bathroom. He admired her flawless skin as he walked to the kitchen to brew a pot of coffee. He picked up his phone to call Ravonne.

Rhonesia found the bathroom and saw a cute little pink terry cloth towel on the edge of a marble sink. On top of the towel was a travel-sized toothbrush, mouthwash and toothpaste. She ran the sink water and rinsed her face. She had the water low, and heard Aramis on the telephone in his bedroom.

"I'm telling you Ravonne, she's not that kind of girl. It was professionally romantic...Sure there is such a thing...We're not co-workers. I am a reporter and she is a 23-year-old college student...What the hell, man, she told me her age in conversation. I'm not going to hurt the girl, man, damn!...Look father, can you get me a reservation at Twenty21...Yes, she's worth it, dammit...You're worse than my foster parents...No we did not have sex, father. I have to go, just make the reservation."

Aramis heard the bathroom door open, and he immediately changed the topic. "You should have heard Cynthia beg me to hold off on the article. Call me after you're done with the fam and your Wydell visit."

He hung up.

Rhonesia sat in the director's chair in front of the kitchen reading the article in the actual paper. She told him, "You didn't have to lie to your best friend, Aramis. I hope he knows that I am not an easy lay. Sure I am a woman with needs, but I am not a queen."

Aramis pushed a mug of coffee in her direction. "I know. Just did not want him to get the wrong image of you. I have been a bachelor for a while. The world is 90% image and 10% wealth, you know?"

"I do. A philosopher, you are, huh?"

"I know a little."

"Did you know that Africans spawned philosophy?"

"I do, and the Greeks stole it."

"You learned something at Harvard, I see," she said with a sarcastic grin.

"I did my undergrad at Clark Atlanta,while Ravonne was at Georgetown."

"Partyville."

"A lot of party, but I did learn."

"A few of my girlfriends had gone down there, but got over all of the partying and stepping. One said that they had charter buses to go to clubs and had step practice at midnight so that the competition could not see them. How do you make an eight a.m. class when you're up until two, three in the a.m. practicing?"

"I did it and I studied. Black schools have a bad party rap, but the Ivy Leagues have drinking reps and high shooting ratings. Keg parties every day."

They fell silent.

Just pure admiration of each other.

The two of them sipped coffee re-reading the words that they had written. He had had enough stories in print. None of them on the front page. His Wydell James article had brought excitement and a little danger. He would need to mind his P's and Q's because ADA Cynthia Thomas and Detective Callaghan would be watching. They stared at each other and then back at the photos of the DA and detective under the bigger picture of Wydell. They both fell into laughter.

* * *

At noon Rhonesia and Aramis sat on his sofa with a box of donuts. The local networks had aired the details of the article as their lead stories. They bounced back and forth between the DA office, the 35th district, and CFCF. Neither, Thomas nor Callaghan had comments. However, Ravonne was mobbed as he tried to get into his car. Ravonne told the press that he would dig deeper into the allegations presented in the article, he would see to Wydell's release, and move to have Thomas and/or Callaghan investigated and reprimanded if the article was true.

"How did the press find him at the jail?" Rhonesia asked, as the news casters moved on to the weather. "I know that he is pissed that he can't even enjoy a day out because the press is hounding him, and he does not want to subject his son to that mess."

Aramis looked at her slyly. "I have no idea how he does it, but trust that he knew this was coming. He's a great actor."

"This is too much fun," she confessed. "What will you cover next?"

"Whatever Thomas and Callaghan eventually says. They have to hold a press conference to tell the taxpayers something."

"Yeah, I suppose so," she said. She then added, "I think that I better get back to my dorm. I forgot my cell phone in your car on purpose. Didn't want to be bothered. My roommate is probably going crazy with worry."

He chuckled. "Let's get you home before I get a kidnapping."

"Thomas and Callaghan would fry you."

He picked up his wallet and keys. "So can we hang out again? Or is this the end of the road?"

They walked out of the door and she replied, "Sure we can hang."

To him it sounded like she was talking to a pal. "How about dinner? Sunday. A nice restaurant downtown. It'll be nice to see you in a gorgeous dress and pumps."

"Something formal you mean? There's more than jeans and sweatshirts in my closet."

He backed out of the parking lot and told her, "I was treading lightly because I know that you are not your average woman."

"I appreciate that. But it appears that you're coming on to me. I think you're being a little presumptuous by assuming that I am interested in you, Mr. Aramis Reed."

The way that she sang his name turned him on. "Well..." he said stammering. She had caught him off guard. He had not been introduced to rejection. Aramis Reed got what he wanted.

Always.

"I am," she said smiling and getting him back on track. "You looked deflated," she said laughing. "What time should I be ready tomorrow?"

"I'll let you know. I'll call you later," he replied and pulled out of the parking lot.

"Oh sure, anything to get me on the phone."

He chuckled, "Maybe."

He loved her confidence. An attractive woman who knew her worth.

"Highly likely."

What he should have been paying closer attention to was Mr. 357 tailing him in a non-descript station wagon.

CHAPTER 77

Wydell sat in front of me with an irritated expression on his face. I really wanted to know what the hell he was perturbed about. After all, he simply had to sit in prison a week, while I wreaked my brain coaching a team to assure his release. He was before me with a long face, as opposed to a smile. Ungrateful ass.

"What's up with the dog face?" I asked. "Haven't you heard the good news?"

"I saw the news and read the paper, but Shannon just told me some stupid shit on the phone."

"Okay, you can get out Tuesday after the hearing and deal with her."

"No, I can't," he said and hung his head low. "Shit is fucked up!"

"Wydell, what the fuck is up with you?" I was more irritated now.

"Man, she told me that the cops found shells in my room and drugs."

"What room?"

"My dorm room."

"Why would you leave that shit there and not tell her to get it when you were arrested. You should have had someone clean that shit out!"

Yes, I just coerced him to commit a crime. What the hell was I thinking?

"It's not mine, crazy damn man," he yelled and jumped to his feet. "I do not fucking sell drugs, Ray-Ray. I hate drug dealers. Somebody planted that shit."

Damn. Now that was a performance. Either he was very innocent or belonged on Broadway. If the drugs weren't his, who planted them? And why did the police just all of a sudden trot into his room a week after his arrest?

"Wydell have a seat."

I was cautious. Had I not known him, I would probably have been on guard with him walking around like a tiger trapped in a cage for the first time.

"Do not fucking tell me to have a seat, Ray-Ray. For the past week, I have had a bunch of overpaid high school grads and former welfare recipients forced to work tell me what to fucking do. I paid you to work for me. I tell you what to do."

Was he kidding me? No one told me, Ravonne Lemmelle, what to do. Especially not my clients.

"I understand that you're upset, but we are on stage. Look at the clowns in guard suits out there looking at us. Sit the fuck down, now!"

He looked at me with his fists balled tightly. Had I been a public defender, he may have rushed me. Instead, he stood there and clasped his hands together and slammed them hard on the table. The windows to the room looked out at the other inmates having personal visits. They now seemed more intrigued by what was going down in legal interview room number one than their own visits.

Officer Lynch tapped on the door, and I signaled for him to come in. He asked was everything okay, and I gave in a nonchalant thumbs up that would have pissed me off. CO's was right up there on my list of people that I disliked for no reason. Lynch looked at me strangely, gave me a tough stare and then told Wydell to have a seat or his official visit would be terminated. He then left as if nothing else needed to be said.

Wydell dropped into the chair and threw his palms over his face. He was becoming increasingly angry that he was being bullied and could not defend himself.

Wydell said, "Somebody is trying to kill my thunder, Ray-Ray. I do not deserve this. I am a good man trying to do all the right things. What the fuck is going on here? Why am I the scapegoat? Why man?"

"Whoever it is lives on that campus. You have to have an idea who the culprit may be. Any idea?"

"I don't," he confirmed. "If I knew, I'd be all over they ass."

"Speaking of ass, any females that you didn't fuck on campus?"

"What?"

"It's well settled that you're a man whore."

"Come on, Ray-Ray. We're talking about a college campus. A majority-white, female student body who were trapped in their sterile homes and now free and dying to get some dick. I happen to supply dick. But that's no reason to frame me to a life or death sentence."

"Any of them get told no?"

"Absolutely not. I don't turn down pussy."

"Ever get into it with a female. I mean a fight."

"Nah, Ray-Ray. My shit was discreet and I kept my mouth shut."

"What does Shannon think about this dick slinging?"

"She didn't know. She did catch me once, which is the reason that we left the party and the campus the night of the shooting. Everyone saw the fight. I was embarrassed."

"One of the shooters was a female. Got any idea who that might be?"

"Hell no. You sure it was a bitch. I mean, that's crazy. Why would a girl kill them? Or want to frame me?"

"Beats me. I do know that if the Barclay kid was involved, he was with a female accomplice, or he wears a man's size seven. Just an angle. Nothing puts the smoking gun in his hand."

"No, he has huge feet. Thirteens, I think."

"I figured as much. Our girl wore a nine."

"If you looked for a specific vagina and asked for the hair color, whether it was shaved or unshaved or bushy, I'd be able to help. But I do not do feet. That's not why I like them."

"You need to think long and hard about a female you've pissed off, hurt, lied to, or something. You're not perfect. I know you've done something on that campus."

"No, but there's some feminists looking to show me a serious lesson."

"This is not the MO of a feminist. Maybe a poster of you calling you a dog posted all around campus, but a death penalty is harsh for them."

"I guess. What about the drugs?"

"That's nothing. They haven't charged you. You've had no access to the room since the first time they searched it. I would get that dismissed easily."

"I thought that Shannon had cleaned my room out."

"So, she forgot the drugs?"

"Nice try. They weren't mine."

"I had to."

"You're dying to know where that retainer came from."

"I am."

"I am not telling you yet."

"Whatever. What's the purpose of having all that money if you're not living life like it's golden?"

"Ray-Ray, I'm comfortable knowing that I need to wait before I make the big move. As long as people perceive me as poor, they'd be scared of me. That's why I hide my new-found wealth. It's common knowledge that a poor man will kill you over a dollar. I have a dollar, and no reason to kill and ruin my life."

"Here's a written summary of everything that I've done thus far and a copy of the Motion to Dismiss that I filed. I'm going to need you to come up with a girl for me to place a microscope up her skirt."

"To bad that I am here, because I have the perfect microscope," he chuckled, which was a good thing. I hated to send him to his cell angry.

"Your dick got you in this mess as is."

"Hey, you keep my dick off your mind," Wydell said and cracked up.

"I quit. Get a PD," I replied laughing.

CHAPTER 78

Despite a few media hounds being outside of the prison when I left, I pulled into my driveway in peace. I parked and walked into the living room. Dajuan was playing the piano and Brandon was teaching the rabbit to two-step.

"What is this, some sort of animal club? Dajuan the DJ and Brandon the dance instructor."

"Nah, we're just having fun, babe," Dajuan said as my cell phone rang.

"Kensan?" I said into the phone. "Come down, I have time, finally. I am at 321 Arch Street."

I hung up and Dajuan asked who I invited over. I had that chat in his face as a way to broach the topic that I thought may be a problem. It wasn't for me, but this was a new area for me.

"Childhood friend. The one who wrote the script that I have been reading."

"Oh, what's for dinner?" Dajuan asked. He then added, "Why do you look all suspicious?"

"Huh?" I replied dumbfounded.

"You look..."

"Okay, here's the deal. Me and Kensan used to...when we were kids. Of course, that's in the past." I paused and gathered my thoughts, before I said, "I only informed you because he thought that I was afraid to invite him here thinking that you'd trip out." I had to talk cryptically to fool Brandon.

"Why would he think that?"

"See, he's just out of prison. He told me that he wanted to get his life together and thought that I would be sensitive to his situation because one, I am...and two, he thought, correctly that I was a true friend."

"And when was the last time that you two...?"

"My freshman year at Georgetown during Christmas break."

"Hell of a Christmas gift for you, I bet," Dajuan said with an air of sardonicism. "Any feelings at all?"

"He's like my brother."

"Don't trip then. Now back to the question at hand, what's for dinner?"

"Let me see," I said going toward the kitchen. "I could make..."

"Does he still get down?" Dajuan asked, not willing to let the Kensan development go away without an investigation.

"He said he had a little shindig in jail. Got hurt, or some bull shit like that. He claims to admire us and hinted that he's tired of women. All he wants is a career and future. I encouraged him to add a wife to that mix."

"That could be a man," he replied and gave me a faux smile. "Does he want you?"

"No, Dajuan. And for the record, he told me so. I do not want him either."

"You just turned out the whole Germantown," he told me chuckling, before he added, "You little freak."

"No, I didn't," I said laughing and shaking my head.

"I hope that he understands that this is not a game. I'd hate for you to defend me for murder."

CHAPTER 80

At 2:30 in the morning, I found myself inside of a twenty-four hour Kinkos, located inside of the downtown Marriott Hotel at 12th and Market. I had had a great evening with Dajuan and Kensan. Kensan was in my office asleep on the pull out sofa when I left for this late night meeting. He was drunk and could not drive home in that condition.

The empty computer station area, if anything, enhanced my mental rejection of that unwanted appearance. It made me brood for my Harvard days. My laptop had been stolen, and I had to use the computer lab to get a major paper done. I did the assignment while I chatted with Dajuan. I turned in a profound paper, too. It was published in the Harvard Law Review. I was so elated that I drank continually for three days until Dajuan came up to Boston and gave me something else to do.

My cell phone rang and I answered it asking, "Where the hell are you?"

It was Aramis's ring tone and he should have beaten me to Kinkos.

"He's a little tied up at the moment," an evil voice told me, "get a computer, log into your AOL account, and I'll see you there. You will not call the police or your home! Or Aramis and your family will die. Including Constance. And I have no problem getting into the Governor's mansion."

The caller hung up and my thoughts were clouded. I began to shake uncontrollably. I was so afraid that I wanted to die trying to save Aramis and warn my family. Who was this monster? My mind swirled to all of my disgruntled clients, which weren't many because I had a great acquittal rate. None of them appeared to be the prototype for an insane ingrate out to kill me.

What about Aramis? Who has he, or hasn't he reported the facts on? The only case that he actually had a pivotal role in solving was my current client: Wydell James.

I sat down and logged into my AOL account. I was enveloped with absurdity. I looked serene on the surface, but I was breaking up inside without ruffling my outer shell. To expect me not to be an absolute monster, too, in the face of this atrocity was a serious miscalculation on my competitor's behalf. There was no excusable or logical explanation either. This had to lead to an increase in the death toll. For it not to was an utter impossibility. Would my anger thaw or melt away as the snow makes way for spring?

Hell no.

Undoubtedly not.

Someone's life expectancy would be arrested. My evil thoughts were interrupted by an instant message:

> TRE57: You will check into the hotel, rent a lap top and stay in the room and wait for further instructions. Be sure your room overlooks Market Street. Any deviation and what I told you moments ago commences.

The man logged off and left me confused. He didn't even let me respond. Before I logged off, I copied the threat and pocketed it. I then cut and paste the threat and E-mailed it to Jonathan Rude, along with a note.

I walked out of Kinkos toward my illegally parked BMW. As I emerged from the store, my cell phone sprang to life. I answered it quickly.

"Get your ass back into that Kinkos. Now!"

"But my wallet is in the car. I need..."

"Screw what the fuck you need. I need your cooperation to keep the body count in Philadelphia from rising a notch or five. Whatever you need better not hinder you from getting that room. I know that much. Get the hotel room and then you may move your car."

Click!

My mind raced. He could see me. My car would be towed if it stayed on Market. My wallet was in there and I had no cash on me, nor a checkbook.

I walked back into the Kinkos to get out of the man's sight. He had to have been in a room at the Lowes Hotel overlooking Market Street. I really had no idea where he was. He could have been a Kinkos employee as far as I knew.

My mind replayed the message: Be sure that your room overlooks Market Street.

He wanted to watch me from the other hotel using binoculars. I was in a grave quandary and my life, amongst my loved ones, hung in the balance. I charged frantically through the Kinkos and went through the opposite door and was in the lobby of the Marriott. I walked around the empty, circular lounge area and passed the check in/out counters. I found the valet stand, hoping one of the guys that I nodded to regularly was on duty. They were not, so I had to become a conniving man to deal with the man's orders.

"Excuse me," I said politely to the valet guy.

I was not calm, but I forced my body not to showcase my shaking.

"Yes, sir."

"I have a BMW 750LI parked on Market Street. Could you collect it while I check in? I don't want to get a ticket."

"Well, couldn't you bring it around, sir? I have to stay on my post. I am the only man here tonight."

"No, sir, I can't."

"That's going to be a problem," the man said and turned to his desk to find something to do.

I had other plans for him, though. "Listen. I am in a dangerous situation that I cannot discuss. Please!" I begged somberly, and showed him the message that I had printed. “Could you please get the car? Pull it around here and do not put it underground, man. Please. This is a matter of life and death.”

“You have to tell the police.”

“No...no. Just please get the car.”

“Okay. Okay. What color is it?”

“Midnight blue/black.”

I walked back through the lobby with the valet. I said to him, “Before you bring it around, please pass me my wallet.”

He looked at me plainly, but he jogged over to the car, grabbed the wallet and then brought it back to me.

I walked back into the Kinkos and went back to the computer station. I had a plan. I made a car rental reservation for myself. And then another for Dajuan and Constance. I was just thinking ahead. Getaway cars. Maybe I would be allowed a fraction of a second to warn them. As I grabbed the reservation from the printer, my eyes played a violent trick on me.

My $75,000 car was scattered all over Market Street. Flames attached to metal matter illuminated the essential Center City corridor. The Septa headquarters was directly across from the Marriott and next door to the Lowes. The front windows were blown out of each building. More importantly, the valet was no longer with us, and there was nothing left for a cremation.

CHAPTER 81

I briskly walked through the Marriott lobby. Sadness and exhaustion overwhelmed me. This was a serious inconvenience. Sure, I care about the valet, but my family was far more important. Sad, but true. No, the poor valet should not have expired that night. What made his death all the more unbearable was that a bomb was set to have me in a coffin. I should've been the valet.

But I wasn't.

And someone would pay. I figured that this TRE57 character figured that I was dead.

But I wasn't.

Ha!

Problem was the police.

I thought that they would put an APB out on me the moment they watched the tapes and saw me on camera escorting the valet across the lobby to the car. They would hopefully check the computer to see what I endured.

I wanted to call Aramis's phone to confront the man who had blown up my car, but he may have perceived that as disrespect. After all, he was a lamebrain who had orchestrated the kidnapping of my best friend and threatened to kill my family. I was terribly shaken and confused. Even angry. I started to blame myself for not taking that blast myself, but that was absurd. I did not wish to seem ungentlemanly, but...

My cell phone rang, and I immediately answered.

"You can't know Ravonne Lemmelle how sorry I am," the caller told me.

"What? That I am alive."

The idiot giggled. I could not stomach the gaul of this clown. "You won't be for long."

"What do you want?"

"For you to be dead!" he said simply, as if he just asked for his fries to be super-sized. He then added, "You're always meddling. Can't keep your arrogance to your goddamn self."

He actually supposed that I should have. It was he who had killed the valet. It was he who had me roaming 13th Street, which, until that moment, I forgot where I was. I walked past an adult book store at Arch Street, and, at three a.m., three male prostitutes lingered outside looking for a date to get a hit of crack cocaine, I surmised. One of the freaks looked at me like I was competition. I was clean and tasty, while he drank a can of beer concealed in a brown paper bag and was noticeably dirty and tired. His knuckles were in need of a drink, also. Like a shot glass of lotion.

I pushed on and walked beside the Pennsylvania Convention Center. It amazed me how Philadelphia's Boys Town (like in many other cities) was perched where visitors had easy access to discrete pleasure.

"Are you hearing me," the man yelled into my earpiece.

"Yes, sir."

"Do not fucking patronize me, faggot. I know all about your subtle sarcasm."

Again, I was speechless, but I knew that I had to stay in that conversation.

"I do not even have an idea about what I've done wrong."

"For starters, being born," the man confirmed for me. "Secondly, getting a law degree and then deciding to practice law. Lastly, you've interfered with my legacy. But you'll fix that."

"Your legacy? Pardon me, but I am lost."

"You've been lost since you sucked your first dick," he said as I crossed Cherry Street.

I walked past a few more hustlers. It was freezing out there. I donned a mink baseball jacket, lambskin gloves, and Timberlands, but the boys were in the bare minimum.

"Why isn't Mark Artis in prison for the rest of his life?"

Instinctively, I replied like I was in a courtroom. "His true name was Donald Marramount. I proved that he was not Mark Artis. The perpetrator of the fake kidnapping was the legendary Mr. 357, that's why."

And then it hit me. Tre57 was 357.

Mr. 357.

"Thanks for the legendary status."

I could not be on the phone with that thug. I immediately remembered the recording feature on my cell phone and activated it.

"So, you're upset that I got him off?"

"Absolutely, dick breath. With him out, the feds are still looking for me. You interfered with my life, now I want to end yours."

"No...no...no," I said, because that was the only thing that I could say.

I walked across Vine Street and tried to register why this man hated me. As I walked, I was still passing male whores. One of them looked like an infant prostitute. He didn't look over 12 years old, despite being about 5'10".

"Yes, yes, yes. And you've already negated from my plan as is. Now, you face arrest for that explosion. I am sure within minutes the police will be looking for you. You better run for your life. I'll be fair telling you that Aramis is not dead, but he is a little tied up at the moment at a very unlikely place. I am not going to get you now. I want you to run frantically for your life from the police while wondering when I am going to strike. And I am. At the precise moment that I feel like. I'll get you. But for now, I have to make an anonymous tip to the police to be sure you're a wanted man."

He hung up on me.

Where the hell was Aramis tied up? Was he really dead? My mind began to replay what he had told me to get me to the Kinkos. He had said that he had an anonymous tip from someone that claimed to know who the Hope Circle murderer was. They wanted to meet me ASAP and I had to be in attendance. That was designed to blow me into pieces like the poor valet. My mind was disturbed by a Chevrolet Caprice Classic that circled me like a piranha for the second time. I could see the silhouette of a male figure, but not the characteristics.

I called Constance, who answered on the first ring.

"Granny," I said. "Listen carefully. Do not argue or ask questions. Just act. Get up now and have a neighbor take you to the airport this very instant. Do not take your car. Do not go in or near your car. Period! Take your cell phone. Keep it charged and take a flight to the hotel that we stayed at to celebrate my law school graduation. Check in under your only dead child's name, and I'll call you later."

"I'm on it, now," she told me as the Caprice passed me again. "Are you and the baby okay?" she asked with love and urgency.

"Yes, but we will be safer with you gone."

"Am I in..."

"Constance, expect the worst and pray for the best, but get out of there, please."

I hung up.

I didn't want to lie to her. Bottom line, we were all in grave danger.

CHAPTER 82

Continuing up 13th Street, I heard sirens wail as I sent a text message to Kensan. I sent it three times to be sure that it woke him, in the event that he was in a deep sleep. I was very glad that Dajuan and I invited him to spend the night as opposed to letting him drive home drunk. I didn't want to call my house phone or Dajuan's phone because I had no idea if they were bugged or traced.

Before I reached Spring Garden Street, I cut through an alley and headed toward 12th Street. I wanted a taxi to pass by, but the Caprice did and slowed to a stop.

The window rolled down and I jumped. I expected a gun to come out, but all I got was a toothy gay-ass smile.

"How big is that dick and how much?" the freak asked me.

I thought a moment before I said, "Can't answer that cause you may be a cop. Pull onto this here little block," I said and pointed to the corner.

He had no chance to sleep with me, but perhaps I could use him for a ride. When I reached the corner I turned and the man had parked three cars from the corner. The block was dark and occupied by a warehouse only. When I was at the driver's side door, I signaled for him to roll down the window.

"What you got?"

He was a skinny, dark man, with to many teeth. It was obvious why he had to pay for tricks.

"I got about twenty bucks," he said.

I pulled my shirt out of my pants, unbuckled my jeans and then unzipped them. I didn't know that I was so cheap. *Twenty bucks, wow.* He looked at me with great anticipation, and I obliged. There I was, the son of the Governor, a Harvard grad, and a male prostitute. Helluva resumé. Brandon would be proud.

The man reached his arm out to touch me and I broke it. One swift motion, and I snapped it at the elbow. He yelled like a woman, and I shut him up with a blow to his temple

He was barely cognizant when he said, "I'm sorry, man. She paid me to keep you busy for an hour. She gave me a grand."

"She? Who the fuck is she?"

I was confused as hell.

"Dunno. I was passing by looking for a date, and she flagged me down. She wanted me to take photos performing oral sex on you and text them to her. I think my arm is broken."

He was whining and held onto his arm.

"What number are you supposed to text?" I asked fixing my clothing.

"It's in the ash tray."

"Thanks," I said and hit him again.

He was asleep when I reached into his car door, pulled the handle and opened it. I pulled the man out by his shirt and dropped him to the ground. I searched his pockets and took his wallet. Next, I hopped into his car and drove off in it.

Assault and carjacking down, murder to go!

CHAPTER 83

I sped out of the alley having noted that I was running for my life, wanted by the PPD, and in a stolen vehicle. Hadn't I worked to avoid this kind of dilemma. Apparently not. I was supposed to represent the crazy men and women who committed these sorts of heinous acts.

At Sixth Street, I made a left off Spring Garden and sent Kensan another text message. I wanted to call my home badly. That Mr. 357 character was an obnoxious dumb ass and capable of garnering a spot in Ripley's Believe It Or Not. I was not familiar with the man, but...Wait! I had an epiphany. The man whose car I took said that he had met a woman. Could Mr. 357 be in drag?

That made sense. Nothing made sense. I was a wreck. This had to be a damn dream.

I pulled out my cell phone and call Jon Rude. He was groggy, but he got right up at the mentioning of the words: blown-up, 357, chasing, carjacking, and dead. Those words in combination with me were insane. Using caution, I asked him to hang up and told him that I would text him in the event my phone or the car that I drove was bugged. I was taking no chances on my life or my family's lives.

I crossed Market Street slowly and briefly looked down six blocks and saw that police cruisers and EMT vehicles had flooded the site of the explosion. I kept driving, though. When I reached Pine Street, I turned right and parked between Sixth and Seventh Streets. I looked fiercely into the mirrors to maintain surveillance of my surroundings. I also looked for my family and Kensan to emerge from the condo. Finally they did.

They walked briskly up the sidewalk and just as they crossed Fifth Street, I saw a truck pull out. A follower, I presumed. Just as I expected.

I had already warned them to be on alert, but I sent Kensan another text to be sure he knew that they were lurking. He knew.

Surprisingly, Brandon held Dajuan's hand, and my boys were moving. I knew that my baby was scared and confused, but he knew that Daddy had a serious job, sometimes dealing with bad guys. He knew that he had to listen to Dajuan no matter what if danger came. It had come.

They crossed Sixth Street and the truck crawled behind them. They got closer to my stolen car, and I rolled down the driver side window. As they passed me, Kensan dropped Dajuan's laptop into the window and they kept walking, without Brandon noticing me. I then pulled off while the truck was unhappily stuck at the light.

The driver was not looking to harm my family at that point. Perhaps, they wanted to be led to me. I planned for them to get their wish, too.

CHAPTER 84

Twenty minutes later, Kensan pulled his car over on a long stretch of Walnut Street between 31st and 34th Streets. It was three city blocks without intersections. I was leaning on the guard rail on a bridge that overlooked a parking lot. I could see the apex of the 30th Street Amtrak station and the Main Philadelphia post office branch.

Two minutes passed before the truck that had followed my family turned onto Walnut Street. It stopped in front of a music cafe. The silhouette in the driver's seat was on a telephone, probably checking in. They sat and watched until Brandon ran up to me and I picked him up. The driver slithered out of the truck. It was a female. I noticed that first. Second was her long hair. Probably a wig. She looked slim. Petite, sort of. Dark shades covered her eyes at 4 a.m. Who was she fooling?

Not, I said, the cat.

She walked slowly and had the audacity to be whistling, as if she was just a tenant out for a stroll to the apartment building up the block.

She approached us and said, "You guys got a light?"

"Naw. We don't smoke," Dajuan said.

"I do," Kensan said and raised a Glock to her face.

He used the tip to knock the shades from her face.

Before she could get her hand out of her pocket where she probably had a gun of her own, Rude came from the shadows and smacked her upside her head with a .45. She lost her gun and bowed over. Blood gushed from her head.

Dajuan grabbed her by the throat and slammed her to the ground. He fell with her using all of his weight, as I picked up her gun.

"Why the fuck are you following us?" Dajuan asked, as Rude handcuffed her.

Dajuan looked angry enough to kill her first and ask questions later.

"Dad," Brandon said. "That's the lady that said that she was my mom at school the other day."

"She paid me to," the woman said.

"Who the hell is she?"

I was tired of this bitch, whoever she was.

"I don't know her name. She hired me to kidnap the boy."

"What?" Dajuan and I asked in unison.

I began to search for her cell phone, which began to ring as I grabbed it from her purse. I looked at the caller ID and the call was from Aramis's phone. I was livid.

I opened it and the caller gleefully said, "Tell me Ravonne shit his pants when you took the boy."

"I did not. I have long ago learned to swim my way out of shit."

"Ahhhh. Ravonne Lemmelle," the caller said.

It was Mr. 357. I'd bet that he grinned uncontrollably.

"You don't sound surprised, but I'd bet that you are."

I pinched the bridge of my nose and could feel steam escaping my pores. My brain worked overtime. I had been involved in the oddest situations, but this took the cake like an 1899 comedy show by a slave before his master. I had no desire to crash and burn, though. My family was in one piece and I intended to keep it that way.

I told Mr. 357, "I read a little about you a moment ago. You are really fond of women. You kill them and you hire them to do your dirty deeds. And you dress like one of them. I bet you're gay. A faggot. You hate women, don't you?"

"You're a genius. Sure I do. With a passion. Your mother included."

Was I really talking to Mr. 357?

Was someone playing with me?

Did any of that matter? My life was in jeopardy.

"Now that I know that you want my son, obviously to use and hold him as bait, I'll assure you that will not happen, pal."

"You're shitten me."

I didn't know myself. That fool had killed over 30 people and managed to thwart arrest that far.

"Listen, Ray-Ray," he said and cracked up.

"No, you listen. I am tossing my phone, so don't bother calling me. I'll call you when I figure out who you are for the record. I am smarter than the FBI. I've beaten them in court every time I defended a case against them. You have played with me long enough, and it's time I fuck you."

"You already have," he said and burst into laughter, before he hung up.

My eyebrows furrowed. Was he speaking literally, or figuratively? I was numb. My heart thudded hard inside my chest. I was locked in the jaws of a vicious thought. I was on stage and it was hard to stay in character to protect my family. Had I cracked, Dajuan and definitely Brandon would, too. I felt bombarded with vulnerability. I looked Brandon directly in his eyes and then walked off with him. Dajuan came along.

I stopped walking and kneeled before Brandon. We were eye to eye.

"Are you scared, King B?"

"Yes," he said, nodding his head up and down.

I could die.

"The lady tried to kidnap me and kill you."

"Yes, but I'm a big boy and Dajuan, Kensan, and Rude stopped her. I have bad friends. But I need you to be bigger and better than all of us, little buddy."

"Like you big?" he asked a little excited.

His eyes had widened with a vision of being grown.

"Bigger than me. Do you trust, Daddy D, too?"

"Yup," he said and held his hand out for a high-five.

Finally, he was acting his age. He had no real idea that a serial killer was after us. High fives were not in order, but he got one.

"Enough to go without me?" I asked.

I had to. My son came first.

"Uh," he said, "why can't we stay with you?"

I knew that the question stung Dajuan a little, but hopefully he understood.

I said, "Yes, you can, but do you trust Daddy D, how you trust me?"

I had to know, because I had no desire to torture him by leaving him with Dajuan or anyone else.

He looked up at Dajuan, and nodded his head up and down.

"I need you to say it, Brandon."

"This is not court," Rude said.

"Yes, Dad," Brandon said and smiled. "I love Daddy D.

"Good, let's get out of here," I said.

I was ready to play!

CHAPTER 85

Brandon, Dajuan and I jogged down the stairs to the 30th Street Station SEPTA blue line. Not many commuters were on the train platform. The early morning crowd was not at its peak, yet, but it was going to be. Despite the cold weather, it was hot in the basement of the city. The walls rattled. Amtrak was connected to the station, so I presumed a Metroliner was arriving or departing that station. The rumble added horror to the dark mood.

That far, Mr. 357 lived up to his reputation. He made every attempt to frighten me, scare me, and hurt me. And it worked. I was sure that the monster was waiting for me to slip, fall, and bump my head on something sharp. I imagined him locked in a basement with black painted walls hanging upside down. He had to be more invested into stealing my son. But why?

What had I really done to this alien? Creature. Chimera. He was not human. No possibility. I was nearly chuckling at my thoughts, but laughing at that point was inappropriate.

Watching the happy train riders parade across the platform, listening to their iPods and having enjoyable conversations angered me. I had to get away from these happy damn people. I stepped up to the yellow line and looked through the tunnel. An east-bound train approached, and I could hear the west-bound train, as well.

Dajuan just paced. He had walked a mile in circles. He didn't look scared, but I knew that he had to be. He was getting closer and closer to exploding. I felt that. I also felt the train platform convulse beneath my feet.

The east-bound train stopped and the doors opened. After a load of passengers disembarked, Brandon and I stepped on. The west-bound train also unloaded passengers. The platform was packed. We walked very quickly to the door leading to the next car. I pulled the handle and the door slid back. As Brandon went onto the platform that led to the next car, my heart quickened.

"Get the fuck out of the way!" I heard a women's voice yell.

I turned and saw that she had a gun raised in the air.

"Move, you assholes."

I heard the ding-dong warning that the train conductor was closing the doors. As the doors slid shut, Dajuan was at the other car holding the door open. Brandon and I ran out of it and it slammed shut.

The train pulled off and the crazed woman sprayed bullets into the train window. It was bullet proof.

I smiled.

She slammed her hand on the door and rode to the 15th Street station pissed.

Thirty seconds later, we emerged onto Market Street and hopped into the car with Kensan. Daylight had arrived. It was officially Sunday. We were headed to Germantown.

"Somebody was shooting at us!" I said, as he pulled off. "Did you get the tickets?"

"Yes, three. Two adults and one kid, just like you told me. All on Dajuan's card. I hope this works, because the police are definitely looking for you."

"How you know that?"

"They were posting pictures of you in the station."

CHAPTER 86

Kensan Pope's cellar was spacious and covered the entire length of the house. The floors were cold and concrete, except where he had throw rugs laid down. Light was allowed into the room, thanks to the windows that ran under the porch. He had actually cordoned off the bedroom from the living room, giving the area a little style. There was a toilet with a sink and a small stand-in shower. He had everything, except a kitchen.

Dajuan and Brandon sat on the sofa, and Kensan turned on his TV for them to watch. I had the laptop call up all of the information on Mr. 357. I asked Kensan to go to the pay phone and make a call for me, as I researched away.

"Whatever you need," he replied without all of the lip service that he had given me at my office.

"Go call 9-1-1 and tell them that reporter Aramis Reed is tied up in his Park Drive Manor apartment number 1007."

"What if he is not there?" Dajuan asked.

"No harm to the police. That's their job," I said. "I can then take the steps to have them searching for him."

* * *

The idea of Aramis being dead was unbearable. I steadily researched and learned that 357 did reference a gun. It also was the number of crimes that he committed in a city.

Three.

Five.

Seven.

He had committed two in Philadelphia according to him, so I was third. Or perhaps, number three on his road to five or seven. He was spiraling out of control, and I planned to help him fall from grace. I would be right there to plant the Ravonne Lemmelle flag on his forehead. I typed in another website, and Aramis Reed marched down the basement stairs in front of Kensan.

I jumped to my feet and embraced him tightly. I was overwhelmed with joy and could not thank God more.

"What the hell happened?" I asked and released him.

"Some crazy bitch put a .357 to my dome, made me call you, and that's after I allowed her to cuff me to the bed," he said and plopped on the sofa.

"What? How'd the hell did you meet her?"

I gave him a blank stare and he volleyed a crazy one, so I said, "The party line." I let that sink in before I said, "Bet that will keep your ass off that chat line now."

I then asked Kensan, "How'd you get him from the police?"

"I never called them. I went to the apartment and had the manager open the door."

"Wow."

I was impressed.

"Yeah, I am not as dumb as I look," Kensan said and grinned.

No one could laugh.

"Maybe," Aramis said. "But what the hell is going on and who is this crazy bitch?"

"She claims to be Mr. 357."

"What! Lies," Aramis said.

"Yes, this bitch is a psycho, too. *The Inquirer* had covered Mr. 357 extensively. Could you get the notes and articles from the library vault, so we can figure out who this is?"

Aramis said, "I suppose I could, but what does Mr. 357 want with you or me? And since when did mister become misses?"

"Since tonight," said I, and then told him the short version of tonight's events.

He replied, "That's bananas. Why would someone want to take Brandon?"

"I guess it is anger at me for having Artis acquitted. Other than that, beats the hell out of me. Call the editors and get the info to see if I crossed this son-of-a-motherless goat."

"They're going to take me through a bunch of red tape, because I am not an official reporter, but I may have a favor due to me."

"Tell them that you may nab Mr. 357. They'd be richer if they published the report. You would be famous and make history. So do whatever you want to do to get their library."

* * *

An hour later, Aramis and I continued to plow through the *Philadelphia Inquirer's* library files on Mr. 357, two hours after they had E-mailed what they had. I had sped read all of the articles twice. There were articles from all of the cities where he had committed crimes. The article titles could not be ignored, either. I could not imagine going out to retrieve the morning paper and having one of these former headlines screaming at me:

HE'S HERE, MR. 357
LOADED .357 LEFT IN THE BOX W/BODY
MURDER CONNOISSEUR IN MIAMI
STAY IN TONIGHT, OR MAYBE GO OUT

If I was not a sane lad, I would believe that other murderers felt second rate when the press announced Mr. 357's arrival to their town. The thought of local Charles Manson's becoming envious of Mr. 357 was repulsive. Hell, I was jealous. His intelligence superseded mine by far.

"I am really on to something here," I announced to Aramis.

He gave me one of those point-blank stares and I explained myself.

"I've outlined a chronology of the crimes and it seems I've been a visitor to all of the cities where they've taken place."

"Good for you. The frequent flyer. Maybe you did literally fuck this animal. If he or she looks like the babe that tied me the hell up, I don't doubt that ya gay ass fucked her. If it's her," Aramis replied.

"You really think Mr. 357 is a broad somehow?" Kensan asked.

"Anything is possible. No gun was used and maybe a woman was scared to shoot," Aramis told him.

"Nah. I'm not buying that," Kensan said. "I know plenty of chicks that are shooters."

"Hood rats, yeah. Ghetto woman," said I.

"Are you implying only hood chicks shoot? Because I know or at least bet that there is a country bumpkin that'll blow your head off."

"Okay, I get it, Kensan. But this is the work of a psychological dysfunctional man."

"Ravonne, you're starting to annoy me. You're sounding dumb. You could be Mr. 357. He does not have to be insane. He could be very sane. The typical soccer dad. By all accounts you're a stable family man, which could be a serious facade."

I was taken aback by the aggression in Aramis's tone.

"Alright, I get it. Let me see what you've been writing."

I began to read his notes as he spoke to me.

"I began an article shell of what has happened from the moment that she cuffed me until the moment Kensan rescued me. Even the things involving you."

Aramis's notes were meticulous and extensive. I found very interesting things that "make you go um" hiding beneath his ideologies. He could've made an acute attorney, but he worked out to be a fine investigative reporter. His hypothesis was doused with hunches and innuendo, but the ideas were fresh, considering he had something no other reporter had, and that was contact.

I stopped reading and said to him, "Something connects me to this monster. I wronged it somewhere."

"Maybe in another lifetime," Kensan joked in an attempt to balm the mood.

"He loved Milan during the summer of 2000," Aramis said.

"True, and I was there for two months as an exchange student at U of Milan."

"How could I forget that? Ariel only visited you once and never took your calls. She called you when she was not busy with Kim. Or was it Daisy at that time?"

"Daisy. You had to hear all about that as my best friend, because I had no one in Italy to really chat to. Okay, so I came back from Milan in mid-August and we ventured off to Harvard Law together."

"Along with your then girlfriend, Ariel, whom I still dislike."

"Whatever. At any rate, I got her pregnant in January/February 2001 and then came Brandon in October."

"But according to the papers, good ol' Mr. 357 was ravaging Boston beginning in September 2001 as Sylvester Bailey the murderer and prolific international hacker. Who, might I add, eclipsed the reputation of the Boston Strangler. In October 2001, Ariel dumped you for Hollywood and never looked back. So, between December 1997 and October 2001, I'm assuming you wronged the clown."

"So Ariel is the connection?" Dajuan said, and opened his eyes.

He had been feigning sleep with Brandon up under him in a deep sleep.

"Well, I have to bring something to the light." Everyone's eyes beamed in on me. I felt like I was about to perform at a Super Bowl half-time show. "Ariel came to see me a week ago."

"What!"

That was Dajuan. He moved Brandon to the side and stood. Kensan and Aramis stared at us.

I went on. "She came to see me on the same day as the Artis acquittal. She refused to meet Brandon, so I walked out of her hotel room. She claimed that she wanted some money. Then she added that she was going to file for divorce and take me for half my worth. And that was because, I told her that if she did not meet Brandon I did not want to talk to her.

"And take note that that night Dave and Busters was robbed and you received a crank call to watch the news that morning. Also note, Dorothy Kincaid, was bagged, tagged, and shipped to the local FBI office that morning," Dajuan said. He went on, and said, "I've actually read most of what you two are now gagging over. I actually had time to read the papers. It seems that Ariel has been around the set of all of the Mr. 357 crimes in Milan, Boston and now Philadelphia. I'm willing to bet that she was at the Salt Lake City Olympic Games. I would also bet she was with the true Mark Artis, too. That explains why she's back or she may be Skylar Juday in drag as a man. You did not get the connection with Artis, so the heat was turned up."

"There you have it folks. Whoever is trying to kill you has a connection to Ariel Greenland," Kensan said.

"Makes sense to me. Why else would they want to blow you up and take Brandon?" Aramis asked.

"He's right," Kensan added. "You were supposed to be blown up and at the same time your condo was being staked out to kidnap Brandon. Only that piece of the plan fell through because I was there and gave you an outlet to warn D and B."

"Oh shit," Aramis and I said together.

I then said, "D and B, as in Dave and Buster's like Dajuan and Brandon. She fuckin' did it! That crazy bitch is Mr. 357. That was a clue to the identity and now that I think about it, her favorite drink is..."

"Don't tell me," Dajuan said. "Let me guess, Louis the damn 13th, which further explains why the women who were raped had no semen or body fluid evidence. She used a dildo."

I bet I looked as ridiculous as I ever have in my life. That couldn't be it. A charming analysis that I could not accept. We were on the right train going down the wrong track.

"Ariel is not Mr. 357."

"Why not?" Dajuan asked.

"She's not!" I growled and jumped to my feet.

I was in no way going to let them badger my wife and son's mother. "Where the hell is she now?" I asked and paced the floor.

"Probably waiting for you to return home, or work, or to the courthouse," Aramis said to my back.

Dajuan walked up to me and touched my shoulder. I gave in and spun and hugged him tightly. Tears fell down my face. How could I have had a baby with Mr. 357? He was a terrorist in the highest form. Could Ariel have fooled me so easily? Why marry and have a baby by me?

"I never wanted to hear myself say this, but I need to go to the FBI."

CHAPTER 87

Armed with a neat, concise legal brief, I barged into the FBI office headquarters like I owned the joint. I would brook no superiority complexes from the agents who would perceive my ideas as wildly unbelievable. My brief was written in very clear layman's terms because I was fully aware that despite the degrees earned by the agents, they had a brutish lack of thoroughly devoting energy to civilian ideas.

I, along with Aramis, sat in what was the war room for the plans to capture Mr. 357. It was 9:20 according to a digital clock on the wall. As three agents consumed the Mr. 357 Brief, I took the free time to steal what information that I could from the pushpin maps and many bulletin boards around the room. Despite Aramis's neutral expression, I was sure as a thirsty reporter he was doing the same as I. The agents should have put us in an empty interview room. Aramis should never, never, never be in a room that confided so many worthy developments.

All of the civilian leads appeared to be verbal descriptions or forensic artist's sketches of alleged eye witnesses. To my supposition, all of those leads were moot. Mr. 357 was not only a master of disguise, he could cross racial lines. That was a compelling skill that many men of the criminal cloak were not privileged to. There was no police or what they called, "trained eye" leads because the only three judicial figures to encounter Mr. 357 were all dead.

The only evidenced personal history were Mr. 357's crimes. Which to me was not personal. Every piece of data on the crimes was public information, and that's hardly a fair description of personal.

There was a lovely photo array of any surveillance which had been used to print a photo of Mr. 357. I looked at the photos very closely to see if I could see any likeness of Ariel Greenland. My mind also rewound and pictured Ariel in my office two weeks prior. Before she left me for Hollywood her canines on both sides of her mouth were slightly off, which forced an appearance of crowding. However, the only thing I noticed was her fabulous veneer job and the enamel was the brightest white. The new look was toothsome, but could they have been faux teeth? Pure theatrical?

So many suppositions needed to morph into facts. I was in a war room inside of the FBI headquarters where facts were to be found and later used to prosecute. I never thought I'd be on this side of the table.

The agents seemed to be eating every word on the page like beef Wellington. I was not fooled one bit, though. I knew a tsunami of questions would follow. First, they'd interrogate the hell out of me with tedious questions about the car bomb. Probably force me to convince them that I did not plant the bomb myself. They could satisfy all of the prongs to try and substantiate it, too.

Carlos Savino, my boss and lead counsel at my firm, would beat the bologna down with a bat, but I imagined them claiming that I had a criminal connection to Mr. 357 as Mark Artis, and I had a means to garner explosives. They could make the motive car insurance. A joke right? The FBI usually cooked up beautiful *con somme* prior to arrest as they did with Mark Artis. However, I added power steering fluid to the soup, so no jury bought it. Now, I had the balls to press upon them a conceivable theory of who the true Mr. 357 was. I imagined the media beating they'd get. Not to mention the deflated egos. One of the agents closed the brief that I had written and the interrogation began.

It was brief, and ended with them kicking me out with two conditions: no contact with Ariel Greenland, and I could not leave Philadelphia.

MONDAY, JANUARY 15, 2007

CHAPTER 88

After leaving the Federal Bureau of Ignoramus office, Kensan drove Dajuan and Brandon to the Amtrak Station at 30th Street. We had planned for them to take an Amtrak train headed to Boston, but they would depart the train in Trenton, NJ, then take a SEPTA train from Trenton back to the Philadelphia Airport and board non-stop flights for LAX to join Constance. Meanwhile, I had work to do.

We drove Aramis to his apartment to grab his laptop and clothing. He would be with me for a while, and needed to be prepared. He also retrieved his car, and Kensan and I followed him back to my home where we had met Jonathan Rude. Rude had swept my condo for bugs and hidden cameras and stayed there until I got there.

At nearly three a.m., I was lying in my waterbed after taking a cat nap. Kensan was in the bed with me when I awoke, when I distinctly recalled going to bed alone. He was in boxers and a tank top and lay on top of the covers. I briefly admired his body, which wasn't perfect, but attractive. I slithered out of the bed because I was afraid to wake him. I was more afraid of what may have ensued when human desires took over.

I headed to my office and found Aramis typing away. He was determined to have an article about the exciting night of attorney, Ravonne Lemmelle, on the presses. We had decided to exclude all references to Ariel Greenland and the FBI. We focused on the car explosion, the attempted kidnapping of Brandon, and the threats that I received via telephone and instant message. We excluded the stolen car portion for obvious reasons. I saw that he was busy and just left him there. I had my own masterpiece to glue together.

Back in my bedroom, I pulled out my notes and the motion to dismiss relevant to Wydell James' case. That did not vanish, despite my drama.

One habit that I had was that I loved rehearsing my lines long before I had to say them. Oftentimes, I prepared a speech for George Bush in the event that I ever met the President. I even edited and revised the words in my head. At that point, I lay in bed and rehearsed my private conversation that I'd hold with the judge to have Wydell's charges dismissed.

I sat up on the bed and grabbed the remote to the stereo. I needed to get pumped. Despite my personal crisis, I had a job, which I could have ignored and postponed for two weeks, but I couldn't subject Mr. James to my problems. That was what my colleagues did, and that was what separated me from them. I had a Motion to Dismiss to prepare for, that would go on as planned, as long as I was not dead or otherwise mentally unable to stand trial.

I did a quick bathroom tour before I tried to recall the last meal that I had. I couldn't. I popped a TV dinner in the microwave and knocked it down. I was eating when the telephone rang. It was Dajuan. He was in a city on a layover. I won't bore you with the details of this conversation. Just know that there were a lot of reservations and tickets purchase to confuse anyone trying to find my family. Had someone tried to track them, they'd be dizzy. I assured that.

I annihilated the Salisbury steak, mash potatoes, and mixed vegetables. Afterward, I dug into my briefcase for my Wydell James file and composition book. After a refresher read, I pulled out my tape recorder and blasted off questions for prosecutorial witnesses and my own. As I brooded, a fascinating development stumbled upon me. At that precise moment a shadowy figure stepped into the kitchen.

CHAPTER 89

He hit me with a ferocious punch. My forehead felt as if I was socked by a Barry Bonds swing of the bat. The back of my head slammed into the wall behind me. Whoever it was had tremendous power. He was absurdly horny-handed. I heard sounds that were unidentifiable. I was sure that I had seen Betsy Ross stitching the flag. I was dizzy. Everything spun faster than Earth.

I assessed my options, which were scarce. Undoubtedly, the intruder had a gun. Had to! They knew that I was thoroughly trained to use my hands in ways only watched on karate flicks. The ones that had the voice-overs that never ran their course with the actors actually speaking. Besides that, my eyes were no longer 20/20, so I nixed a toe-to-toe battle. If I had charged the man, he would have shot me in the process. However, if I somehow got through the man's zone and got my hands on him, I would have been able to tear his ass apart. All of my thoughts were arrested when the intruder parked in a chair opposite me. Very casually, by the way.

Through blurred vision, I saw that man, Prince Charming, that was with Ariel at Sole Food. His hair was long as far as I could tell. To fully open my eyes burned terribly. I saw a full beard and mustache. Dark brown. No coat. There was a scarf, though. Wrapped casually as if he never intended to be in a fight.

Aramis lay on the sofa, totally oblivious to what happened. And, where the hell was Kensan? Certainly, both of them had to be sleeping lightly considering the danger that we were exposed to over the past hours. I placed my hands on the table to use as leverage to push my chair back to free my legs from under the table.

The man wiggled a long, slim finger at me, indicating, no.

He said, "I guarantee you that I have a gun. A very big gun. Before you decide to do anything other than sit quietly, know that it'll take two seconds for you to hit the ground, and you'd never even know."

I knew the answer to my next question, but I still asked, "Why the hell not?"

"Because you'd be dead in a nano-second," the man confirmed.

I tried to place the accent to no avail. His voice was deep and dark, and he may have made the accent up.

"Now that we are clear, allow me to formally introduce myself. My name is Skylar Juday, and your beloved media simpletons refer to me as Mr. 357."

This was going to be a poignant *tete-a-tete*. By far, the most unwelcomed one that I had ever engaged in during my life. However, I was prepared for it and that scared me. I had spent countless minutes devoted to this encounter. It would've been better, had it been under my terms, but I had to settle for being on my turf. Somehow, I didn't think that I had home advantage, though. I had no doubt that Mr. 357 had been in my domicile many times when no one was home.

I sat silent and waited for him to speak because I did not want to start off on the wrong foot. He had warned me not to patronize him. He also knew all about my subtle sardonism. He knew a zillion other things about me, too, probably. Like which hand I used to scratch my ass.

"I must say that you are a clever fellow. I genuinely applaud you. Make no error that I vehemently hate you, too."

His voice was robotic and it seemed that the lines were rehearsed.

"For what reason?" I asked without a touch of anger or sarcasm.

I was no dummy. On my best behavior.

"Which one? The applause or the hate?" he asked. On top of that, he stacked, "With your disrespectful arrogance, I am sure you want both, starting with the praise. Your trickery to get Constance, Dajuan, and Brandon to safety was brilliant. My people haven't nabbed them, but I will personally after I am done with you."

Gee thanks, I refrained from saying. The escape system that we had set up was very slick. I had read too many espionage novels not to know how to get away. When I told Constance to go to the hotel that we stayed at for my law school graduation, anyone listening would go to the MGM Grand in Las Vegas, Nevada, but she would go to the LeMeridien in Las Angeles, California. She would later meet Dajuan and Brandon at LAX and board a non-stop flight back to Philly. They would check into the Lowes Hotel, my favorite hotel, and be taken care of.

He interrupted my thoughts by saying, "There are so many reasons that I hate you. I'll recap the ones I told you before, you being born and studying law."

He confirmed for me that he had indeed called me and tried to kill me.

"What does that mean? I did not request that."

"You'd better lose that base in your voice, quickly, Mr. Lemmelle."

"Sorry."

I was a patsy at that moment.

"You're not," he said. "Let's cut to the chase. You were always the smart one. The one with the BMW at seventeen, thanks to mom. Best graduation gift after law school, Las Vegas. You even won a three million dollar jackpot. Married the prettiest girl, who by chance, was bi-sexual like you. Your mother gave you everything, and she was afforded that luxury thanks to your father's salary. Guess what my father gave me? A fare-the-well when I was an embryo and never looked back. Well, once, but it didn't matter."

I frowned up my face and tried to figure out where the hell I knew this guy from. Where the hell did I fit into all of this? There were so many more kids to stalk. They were richer and smarter than me. Why me?

"You're trying to figure where do you fit into this Algebraic equation. It's simple. We have the same father."

CHAPTER 90

From his pocket, Mr. 357 pulled a five-by-seven envelope and tossed it at me. My heart beat at a range hovering between eighty and ninety beats per minute. My hands shook uncontrollably, and I could barely snatch up the envelope, but I had to see the proof to the man's claim.

Inside, I found a New Jersey birth record for Sirius Bates. The date of birth read: March 12, 1972. The father was listed as Joshua Lemmelle. My mind raced trying to pull together a film of 1972 in my mind. I was not even born. As I tried to recall it, I sat the birth record, which was laminated and could've been fake, aside. In the envelope was a birth certificate stamped with the raised New Jersey seal. The information matched the birth record.

I raised my head to look at the character as he removed items from a small bag. He then began to remove his make-up. I watched in awe as I recalled my father was stationed at Fort Dix in New Jersey. It was perfectly plausible that he knocked up some wench and left her to return to Philly. Constance would've been livid had he borne a child out of wedlock. Hell, even with my sexuality, she did not approve of me having a bastard. So I married dumb ass, Ariel Greenland.

As the face paint revealed what I believed was real flesh, I wanted him to re-apply the makeup. His skin looked terrible, having been marred by years of gluing on beards and mustaches. He needed a dermabrasion expert (several) to clear his skin. I looked horror struck.

"It gets worse," he warned.

The hair piece was removed, and the scalp was equally damaged. Amazingly, I had momentarily forgotten I was in the kitchen with a bona fide monster. He raised his sweater over his head and his T shirt went next. His over-developed, masculine chest had scars and bruises everywhere. It looked as if he had been beaten profusely with an extension cord while in a bath tub. Despite the scars, I saw the same fungus spread in patches throughout his chest. If he was going for the shock effect, it worked.

"This is what dermatologist call acute dermatophyte. It's a fungus parasite on the skin, and in my case, hair, too. Our father called me a freak of nature when my mother notified him of my arrival and he visited me. I was a one-year-old. He denied being the father of the monstrosity and walked out never looking back. But I looked for him, though. And my revenge begins with you. Well not exactly, my mom went first because she never pursued him for child support. She told me that he was from Dallas, Texas. Got all that?"

I nodded my head in disbelief. I did not want to believe him, but I knew how calloused my father was. I was sick to my stomach and tasted bile in my throat.

"When I got to be sixteen, after being tortured as you can see, thanks to my adoptive parents, I set out to find, Mr. Lemmelle. My abnormality had taunted my adoptive parents so they tortured me while collecting money from the state to take care of me. Girls hated me and teased me, which is why I kill them and have them do filthy things. But they love me in costumes and are hard up to fuck me until they see my dick."

I cut in, "Are you sure that we are talking about the same Joshua Lemmelle? The one I know created meanness and I surmise that he would have paid you to stay away from his political aspirations."

"No one asked you to guess. This is not a courtroom, little brother."

He found that hilarious.

"Haven't you wondered why he hates you?"

"No, because I know that he hates that I am gay."

The man stood and I thought he was going to attack me. He unbuckled his pants and pulled his zipper down the track before he shimmied his pants to his mid-thigh. Next went his boxers.

CHAPTER 91

Male and female reproductive organs stared back at me. Then it hit me. I blurted, "He hates me because both of his off-springs..." I couldn't form the words to say what I felt.

"Finally, something to render the great Ravonne Lemmelle speechless."

I certainly was.

"Please pull your pants up."

"I do not know why you are all out of shape. You love both. I have you on camera with Ariel and Dajuan. You look good on top and bottom."

"You've been spying on me while wanting to kill me and my dad."

"See, your dad. He's our dad. It's not all about you."

He had nerve. I couldn't think straight. I was staring at the sex organs of a hermaphrodite.

"I am smarter than you, brother. You probably want to kill me. I don't blame you, but, be nice. I am also smarter than the FBI and other agencies. I love to prove them ineffective. I do. And you fucked up my plan with the Artis acquittal."

"So that's why you want to kill me?"

"That, and to hurt dear old Dad. See, I've learned that the more evil and hateful people are toward someone they really love, the deeper the love hurts. I've sat at the funerals of all my vics. I'm going to get dear old Dad and pin it on you."

The door bell chimed.

"That should be your wife," he said and slipped into a sweater.

He held his other belongings and disappeared into the living room.

The doorbell rang again. As the monster unlocked the door, I saw Kensan glimpse out of the office. His weapon shimmered. My heart pounded crazily. I didn't want Kensan to kill Mr. 357 at that point.

I battled to maintain control of my emotions. I had to calm myself. While I disliked Ariel I did not want her dead.

The door swung open and Ariel was there.

"Don't move!"

That was Kensan finally making his presence known. Stupidly, by the way. Why not just shoot?

Everybody but Mr. 357 turned to face Kensan. He grabbed a fistful of Ariel's hair and snatched her into the living room from the doorway. She screamed, and Mr. 357 shoved his gun violently into her mouth.

"What are you doing?" Ariel mumbled.

"Oh, shut up bitch. You didn't think that I really wanted you, did you?" Mr. 357 asked in his fake South American voice. He switched back to his sinister voice and said, "Now, Mr. Lemmelle, if you desire your son having any relationship with this runaway mom, you'll have the man with this gun in my little production put it on the carpet. Easily. Or Brandon loses his mother."

I looked deeply into her eyes. I looked forward to a sinister ending for my unbearably haughty wife in court, but not her death.

Mr. 357 interrupted my train of thought and said, "So what's it going to be?"

Considering the man never gave options, I didn't have time to over think. Just pure balls. I encouraged myself. I motioned for Kensan to put the weapon down. As he did, Mr. 357 threw Ariel at me and we went crashing to the floor. She screamed, and I pushed her aside and bounced back to my feet.

"What are you going to do, pussy?"

Mr. 357 had challenged me. He wanted a piece of me.

"I got this," Aramis said and then sucker pinched Mr. 357 on his right temple. The forceful shot sent Mr. 357 to his knees--the first sign that he was human. He jumped back up having lost his .357 Magnum.

Next, Aramis threw a speedy roundhouse punch that connected, and I followed up with a nasty upper cut that fell deep into his stomach. Mr. 357 gave me a stomach shot in return. My stomach hurt like hell, but I gave him a two-piece that forced him to slam against wall.

"That's all you got, faggot?" Mr. 357 said and threw a sloppy punch.

It landed. Meant nothing. He was disoriented and missed Kensan approaching him. He had the Glock aimed at Mr. 357's chest. Aramis had picked up Mr. 357's Magnum .357.

"Ain't no fun when the rabbit got the gun," Kensan said. "Get the fuck down, clown."

Mr. 357 chuckled and said, "You got balls," to Kensan.

So did I. I slammed my fist into Mr. 357's face. That forced him down. Adrenaline forced him to jump back up and attempt to charge toward me. He was stopped by a bullet.

My wife had saved the day.

CHAPTER 92

I ignored the FBI orders to report to their office. I went to the Lowes Hotel with my wife. They had Mr. 357's makeup bag, the recording of his confession on my tape recorder, and the birth records that I prayed were fake.

I was absolutely wrong about Ariel and that hurt. How could I assume she was such a heinous character? I prayed she never found out how I bad mouthed her.

With the Associated Press asleep, I was able to stroll through the lobby without a mob of reporters on me. Aramis was at *the Inquirer* office preparing to tell the world that Mr. 357 lay in the morgue with a gaping hole in his chest, thanks to Ariel Greenland. I remained shocked that she had a gun and shot him dead center.

When the door to the hotel room opened, Constance pulled me into her arms. She didn't look well. She was haggard and tired.

"I thought you got rid of the bad guys." Granny said, letting me go and sizing up Ariel.

"Not right now, Granny. We've been through a lot."

"Sure."

Granny rolled her eyes and stepped aside to let us into the room.

Brandon was asleep. Dajuan looked up at me, jumped up, and grabbed me into his arms. The kiss that we shared was soft and passionate. First time that Granny had seen that. We pulled apart.

"Sorry," Dajuan said to Granny.

"Boy, I know you two kiss. What I don't know is why is she here?"

"This is crazy. I do not belong here. She never liked me," Ariel said.

Ariel was turning red.

"Still don't, bitch!" Granny said, and then added, "FYI you can leave."

"Come on, Granny, she's been through a lot. The bad guy put a gun into her mouth."

"Brandon has been through a lot, too," Granny replied and waved at my son. "And so have you."

"Ravonne, I'll deal with you later," Ariel said to me and then left the room.

That was not how I expected it to be. I could not focus on Ariel, so I skated across the room to my son and woke him up. He was groggy and crawled right into my arms.

"Did you get the bad guy, Dad?"

"Yep."

"I had a dream that you did. Thanks."

"Anytime, lil' buddy."

At that point, my cell phone chimed. It was a call from Aramis's cell phone. How could that be with Mr. 357 very dead? I flipped it open.

"You do not think it's over, do you?" the caller asked. I knew the female voice.

If I ever had to act, that was the moment. My family couldn't take knowing that Mr. 357 was alive and well.

"Do you think Mr. 357 would fail that miserably? I am shocked you really believed you had that sort of clout. Shame on your arrogant ass. I killed that man that I hired at your home to take care of the loose ends. Did you believe any of that bullshit that he spat out of his mouth? What a pity if you did? But as I said before I left your room, I will deal with you later."

CHAPTER 93

Like a bullet racing out of a .357, I shot out onto Market Street. I squinted up the block trying to put crosshairs on my target. I had my cellular to my ear coordinating a search plan with Agent Gibson, who was eager to get in on the chase. There were a few drunken bodies, who spent their day off celebrating MLK Day with cocktails. I demanded that they clear my path as I headed toward 12th Street. When I arrived there, some inebriated bitch swayed on her boyfriend's shoulders, her head lopsided, and a bottle of cheap cognac was tucked in her hand.

I did an about face and caught Ariel making a left down 13th Street. I had the advantage, considering she had no idea that I was on to her. I hastily headed south on 12th Street to prevent her from putting too much geography between us. As I plunged down 12th, I spotted her through an alley behind the hotel. She walked briskly down 13th while doing something with her hair.

Bulldozing my way through the small crowds of people, I pissed several people off. I was badge-less and in pursuit of a monster that could've made one of them a victim next. It was wise of them to get the hell out of my way. Crossing Chestnut Street, I saw that Ariel had thrown on a ball cap. She was altering her identity.

Shoving and pushing and avoiding eye contact with the people, I managed to get Agent Gibson back on the line. I passed along her wardrobe change to the FBI. To my amazement, Ariel was coming my way. She wiggled out of her blouse, and obviously lost her coat on 13th Street.

Peeking around the corner, I promised Agent Gibson that I would have my wife contained on the corner of 12th and Samson. I watched the ball cap bounce down the block. Faintly, I saw a mustache perched on her face. This had been the most horrifying sight of my life. What I did next was worse, though.

CHAPTER 94

I slugged Ariel with enough force to stop a freight train. Her head snapped sideways. A tooth darted out of her mouth and skirted the concrete. She landed next to the tooth. Going for the kill, I grabbed a handful of her hair which lifted in my hands. Ariel had a close cropped Cesare with waves that rivaled mine under her wig.

Heat consumed me along with admonishing stares from patrons standing outside of the corner bar.

"What the fuck? Are you crazy?" one of them yelled at me.

He was a buff white man. Probably the bouncer with a gun, and he walked toward me.

I pulled out my weapon.

Blood pounded inside my temples. I was in front of a bar with black people celebrating a day of peace. And there I was having knocked out a woman and taken off her wig.

"I'm calling the cops," a loud mouth woman said.

The moment that I lent the bar patrons some attention, Ariel had a gun pointed at me. I was at gunpoint again.

So was she, though.

"Is that Dajuan Jones?" I heard that sassy woman call out.

First came the siren. Moments later, the lights, flashing blue and red. Un. Be. Fucking. Lievable. A standoff all about me.

I heard a sinister voice and the crowd outside of the bar raced for cover. The voice belonged to the calvary: Agent Quadir Gibson. Neither of them complied. I didn't either.

"Dajuan, do not do anything crazy," I slowly told him.

"That's all you're worried about," Ariel said to me.

Droplets of blood escaped the gap that I lodged in her mouth.

"Put your fucking weapons down, now!" Gibson barked as backup arrived.

I watched SWAT team officers scatter everywhere and I dropped my head. I was lost and confused.

"Don't look all crazy now," she said from the ground. "Your man and woman are fighting over you. Aren't you special? Everybody fighting over that dick."

Dajuan was silent with his gun hand steady and trained on her. He understood that this was no fight over me. He had me. She used to have me.

"Ms. Greenland, please put your weapon down. You have a little boy."

"Fuck that boy," she said violently.

"No fuck you, you stupid bitch!" I told her.

"I've never been stupid. Got away with all of the crimes. I'll get away with this one, too."

"You're no killer. You're a wannabe."

"Please! Do you believe that your stuck up ass father cheated on your mom. Not with the man's mother that I shot in your condo anyway. He was an easy hire, but investigated too much. He had to go."

"Poignant," the agent yelled. "But, I need the guns down."

"You want me dead, why?" I asked her.

"That's an easy one, counselor. Perfection. You helped the man who raped my mother to give birth to me get off scott free."

"That's the stupidest thing I ever heard," Dajuan said.

He had a voice after all.

"How poetic," Ariel said, and in one swift motion, she aimed her gun at Dajuan.

By the time her trigger was aimed at him she had a hole in the center of her chest.

I silently thanked Dajuan, and was prepared to defend him if necessary.

EPILOGUE

TUESDAY, JANUARY 16, 2007

CHAPTER 88

I sat at my desk with the most absurd smirk on my face. I had won. I beat Ariel Greenland. I hoped that she rots in hell for the pain and suffering that she brought my family, chiefly, her son. Despite the death of my wife just the day before, I reported to the firm the next day, as if nothing had happened. After all, nothing really had happened as far as I, Ravonne Lemmelle, was concerned. I would never understand Ariel's motive and her poor decision making, because I did not believe that it had anything to do with money. Hence, it wasn't worth trying to figure out, so there I was in the office when my fine legal secretary burst in my office with an invitation.

It was 8 a.m. and I was putting the final touches on questions for my witnesses. This would prove the Motion to Dismiss that made my career, and I wouldn't miss a beat. If I was able to beat a murder case at the preliminary hearing, I would be pushed into Philadelphia lawyer heaven--a place where the richest criminals fought to get the best representation for the right price. It would define me, and I was prepared to be described as excellent.

I had been requested to meet the assistant district attorney assigned to convict Wydell James at a low key breakfast spot in Center City. I didn't hesitate to take ol' Cynthia up on her offer.

I was a tad hesitant as I walked along Market Street, where remnants of my BMW remained scattered about. Yellow crime scene tape blanketed the street, and I pushed past it as if I wasn't the root of its placement. I was on a peculiar mission, and no doubt one that had to be beneficial to me. I was prepared to deliver something to the Commonwealth's prosecutor's office that they hadn't experienced often.

Defeat.

My problem was, what they would do to me in return, but I'd cross that bridge when they tried to force one into my country. And, I was not meeting for any sort of *quid pro quo*. Later for that. I was not bargaining a guilty plea in exchange for anything. If that was her motive, she could have hung that up. I was a little sure that Lady Cynthia had been smarter than that, so perhaps this would be a more interesting meeting, and that thought scared me.

I did accept this meeting, because I understood the DA's office's tenuous position with the public. A murderer would be on the loose, if Wydell was let out. They had to pin this on someone. And that was nice, but it wouldn't be my client.

CHAPTER 89

Cynthia sat in a raucous mid-morning diner and that was a bit much for me. I walked in and immediately noticed her standard lawyer coif and scoffed. I walked over to her and asked to have a seat.

"Sure, this won't take but a second," she said and signaled for the waitress. "Coffee?"

"Sure," I said, and then added, "but I thought this would be fast."

"We're dismissing our claims against Wydell for murder," she said and pushed the Commonwealth's response to my Motion to Dismiss across the table.

I looked at the document as if it was war plans of the Iraqis to attack Americans in the Middle East. I picked it up, and skimmed through it. Essentially, the government contended that what was outlined in the motion that I submitted casted a significant amount of doubt on their case, and they decided to drop the charges.

"This nice of you, but let's say that I oppose this subtle written dismissal and ask for a full hearing to really highlight that you have no case, and never did," I said very boldly. "I may need to block you from ever charging my client again."

I was in control, right?

She candidly slid another document over to me.

"What now?" I asked and snatched it up.

I read the heading and smiled.

"You wouldn't?"

She folded her hands on the table and cocked her head to the side, and smiled.

"Try me."

I sat there and flipped through the charging documents. She interrupted me, and said, "Come on, Ravonne. Of course you had to know that I would pounce on this, sir."

Wrong, I thought. She was so very wrong. I had no idea that Dajuan had been convicted of tax evasion three years earlier. Which also meant, I had no idea that he was a convicted felon in possession of a fire arm last night.

"Now, we have given him a pass for shooting her, despite not having a self-defense rule in our laws. However, that mandatory term of five years in prison, would be pretty open and shut, don't ya think? I mean, how many news broadcasts have him shooting the woman center mass. Hell, we've seen it on YouTube over at the office. Would you like the link? It has over a million views."

"Hell no, creep! This is low, even for you."

I wanted to slap the shit out of her!

"But you get it," she said and stood. She shimmied into her coat, and said, "I am sure you can pay for your own coffee," and then walked away.

"But what about the Barclay's committing the murders and framing my client," I said to her back.

She ignored me.

ABOUT THE AUTHOR

Rahiem Jerome Brooks is the breakout novelist with an overwhelming reservoir of criminal tales that motivate American denizen to be overprotective with their personal data, i.e. social security number, pin number, and account number. He is a member of the Mystery Writer's of America, and his debut street thriller, LAUGH NOW won 2010 African-Americans on the Move Book Club's Book of the Year & he earned 2011 AAMBC Author of the Year. LAUGH NOW also the Most Creative Plot at the DMV Expo's Creative Excellent Awards. Rahiem was also nominated as Self-Published Author of the Year at the 2011 African-American Literary Awards.

www.rahiembrooks.com

LAUGH
RAHIEM BROOKS

THE ANTICIPATED SEQUEL TO LAUGH NOW
2010 AAMBC Book of the Year
DIE
LATER
RAHIEM BROOKS

Last
Laugh
RAHIEM BROOKS

KEVIN WOODARD
TRUTH, LIES AND
CONFESSIONS
RAHIEM BROOKS

CON TEST

PRODIGY PUBLISHING GROUP
Coming of Age
JIBRAIL JONES

Second
Thoughts

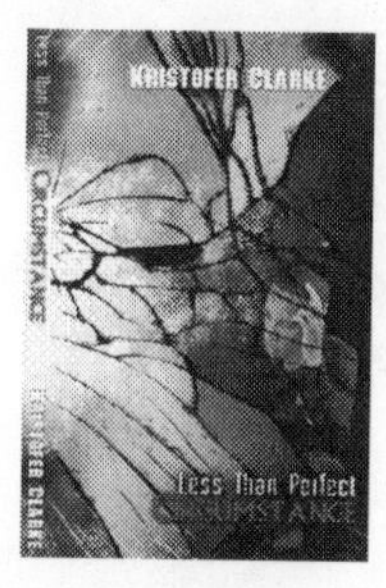
KRISTOFER CLARKE
Less Than Perfect
CIRCUMSTANCE

KRISTOFER CLARKE
'TIL IT
HAPPENS
TO YOU

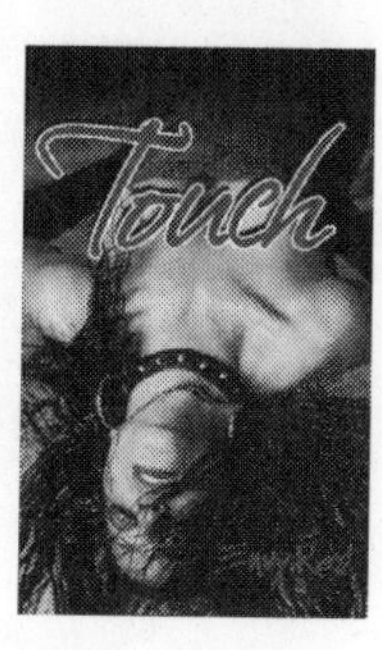
Touch

JADED
EnvyRed

SESSION 1
A novel by
EnvyRed

PRISON ORDER FORM

Rahiem Brooks	Laugh Now	$11.25
	Die Later	$11.25
	Con Test	$11.25
	Murder in Germantown	$11.25
	Last Laugh	$11.25
	Truth, Lies, & Confessions (w/Kevin Woodard)	$11.25
Jibrail Jones	Coming of Age	$11.25
Envy Red	Touch	$11.25
	Jaded	$11.25
	High Rollers	$11.25
Kristofer Clarke	Second Thoughts	$11.25
	Til It Happens To You	$11.25
	Less Than Perfect Circumstance	$11.25
	Total Books Ordered	Sub Total
	Add $1 for each book after 2	Shipping $6
	Total	
	Mail Prison Checks to:	
	Book Orders	
	P.O. Box 25746	
	Philadelphia, PA 19144-9998	

Connect with the publisher, Rahiem Brooks
rahiemthewriter@aol.com

Made in the USA
Lexington, KY
11 February 2013